For Team Kress
(or as I like to call them, Mom and Dad)

CONTENTS

THE NOT-QUITE-FIRST CHAPTER — 1
In which we begin the story

THE FIRST CHAPTER — 4
In which we meet Alex Morningside, her uncle and her year-six teacher

THE SECOND CHAPTER — 16
In which Alex has the most enjoyable PE lesson

THE THIRD CHAPTER — 24
In which we meet some Very Dangerous Men, and witness an act of arson

THE FOURTH CHAPTER — 31
In which we learn some Very Interesting Things about Mr Underwood and his family

THE FIFTH CHAPTER — 38
In which Mr Underwood moves in

THE SIXTH CHAPTER — 42
In which we visit the manor house on the hill and meet the Daughters
of the Founding Fathers' Preservation Society

THE SEVENTH CHAPTER — 53
In which we learn the nature of the coffee-table books and return to the Steele Estate

THE EIGHTH CHAPTER — 62
In which Alex suffers a number of Strange and Unusual Punishments

THE NINTH CHAPTER — 74
In which Alex finds the map

THE TENTH CHAPTER — 81
In which Alex is rather impressive

THE ELEVENTH CHAPTER — 86
In which a very unpleasant discovery is made

THE TWELFTH CHAPTER — 96
In which Alex has to fill out a form and is interrogated

THE THIRTEENTH CHAPTER — 105
In which Alex meets a very old man with a mop

THE FOURTEENTH CHAPTER — 111
In which Alex explores the train

Alex
& the
Wigpowder
Treasure

Adrienne Kress

SCHOLASTIC

First published in the UK in 2007 by
Scholastic Children's Books,
An imprint of Scholastic Ltd
Euston House, 24 Eversholt Street
London, NW1 1DB, UK
Registered office: Westfield Road, Southam, Warwickshire, CV47 0RA
SCHOLASTIC and associated logos are trademarks and or registered trademarks of
Scholastic Inc.

Text copyright © Adrienne Kress, 2007
The right of Adrienne Kress to be identified as the author of this work
has been asserted by her.
Cover illustration by Paul Bommer, 2007
Inside illustrations Paul Bommer/Atomic Squib

10 digit ISBN 1 407 10232 X
13 digit ISBN 978 1407 10232 0

A CIP catalogue record for this book
is available from the British Library

Printed and bound in Great Britain by CPI Mackays of Chatham plc
Papers used by Scholastic Children's Books are made from wood
grown in sustainable forests.

1 3 5 7 9 10 8 6 4 2

This is a work of fiction. Names, characters, places, incidents and dialogues are
products of the author's imagination or are used fictitiously. Any resemblance to actual
people, living or dead, events or locales is entirely coincidental.

www.scholastic.co.uk/zone

THE FIFTEENTH CHAPTER
In which Alex experiences some good food, good company and good dancing
121

THE SIXTEENTH CHAPTER
In which Alex experiences some good food, good company and good dancing
127

THE SEVENTEENTH CHAPTER
In which Alex meets Giggles
136

THE EIGHTEENTH CHAPTER
In which Alex learns something interesting about champagne
144

THE NINETEENTH CHAPTER
In which Alex stumbles upon *The Emperor and the Necklace*
156

THE TWENTIETH CHAPTER
In which we learn about motion capture and visit the Duke's Elbow
164

THE TWENTY-FIRST CHAPTER
In which Alex reasons with the Extremely Ginormous Octopus
170

THE TWENTY-SECOND CHAPTER
In which Alex finds herself trapped
183

THE TWENTY-THIRD CHAPTER
In which we come across a very Illustrious Hotel
189

THE TWENTY-FOURTH CHAPTER
In which Alex meets the MakeCold 6000
199

THE TWENTY-FIFTH CHAPTER
In which we watch a spontaneous musical number and the expedition prepares to depart
209

THE TWENTY-SIXTH CHAPTER
In which Alex is trapped. Again
220

THE TWENTY-SEVENTH CHAPTER
In which we finally get to Port Cullis and visit the Gangrene
227

THE TWENTY-EIGHTH CHAPTER
In which Alex meets Coriander the Conjuror
234

THE TWENTY-NINTH CHAPTER
In which the map is analysed and Alex has a strange dream
243

THE THIRTIETH CHAPTER
In which we meet Captain Magnanimous and a plan is hatched
251

THE THIRTY-FIRST CHAPTER
In which Alex boards the HMS *Valiant*
260

THE THIRTY-SECOND CHAPTER
In which Alex experiences life at sea
270

THE THIRTY-THIRD CHAPTER
In which we anchor at the Cave of the Dislocated Thumb and something unexpected happens
280

THE THIRTY-FOURTH CHAPTER
In which a fierce battle is fought
288

THE THIRTY-FIFTH CHAPTER
In which Alex meets the crew of the *Ironic Gentleman*
295

THE THIRTY-SIXTH CHAPTER
In which Alex and the captain meet
303

THE THIRTY-SEVENTH CHAPTER
In which we witness a reunion
316

THE THIRTY-EIGHTH CHAPTER
In which Alex is made an offer
322

THE THIRTY-NINTH CHAPTER
In which Alex makes an important decision
330

THE FORTIETH CHAPTER
In which we get to go on a treasure hunt
337

THE FORTY-FIRST CHAPTER
In which Alex uses her problem-solving skills to great effect
346

THE FORTY-SECOND CHAPTER
In which Alex has a revelation
355

THE PENULTIMATE CHAPTER
In which everything comes to a head
362

THE LAST CHAPTER
In which loose ends are tied
377

THE NOT-QUITE-FIRST CHAPTER

In which we begin the story

Headmaster Doosy felt extremely small in his chair. He didn't feel small usually. Usually he felt magnificent and powerful, as most headmasters do, but sitting opposite the bearded gentleman that he was sitting opposite made him feel insignificant.

"I understand you are interested in our year-six teacher, Mr Underwood," said Headmaster Doosy, trying to sound magnificent and powerful.

"Yes," growled the very large man.

"Well, I'm afraid he's transferred, just last Thursday, actually." Headmaster Doosy passed over a file folder. The large gentleman took the file in his large hand and opened it.

"Does this say 'Wigpowder-Steele'?" he asked. He was visibly shocked.

"Yes, the Wigpowder-Steele Academy," replied Headmaster Doosy. "One of the most prestigious schools in our district. It's two towns over." He was starting to feel slightly more at ease.

Suddenly, the big man stood up with such force that his chair flew across the floor. He reached over the desk and grabbed hold of the collar of Headmaster Doosy's shirt, lifting him up so that his feet were dangling in the air.

"You'd better not be messing with me, because I'm a doctor," he said softly.

Headmaster Doosy did his best to maintain his composure. "I am a friend of many doctors, sir. That doesn't frighten me."

"Do these doctors sneak into your room at night and put your arm where your leg is and vice versa?"

"Not to my knowledge, no," squeaked Headmaster Doosy.

"Then you had better not be messing with me," repeated the big man, and he dropped Headmaster Doosy back into his chair.

The headmaster sat, shaking with fear and rage. "I have half a mind, sir, to report you to the proper authorities. That is most definitely not the way to treat a headmaster." His voice cracked. "I'm sure there must be a rule . . . or something. . ." Headmaster Doosy looked around his office as if searching for some sort of book of rules on the correct treatment and care of headmasters.

The large man took off his monocle and wiped it. "I don't care much for your 'authorities', as you call them." He replaced the monocle, keeping firm eye contact with the headmaster. "I answer to my Captain. And my Captain alone." He turned his great bulk, inadvertently knocking Headmaster Doosy's desk lamp off the table. The large man sighed fiercely, picked up the lamp and threw it across the room, where it shattered against a framed photograph of the headmaster shaking hands with the local dog catcher. The large man turned one last time to face the cowering Doosy, then with a slight squint, left the room.

Headmaster Doosy sat, dazed. When it seemed clear the gentleman would not be returning, he quickly turned to the school intercom and spoke. "Good afternoon, this is your headmaster speaking." His voice shook slightly. "All students with a last name beginning with 'S' will have detention for the next two weeks. Thank you."

Headmaster Doosy sighed and leaned back in his seat. He was starting to feel magnificent and powerful again.

THE FIRST CHAPTER

In which we meet Alex Morningside, her uncle and her year-six teacher

Y ou would be forgiven for thinking Alex Morningside was a boy. In fact, she would be the first to laugh at this, because, for one thing, she wasn't, and for another, she didn't mind people thinking otherwise. This was because she had an Excellent Sense of Humour. It wasn't that she wanted to be a boy or anything, it was simply that she didn't see much difference in being treated as a girl or boy. Because, after all, everyone is just people.

One of the reasons people thought she was a boy was her haircut. Her haircut looked like someone had put a bowl on her head and cut around it. Which is exactly what her uncle had done. Also, they thought she was a boy because her name was Alex. Of course, Alex was short for Alexandra, but neither Alex nor her uncle liked that very much, so they shortened the name. They could have shortened it the other way, I suppose – Andra – but she and her uncle preferred Alex.

Anyway, as you may already have guessed, Alex lived with her uncle. This was because, when she was very young, he had become her legal guardian after Alex's parents had perished while spelunking in Iceland. Together they lived above his shop. The shop was very special because it was on the side of a bridge. It was also very special because it was very useful. A useful shop is a shop that sells something like fruit and vegetables, because you need fruit and vegetables to stay healthy and therefore they are necessary. Whereas a non-useful shop is a shop that sells things like antiques or jewellery, which are both lovely things, but are definitely not something you need to stay healthy, no matter what people tell you.

Alex's uncle's shop was useful because Alex's uncle sold doorknobs, and what could be more necessary than that? If you didn't have doorknobs you would find yourself trapped in your own home, or worse, unable to get into your own home, and you'd have to sleep outside on the street. And then your own home itself would become useless. Which would be horrible. At this point in her life Alex could only imagine the horribleness of not having a home to return to. Unfortunately, she would learn all too soon what being without a home was really like.

But back to the doorknobs because there is so much more to tell about doorknobs. For example, your personal favourite kind of doorknob might be brass because you like the smell of brass and the fact that it's always cold, but Alex's favourite kind of doorknob was crystal because when the sun shone through it, it would make rainbows. Her uncle had all other kinds of doorknobs as well, though. Some looked like clear glass balls with butterflies trapped in the middle and some were shaped like letters from the alphabet and some were made of fluffy fabric. And because it was a small shop, there was barely any room for all the different types of doorknobs, so it looked rather magnificent, and Alex would always feel very special that she lived with her uncle in his shop.

To be perfectly accurate, Alex didn't live in the shop, but above it. And even better, she lived in a tiny turret at the very top. And even though it was tiny, Alex just loved her turret and would spend much time up there developing   photographs.   Alex   was   a   keen photographer – she had been ever since she was really little. She also liked making up stories, though she wasn't sure if the Alex in her stories was as brave as the Alex in real life. Well, it didn't matter, because her imagination was her own, and she could do with it whatever she wanted. Except of course when she had to go to school. Which I would like to tell you about. . .

. . .Now.

This school Alex attended was called The Wigpowder-Steele Academy, and it was very prestigious. What made it so prestigious was the fact that it had the word "Academy" in the title and the fact that it was one of those schools you pay to go to. This ensured a Higher Quality of Education and, more importantly, a Higher Quality of Pupil, because if you spend all that money it means that your child is therefore really special. Of course "special" doesn't always mean "intelligent", and in this case, as Alex had most definitely concluded after careful research, "special" seemed to mean, simply, "rich". Anyway, because The Wigpowder-Steele Academy was so prestigious, it had a board of directors who got to meet and discuss things and eat iced pastries around a large wooden table. Alex's uncle sat on this board. And for this reason, even though she and her uncle wouldn't otherwise have been able to afford it, Alex got to go to Wigpowder-Steele for free.

As much as she enjoyed learning, which she did – a lot – Alex did not enjoy Wigpowder-Steele. She didn't enjoy wearing a uniform with a skirt. She didn't enjoy her teachers, who were all very old and smelled funny and didn't seem to know about any of the developments that had happened in the world in the last thirty years. And she most definitely did not enjoy her peers, who were more concerned with how their hair looked than listening in class, and who were quite simply ridiculous. However, that was OK because her peers didn't enjoy her much either, and she spent most of her time on her own.

So you can understand why, on her first day back at school, despite her fondness for all things educational, Alex remained ever so slightly anxious.

"So, Alex," said her uncle as they sat at the kitchen table for breakfast, "are you excited about your first day of school?"

Alex swallowed the bite of breakfast she had been chewing and thought carefully. "Well," she said, "I am excited to be in year six, and I am excited to learn synchronized swimming. And I definitely can't wait for maths this year. But I am not looking forward to Mrs Swinsky."

Her uncle looked up and nodded seriously.

Mrs Swinsky was not only the year-six teacher but

the vice president of the board. She was very, very old and she had very, very old-fashioned ideas. For example, she was quite fond of the ruler – that is, taking a ruler and smacking the hands of her students when they misbehaved. She would even smack the hands of the board members if they misbehaved, but Alex's uncle had never been smacked because everyone liked him.

"You don't worry about her, and you just focus on learning," he said, playing with the tip of his long white beard. "And if she does anything to you, all you have to do is tell me and I'll talk to her." He leaned over the small table and with a devilish grin added, "I think she fancies me."

Alex smiled because it was probably true. She also smiled because her uncle did not exactly look like a movie star. For one thing, he was very old, probably the same age as Mrs Swinsky, but instead of being old-fashioned, he behaved more like a kid. It meant that he liked to play hide-and-seek and tag. It also meant he appreciated really good stories, especially made-up ones. But he was also very well respected by adults. And anyone who ever met him found him Very Interesting because he knew a lot about many different things. He looked Very Interesting as well. He was very small and skinny with a long white beard and wore tiny spectacles for examining doorknobs. And he always dressed very well in a suit and tie and brown shoes.

"I tell you everything anyway." Alex smiled, wiped her mouth, said, "Excuse me", and stood up and left the table to brush her teeth.

Having braces meant Alex needed to brush her teeth often and good dental hygiene was of primary importance to her. For that reason, wherever she went, she always carried her toothbrush with her in a little plastic oblong container to keep it clean. The container was blue and had her name written in thick black marker on it. Alex wondered if maybe it was because she brushed her teeth at school that her peers didn't much like her. It was quite possible because, after all, they were ridiculous.

Once she finished brushing her teeth, she packed up her rucksack, said goodbye to her uncle and headed off to school. The walk to school was quite pleasant because the town she lived in was quite pleasant. Some people might have called it quaint. Some others might even have called it claustrophobic. Still others would have called it burnt sienna because the houses were all made of reddish brick. In her town there were ten small churches and one large cathedral that was incredibly beautiful. There was one outdoor market for textiles and one for food. There were also three schools and one large department store. On the other side of town was where the rich people lived in terraced houses. And the grandest home of all was up on the hill just beyond that.

It was a giant manor house that had once been privately owned but had been bought by the local authority. This was a Good Thing because instead of the house being destroyed to make a parking lot, it was preserved in its Original Condition. Which meant little old ladies would give guided tours to tourists and school groups through roped-off rooms. And in that manner Alex had already, even at her tender age of ten-and-a-half, visited the place on three occasions.

In no time at all Alex found herself standing in front of the imposing entrance gates that framed the drive up to the school. Wigpowder-Steele was a very impressive-looking building made of red brick with a curved tree-lined drive. It was four storeys tall and sixteen windows wide, and written across the front in Latin was *Graviora Manent* which loosely translated as "Greater Dangers Await".

This morning, like every other morning at the school, the drive was in chaos. Very posh cars were swerving this way and that, cutting in front of each other and lining up to stop in front of the school, where each would eject a very posh child from the passenger-side seat, all neat and pressed and in uniform. Alex's uniform was wrinkled. And there isn't much more to add about that.

She decided to walk on the grass as the drive was quite dangerous, what with all the speeding cars of parents who were not actually late for work but were too important not to think otherwise. Walking on the grass was actually quite rebellious of Alex since there was a sign clearly marked "Do not walk on the grass", but, as it was the first day of term, everyone was too flustered to notice.

As is so often the case, however, when we think we are doing a harmless thing, it can turn out to be quite the opposite. And in this particular circumstance the grass was entirely the wrong place to be walking. But one could also just as easily point out that it was entirely the wrong place for a bicycle as well. Fortunately, Alex had excellent hearing, and the bicycle had an excellent bell, and the two put together meant that Alex managed to jump out of the way just as the bicycle was about to run her over.

"Oh my goodness! Are you all right?" said the young man riding the bicycle as he skidded to a stop. He jumped off and ran over to her in a panic. He was a thin young man with floppy short brown hair. He was wearing khaki trousers and an argyle-knit sweater and white tennis shoes. And goggles, which would have been more appropriate for riding a motorbike.

"Yes, I'm fine. But you shouldn't have been riding on the grass," she replied, catching her breath.

"No, I suppose you're right. I was just worried about being late for my first day. But it was completely irresponsible of me, and I am so sorry." And he stuck out his hand for Alex to shake. Alex was quite taken aback by this gesture, being offered a hand like a grown-up. But, she reasoned, this could only be a good thing, and she took his hand in hers.

"My name is Alex."

"My name is Mr Underwood."

Alex could see herself reflected in his goggles. Her mousy brown hair (which her uncle insisted was ash blonde) was almost covering her eyes, and she could see she would need to ask her uncle for a haircut soon. And then she realized . . . "I'm a girl," she said because she didn't want to embarrass him.

"Yes, I know," he replied, releasing her hand.

"Oh. But how?"

"You're wearing a skirt."

"Oh, of course." She looked down at her grey pleated uniform. "I don't usually wear a skirt, I just have to for school. Usually I wear trousers, and people think I'm a boy." Mr Underwood nodded. They stood there quietly for a few seconds.

"Well, Alex, perhaps you could do me a favour. I need to find the year-six class, and, well, I haven't a clue where that would be." He looked at the towering building in front of him.

"Why do you need to find the year-six class?" Alex asked suspiciously.

"Well, because that is supposed to be my class." Just as he said it the loud school bell went, making him jump. He instinctively glanced over his shoulder. Alex followed his gaze.

"What are you looking at?"

"What? Oh, nothing," replied Mr Underwood, turning back.

"Gosh, you're paranoid," said Alex, shaking her head. "It was just the school bell."

"Well, ah, the fact that you're paranoid doesn't mean they're not after you," Mr Underwood pointed out and laughed nervously.

"I guess." The two of them stood in uncomfortable silence for another moment. Alex saw that she would have to be the one to defuse the awkwardness. "So . . . ah . . . what happened to Mrs Swinsky?"

"Who? Oh, Mrs Swinsky. Yes. I believe she went to Portugal for the summer and never came back."

"Oh." Alex thought for a moment. "That's odd."

"Yes," replied Mr Underwood, "I suppose it is."

Alex shrugged, and started walking towards the school. "Well, let me show you the way," she said. "Year six is my class."

"Thank you very much, Alex." He followed her up into the school, his bike in tow.

Alex smiled to herself. Year six at Wigpowder-Steele was going to be a good one. A little weird, but good.

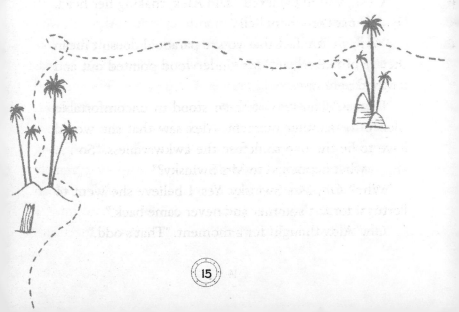

THE SECOND CHAPTER

In which Alex has the most enjoyable PE lesson

What an exciting few months of school Alex had with Mr Underwood as her teacher. He was nothing like any of her other teachers had been. First of all, he was intelligent. He could answer any question. If you asked him about Zimbabwe he would tell you all about Zimbabwe and not, "Alexandra Morningside, we are studying the feeding habits of fruit flies. Stop asking pointless questions." Secondly, he made learning extremely entertaining. Like when they were learning all about Joan of Arc, and they staged a trial and Alex got to play juror number two, and she wore a pair of her uncle's spectacles to make her look like an adult. (The best bit was the bonfire at the end when they got to roast marshmallows.)

Mr Underwood was also young, which was just plain refreshing. It was also a bit frustrating for Alex because many of the ridiculous girls in her class thought that he was "fit" and they would wear make-up (because even when you are ten or eleven, certain parents don't mind you wearing make-up) or do their hair in a different way. And they would always laugh at his jokes, even though they didn't really understand what they meant, unlike Alex, who picked up most of his references.

Alex had also been correct, though, in assuming the year ahead was going to be slightly weird. Mr Underwood did have some awfully strange ticks. For example he was very particular about grammar, which I suppose is important for a year-six teacher. However, Alex had never seen anyone react so strangely when people didn't use the words "I" and "me" correctly.

"The best way of knowing if you should use 'I' or 'me'," he had explained, "is to say the sentence just referring to yourself. So you say, 'Could you help me with the dishes?' in order to realize that it is 'Could you help John and me with the dishes?' and not 'John and I'."

This was all well and good, and very educational, but things got a bit complicated when Douglas Gerald, who consistently flouted the rule, was finally given detention.

This seemed awfully harsh even for Douglas Gerald, and there had been many letters from angry parents who wrote in to complain and Mr Underwood had been forced to apologize.

"What does it really matter anyway, whether you say 'me' or 'I'?" Terri Little had asked, with a flip of her hair, of a rather disheartened Mr Underwood once he had finished his apology.

Mr Underwood sighed. It was obvious he didn't want to discuss the subject any further, but he never refused to answer a student's question. "It matters because many people, when they are forced to choose between 'me' and 'I', choose 'I'. They do this because, for some strange reason, 'I' sounds more intelligent than the word 'me'. And so they think it makes them seem intelligent, when really using the word 'I' when it should be 'me' just shows that they are not as intelligent as they think they are – and that, worst of all, they are trying to show the person they are talking to that they are someone they aren't."

Alex had watched Douglas as he turned a slight shade of pink.

Well, anyway, I digress. The point was that Mr Underwood was a marvellous teacher despite being ever so distinctly odd. And sometimes, these two attributes together could make for some surprising and wonderful lessons as well.

Take Mr Underwood's PE lessons, for instance. Alex, although she liked playing outside and walking, did not tend to enjoy PE. Normally the class was made to do calisthenics, or circuits, or something pointless like that. But Mr Underwood was having none of it.

Alex always had complete confidence in Mr Underwood, but even she could not imagine how it was possible to make PE enjoyable. So in their first lesson she was, as always, the last one changed and entering the gym. What she saw was most startling. Mr Underwood was dressed entirely in white from head to toe, and this is a literal description because covering his head was a white mask with a fine wire mesh where the face was. In fact, she only knew it was Mr Underwood when he lifted it up and said, "No dawdling now, Alex, class has already started." And as she sat she saw the most startling thing of all. Mr Underwood was brandishing a sword. This seemed awfully dangerous, even – or perhaps especially – in a prestigious school like Wigpowder-Steele.

"I've got the go-ahead from the board of directors to teach you my favourite form of exercise. Can anyone guess what it is?" And it seemed rather obvious it would have to be something involving swordplay, but just in case they hadn't figured it out, he sliced the air with the sword, making a swooshing noise. "Well, it's called fencing. Fencing looks as if it's dangerous, but it's actually a sport, and I can guarantee that no one gets hurt. First of all, you all wear these masks," and he pointed to the one on his head, "and, second, you'll see that the tip of the sword is blunted. That is called a button because it looks like someone has stuck a small button on to the point. The swords themselves are called fencing foils. Now, I thought it would be fun to learn something a bit different, and fencing is a most excellent form of exercise. So, let's get started."

What followed was fifteen minutes of stretching and a half hour of "lunging", which is when you keep your left foot on the ground and take a giant step forward with the right, so you find yourself in a lunge, which is incredibly painful, especially when you do it over and over again. And then class was finished, and they didn't even get to touch the swords at all. Nonetheless, no one could talk of anything else, and during lunch every other student in the school wanted to ask them all about it.

After that initial fencing class, things got a bit better, and they even got to use the swords eventually. And once they got to do that, well, then, things got very exciting indeed. They were paired off, and they each got a mask, and then they had to fight. By then they had learned how to hold their swords *en garde*, and they knew how to advance and retreat and how to beat away a sword, and they constantly learned new techniques at the start of each class.

Alex discovered that she was quite adept at it and got quite good. In fact she got so good that she couldn't really fight with many other people in her class, so if he wasn't busy teaching, she got to fight Mr Underwood personally. Sort of like this:

Mr Underwood	Alex
en garde in *prime*	*en garde* in *seconde*
refuse the blade with a *dégagé*	*appel*, change beat

[Both re-engage in tierce]

froissement, thrust chest	parry *tierce*
retreat back, parry *quarte*	bind into *patinando*
riposte into lunge	retreat, parry *seconde*
recover, parry high *seconde*	*punto reverso*
bind over, thrust centre	*demi volte*, hand parry into Angelo's deceit
attempt parry *tierce*,	*dégagé* into spin, feint thrust
rassemblement	centre
evade with a *passata-sotto*	slash head
thrust centre, "Ah ha! I have you!"	

. . .which I'm sure you'll find pretty self-explanatory.

Of course, Alex, despite having quite a good *punto reverso*, tended to lose when she fought Mr Underwood because he was very, very good and wouldn't pull his attacks. Yes, it was slightly odd that a year-six teacher should be quite that good at fencing. But Alex reasoned that maybe he had been on the team in university or something. By fighting Mr Underwood in this manner, she got better quite quickly, and soon she was helping him teach the class. What this meant was that she was even less popular than she had been before. But what it also meant was that she got to become better friends with Mr Underwood than anyone else.

Interestingly, at the same time, while Alex was becoming friends with Mr Underwood, Mr Underwood was becoming friends with her uncle, who had grown to be his most avid supporter on the board since the "I/me" detention scandal. And so, Alex's uncle had begun to invite her teacher over after school for dinner occasionally. Now it may seem odd to have your teacher around all the time, but Alex thought Mr Underwood was just as interesting as her uncle, and really enjoyed listening to the two of them talk. Besides, she had no friends anyway, so she didn't care that her peers thought it was strange that Mr Underwood hung out with her family. And even though they also thought this gave her an advantage in school with grades and stuff, Alex knew that, in fact, the opposite was true, that she was graded all the more carefully. Besides, it wasn't as if Clarissa Fairfield's mum wasn't bridge partners with the headmistress, and Brent Snoutford wasn't best friends with the son of the academic examiner.

So Mr Underwood would come over after school and help her uncle with fixing doorknobs and even invented a Special Technique for gluing together shattered glass ones. Other times he and her uncle would have quiet grown-up conversations about the Current State of Government or literature over a bottle of wine. But then he would spend time with Alex as well, for example showing her new and interesting photography techniques.

And this was how Mr Underwood became a Family Friend, because he could get along with both Alex and her uncle, and the three of them would sit up until Alex's bedtime, listening to her stories. Then Alex would go to bed, and shortly afterwards she would hear the sound of Mr Underwood's bicycle clanking away into the distance, along the bridge and down the street, until the sound disappeared altogether.

THE THIRD CHAPTER

In which we meet some Very Dangerous
Men, and witness an act of arson

So let's say many weeks have passed since the family
friendship between Alex and her uncle and Mr
Underwood had been solidified, so that we can get the
story moving and tell you of a Very Important Night.

Strange things can happen in the middle of the night.
The reason for this is that, typically, this time of night
tends to be very dark. This means that there is lots of
blackness to hide in or escape to after having done
something sinister. And this is why most movies have
their scariest moments late at night. Also the street lights
can cast ominous shadows, so you can fool yourself into

thinking things are more dangerous than they are.

However, I should point out that the two men walking down that alley over there were exactly as dangerous as, if you could see them properly in the day and not in the middle of the night, they looked. Which was rather dangerous.

And if you could have seen them in the daylight you would have noticed how one man was very tall and looked very strong, and one man was short and looked very weak. You would have also noticed that the small man had a very pointy nose, greasy red hair that fell lank to his shoulders, and no eyebrows. Although you might not have noticed he didn't have any eyebrows because that isn't the sort of thing one notices. You might have noticed that he looked Odd, or Unsettling, without quite knowing why, as often we cannot place exactly the reason we don't like a person. And we think it is because of who they are or how they behave, when really it is all down to a lack of facial hair. The short man with the pointy nose, greasy red hair that fell lank to his shoulders and no eyebrows was also wearing a black trench coat and black leather gloves. And black leather shoes with buckles. And he carried around a hammer close to him like a security blanket. He called his hammer "Hammer". He called himself Jack.

The bigger man had more than enough facial hair for

the both of them. But, if he hadn't been wearing a bowler hat, you would have noticed he had none on his head. Interestingly, he wore a monocle. This is interesting because it is very annoying to wear a monocle as you have to hold it in place with the muscles around your eye. So it is a very definite Choice to wear a monocle instead of glasses, which are much easier to deal with, but what that Choice meant for that man, I haven't the foggiest.

The bigger man with the hairy face and bowler cap and monocle was wearing a three-piece suit. He liked to look professional because he was very proud that he was a doctor. People called him Dr Brunswick. Because that was his name. Dr Brunswick was also wearing rubber boots.

The two men had one map between them, which had caused them to argue over who got to carry it. Of course the doctor had won, because he was bigger, and bigger men usually win things. He had also won because he was much smarter than Jack and much more adept at reading maps. And he had drawn the map in the first place.

The map was of the town, the same town that Alex lived in with her uncle and her year-six teacher, Mr Underwood. And it was leading the two men down a small alley that opened on to a pleasant cobblestone mews.

This mews was lit by street lights and the two men were very cautious in approaching number eighteen, which was where the map had been leading them. They stood in the shadow of the doorway, and Jack, after a quick look around, opened his trench coat. Being so skinny, he was able to hide all manner of things under there and still not make a bulge. In this instance, he had a can of kerosene with the name "Dude Hector" etched into the side, a book of matches, a bundle of material and the complete works of Dickens. Dr Brunswick silently watched (and by "silently" I mean accidentally knocking over a garbage bin and then kicking it in rage) as Jack drenched the cloth in kerosene and then set it on fire. Then the doctor smashed number eighteen's front-room window and Jack threw the ball of fire into the house. And then they ran away into the shadows.

They ran far from the house, now entirely swallowed by flames. They ran till they were very far away and then stopped. They stopped because this is where they were supposed to meet the third man. I'm sorry, I just realized I forgot to tell you that there was a third man, and the third man was the most frightening and dangerous one of the lot. If you looked at him you could be forgiven for assuming he had no eyebrows because you would definitely not have liked the sight of him. But he had eyebrows. He just didn't have eyes.

Now you shouldn't feel sorry for him because he had never had eyes and had been born that way. And if you have never had something you can't really miss it. Once upon a time, he had had his nose, however, and he missed that terribly. Even more than he missed his ears, and definitely more than he missed his hands. Again though, you shouldn't feel bad for him because though this all sounds unpleasant, and it really is, he could still hear things through the holes in the side of his head, and he could still grab things with the elegant wooden hands designed to replace the originals.

But the reason he missed his nose most of all was that in losing his nose he had lost his sense of smell, and while his sense of smell was no great loss to him, there was one thing that was. I don't know if you know this, but when you lose your sense of smell, you lose most of your sense of taste. And that was, if you insist on feeling sorry for this most dangerous man, what made him the saddest. Because what he liked more than anything in the world was a good whisky. And since he had lost his nose, he had not been able to taste the flavour of a good whisky at all.

Now if you had seen this man in this way, you might have fainted from fright. And you may wonder exactly how he would go about in the daytime with everyone fainting around him. "How," for example, "would he be able to buy a hot chocolate?" you may ask. Well, he had solved that problem by wrapping a long black silk cloth around his head just above his mouth (which was entirely intact, by the way) and tying it neatly at the back of his head. The silk meant he could still hear through the material, and it also felt very nice against the skin. He wore a matching black silk shirt tied with strings at the front and soft dark red leather trousers with black boots. And when he walked down the street, instead of everyone fainting, they would whisper, "What a dashing young man that dashing young man is. I wonder why he wears a scarf around his face?" (There was in fact a small town that he had passed through once that so admired his appearance that he had started a trend of people wrapping silk scarves around their faces – which caused no end of accidents but greatly benefited the silk scarf industry in that region.)

So. . .

This third man arrived from behind the other two, which made them jump. What made them jump was not so much his arrival but the bark that the third man's dog made. It was a very loud bark, and when you are not expecting it, a very loud bark can easily make you jump. Oh yes, I meant to tell you that the third man had a large scraggily grey guide dog who drooled constantly. And the dog's name was Walter. And he could probably bite you in half with one snap.

"So where is he?" asked the third man quietly.

There was a silence broken by the sound of fire engines roaring somewhere off in the far distance.

Then the doctor said, "I knew we forgot something."

So number eighteen was on fire, but this was not very dangerous to Alex or her uncle because they lived on the other side of town from number eighteen. And it wasn't dangerous to Mr Underwood either because he hadn't been home at the time. He had been out for one of the midnight strolls he sometimes took when he couldn't sleep. Of course, when he got back and found his home burned to the ground, he thanked his lucky stars that he had had one too many coffees before going to bed.

And all of this, the dangerous men, Mr Underwood's caffeine addiction along with his home being destroyed, and Alex and her uncle's not, is all leading to an Important Development in our story. For, late that same night, having nowhere else to go, and not enough money to stay in a hotel, Mr Underwood arrived at Alex's uncle's doorknob shop and asked if he could stay. And this is an Important Development because I suppose you could say that this is where our story Truly Begins.

THE FOURTH CHAPTER

In which we learn some Very Interesting Things about Mr Underwood and his family

The three of them, Alex, her uncle and Mr Underwood, sat around the small kitchen table, which was lit only by a small lantern. In each of their hands was a cup of hot cocoa. Mr Underwood had just finished explaining about his walk and finding his home burned to cinders, and they were sitting in the silence that always follows an extraordinary story. However, it didn't last long because Alex's uncle, being an intelligent man, said, "But who would do such a thing?"

Now, there were a few responses that Mr Underwood

could have given but not that many. Either he did know, or he didn't, or he might have known. But none of those required the amount of time it took for him to answer Alex's uncle.

"I have one guess," he said, pushing back his floppy hair from his forehead. "I don't know if the members of the board of directors know this, but one reason I was hired at the Academy was that my great-great-great-grandfather was Wigpowder himself."

"Was he really?" replied Alex's uncle.

It's strange, but when one goes to a school with a name like Wigpowder-Steele, the name becomes the school's name, and one can often forget it was named after someone in the first place. Alex had never really considered the possibility that Wigpowder could have been a real person.

"Who was Wigpowder?" she asked, intensely curious.

"Ah," replied her uncle with that devilish spark in his eye again. "The Infamous Wigpowder was what he was known as." He stopped and thought about it for a moment. "Which was admittedly a rather odd name. At any rate, the Infamous Wigpowder was a very notorious pirate."

"You're related to a pirate!" exclaimed Alex.

"I guess so," replied Mr Underwood with a smile. And then added, "On my mother's side." Whether this was supposed to make it better or worse was not exactly clear.

"Well, the Infamous Wigpowder amassed a huge fortune over his lifetime of pillaging ships. And on his deathbed he dictated his last will and testament. This consisted of instructions for two things. The first was to donate half of his treasure to the town in the hopes of starting a quality institution to further the education of our young people. And the second was that the remainder was to be left to his eldest son, not yet of age," continued her uncle.

"So far so good," said Alex, following carefully.

"Now you have to understand that pirates are not very trusting. This is why they bury their treasure on islands instead of putting it in banks or investing in bonds. And it was all very well and good for Wigpowder to request that his money be handled in a certain way; but it was another thing actually to get hold of the money itself and yet another thing then to persuade whoever did get hold of the money to part with it."

"Well, what did he do?"

"He asked the wealthiest man in town, Alistair Steele, to execute his will. This was a very clever idea because Alistair Steele was not only the wealthiest man in town, but he was also a philanthropist, meaning he often gave to charitable organizations, and therefore he was the least likely person to want to keep the fortune for himself. It was he whom Wigpowder entrusted with his treasure island's map, and it was he who sailed off to retrieve the treasure.

"Alistair Steele was indeed a good man. He followed Wigpowder's will to the letter, using half of the money to create the Academy, and leaving the other half on the island for when Wigpowder's son came of age. But unfortunately, Steele became very ill all of a sudden and passed away before Wigpowder's son had fully grown up." Alex's uncle looked at Alex to make sure she was still following. Alex nodded for him to continue.

"However, he did manage to leave instructions with his wife to make sure Wigpowder's son was given the treasure map when the time came. But Steele, though an excellent man, had not made an excellent choice in his bride, and his wife could not think of a reason why she shouldn't keep the fortune for herself. Of course, being of a sickly constitution, she never actually went in search of the treasure, but kept the map secretly in her possession until her eldest son was old enough to seek it out himself. And so the two sons of the two men grew up, and then, one fateful day, Wigpowder's son finally came to claim it, and of course he was refused."

"What did he do?" asked Alex, breathless.

"He did what any young man of the time would do.

He challenged the young Steele to a duel. Unfortunately, neither man was very good at duelling and in some way or other they managed to kill each other. Steele's mother, seeing her son dead, herself perished on the spot. However, the feud didn't end with their deaths, and their younger siblings continued to fight over to whom the treasure belonged.

"Now the only one who knew where the map was hidden was Steele's wife. Both families set about trying to find it, and eventually the feud got quite out of control. The Steeles and the Wigpowders were banished from the town, and the whole thing eventually was forgotten about."

"Then why did the school want Mr Underwood to teach if he was banished?"

"Good question. Mr Underwood?"

Mr Underwood shrugged. "Time passes. And my great-great-great-grandfather's generous contribution was never forgotten. Nor, I suppose, was the fact that the money belonged to the Wigpowders and not the Steeles, so I guess, I'm a good guy."

"OK. That's the story, then. But who burned down your house?" asked Alex.

"I think it must have been Steele or his men," answered Mr Underwood thoughtfully.

"His men?"

"Well, here is the twist to everything. The latest Steele, it turns out, is a pirate. And not only a pirate, but the captain of one of the most infamous pirate ships this side of the equator. The *Ironic Gentleman*."

Alex thought really hard, so hard that she needed to squint her eyes. She said slowly, "So the great-great-great-grandchild of the Infamous Wigpowder grew up to become a respectable year-six teacher, and the great-great-great-grandchild of the philanthropist Alistair Steele became a pirate captain."

"Yes," replied Mr Underwood.

"Neat."

"That's all well and good, but why would Steele attack now? Why would he burn down your house?" said Alex's uncle.

"They must have assumed that, because I was in town, I was coming back to reclaim my inheritance. They must have thought I either knew where the map was or knew where the treasure was, and they wanted me out of the way. I am, after all, the last Wigpowder in the line."

"Gracious," said Alex's uncle and leaned back in his chair.

"Is that why you came back? To reclaim your inheritance?" Alex was wide-eyed.

"Yes," replied Mr Underwood simply. "And they were also right about the map. I do know where it is. Though why they should want to kill me instead of questioning me is something I don't understand."

"Where is it?" asked Alex, hopping up and down in her seat.

"Where is what?"

"The map!"

"Well . . . before my mother passed on, she shared with me the only bit of information that the Wigpowders knew and the Steeles could never be sure of. The map was somewhere in Alistair's home."

"But where is that?"

"You should know, Alex," said her uncle. "You've visited it three times with your school already."

THE FIFTH CHAPTER

In which Mr Underwood moves in

It came to pass that the reconstruction of his home was going to take several months, so after asking her permission, Alex's uncle invited Mr Underwood to stay with them in the interim.

Now I would imagine that the idea of having your year-six teacher move into your home might not be a pleasant one. You would assume you would probably have to be on your best behaviour all the time. And you probably couldn't do things like multiply twelve times three hundred and sixty-four incorrectly. Fortunately, however, since they were already Family Friends, Alex was very happy to be living with Mr Underwood under their roof all of a sudden. And she didn't worry that this solidified her reputation once and for all as teacher's pet in the eyes of her classmates, because she knew deep down that she wasn't one. Besides, what else were you supposed to do when your uncle's best friend's house gets burned down by pirates? Honestly!

Though she enjoyed the new living arrangement, it wasn't perfect. For one thing, her uncle and Mr Underwood began to have more and more complicated conversations about things Alex didn't understand. And while they never ignored her, she kind of felt left out at times. She also was tremendously frustrated that, since the night of the fire, they had not made one mention of the treasure map, nor any plans to find it. Alex, on the other hand, had spent the last two weeks thinking of nothing else and had puzzled over this behaviour. She knew that Mr Underwood wanted to reclaim his fortune. And she knew that Mr Underwood knew where the map was. But he didn't seem at all bothered about going to look for it. She knew this because when he wasn't teaching, he seemed more interested in marking three-page essays on "What I Want to Be When I Grow Up" than treasure hunting, no matter what he said.

"Are you frightened of being burned alive?" Alex finally asked him quietly one afternoon in class, pretending she needed help with a maths problem.

"Alex, we are studying fractions."

"I was thinking that you might be frightened of being burned alive. Like Joan of Arc. Except that I don't think you have to worry about that."

"Alex, please sit down and do your work."

"I've finished my work. Here." She passed him her workbook and he glanced over it. "Listen, I think there's more to this than meets the eye. That burning your house down was a mistake. I think that if Steele wants the map and thinks you have found it, he wants you alive."

"I hardly think this is the time or place to discuss such things. And anyway, who says I am frightened of being burned alive?" he whispered back.

"Oh, come on, Mr Underwood, you know exactly where the map is and you haven't even once left the house to go looking for it. If I were looking for a treasure, I would be more proactive."

"Yes, well, thank you for the advice, Alex. Now please sit down and we'll discuss this at your uncle's," and he passed her back her book. "You got number fourteen wrong."

Poor Mr Underwood. There is nothing more difficult to avoid than the questions of an inquisitive child. He had spent two weeks tiptoeing around the subject, but Alex was too headstrong to give up. She just couldn't see why Mr Underwood wouldn't want to work harder at finding what was rightfully his.

The only good thing in putting off searching for the map thus far was that Alex was able to use the time to formulate a plan. It wasn't much of a plan, really. It consisted mostly of Alex going to the old mansion on the hill and searching the library. After all, that seemed the most likely of places a person was going to keep a map. Unless, of course, Steele had had a room dedicated entirely to cartography, which then would have been even more likely. But he didn't. Of course the most crucial element for this plan to succeed was going to the old Steele House in the first place. And so finally what it came to was Alex giving Mr Underwood a direct order: "This Saturday you are going to take me to the manor house on the hill and we are going to do some reconnaissance."

THE SIXTH CHAPTER

In which we visit the manor house on the hill and meet the Daughters of the Founding Fathers' Preservation Society

That is how it came to be that Alex and her year-six teacher, Mr Underwood, on a wet Saturday morning, finally found themselves trudging up the muddy hill to the manor house.

"Now, Mr Underwood," Alex said as they were climbing, "I think what we ought to do is split up. You can take the bottom floor and the kitchens, and I'll take the top two floors. We will meet back in the shop in an hour."

Mr Underwood nodded.

They passed through the doors and approached the little old lady at the desk.

"Why, hello, dears!" she said, her voice cracking. "My name is Poppy." And she pointed to her name on her nametag. Underneath her name was printed "Daughters of the Founding Fathers' Preservation Society". The tag was pinned to a cable-knit sweater with pink roses sewn into the spaces.

"Lovely to meet you, Poppy," said Mr Underwood. "Two tickets, please." And he handed her a fiver.

"Oh, I am sorry, my dear, but I am afraid the price has gone up to four for adults and two for children." She smiled, revealing a set of rotting yellow teeth.

"Oh." Mr Underwood dug out a dusty coin from his pocket.

"Thank you ever so much, my dear. It is a shame, isn't it? But it takes so much work to keep this beautiful old building ship-shape. Now, here are your maps, and there are guides in each room, so you can ask them anything you want, and remember: don't touch anything, and stay behind the red ropes." She was addressing Alex, who nodded. She had been told this three times before. "Of course, I'm sure you already know this. You look," she said to Alex, "like a very responsible young man." She smiled again, the skin around her eyes and mouth contracting in dry flaking wrinkles. Alex shivered, though she wasn't exactly sure why.

"Thank you," she muttered, and she and Mr Underwood headed into the main hall.

They stood there in the decaying room and thought the same thing, which was: "What exactly are the Daughters of the Founding Fathers' Preservation Society spending the extra money on?"

The place had definitely deteriorated since Alex's last visit. Cobwebs hung in dusty dark corners, the carpets were worn through, and a horrible musty dank smell hung heavy in the air.

"I guess I'll go upstairs, then," said Alex. Mr Underwood nodded, again.

Alex headed up the large wooden stairs to the first floor and quickly entered the library.

"Hello, dear." Alex looked up and saw another Daughter of the Founding Fathers' Preservation Society. "Please ask me any questions you have." She grinned, her upper teeth falling down to meet her bottom teeth.

"Uh, thanks." Alex looked at the room and felt immediately frustrated, the way she would feel faced with a particularly challenging maths question. Her obstacle was, of course, the red rope. It ran along from the door across the whole room so that the tiny crowd could only squeeze in at one end. It was a beautiful library, despite the peeling wallpaper and obvious traces of woodworm. On the far wall was a desk and on the desk piles of papers. And there was also a locked cabinet. And somewhere in all the mess, Alex knew there lay a treasure map just waiting to be found.

"So to get away from his family, often the master of the house would come up to his study," the little old lady squeaked, "and I think you gentlemen would appreciate this," she added, winking at the two older men in the room. She stepped over the rope and went to the bookshelf on the right-hand side. She pressed a button and the whole shelf opened like a door. "Now this was the master's secret entrance for his mistress." There were a few giggles. "So, ladies, I would advise looking for a secret button like this around your house!" And she laughed until she coughed. "Or you could," she continued hoarsely, "do what the lady of the house did and have a portrait of yourself hung over his desk to remind him where his loyalty lies."

Alex was shocked. She had seen the door many times before, and had made up many a story of her discovering a secret door like it somewhere in her uncle's doorknob shop. But she had somehow completely forgotten this one existed. She now felt she knew for certain that the map must be somewhere behind that door. She stood silently watching as people moved in and out of the library. There was not going to be any opportunity to get through that door today, that was certain. The thought was incredibly frustrating. Suddenly she was almost knocked off her feet.

"Ow!" exclaimed the little old lady, who had bumped into her. "What do you think you are doing, standing so quietly like that! You really must be far more careful. I could have been seriously injured! Have you no respect for your elders?"

Alex apologized as she steadied herself. But she wondered exactly what she was meant to be doing. Jumping up and down and yelling, "Look at me, I'm over here, be careful not to walk into me!"?

She sighed heavily. Since there was nothing more she could do in the library, and since she just seemed to be in the way, she moved out into the next room, which was the lady's boudoir. Maybe there is a clue here, she thought, rallying her spirits. She smiled at the new old lady who was much shorter than the rest, with bright blue hair.

"Please ask me any questions you have," she said, her breath smelling of garlic. Alex looked around the room and stopped. There on the wall, just above the desk with the little pots of make-up and a fan and embroidery, was a large framed painting of an island.

"Um, could you tell me about that painting?"

"Oh, I am so glad you asked, dear," replied the little old lady, spit flying out of her mouth. "It is of an uncharted island, somewhere far out to sea. Now, I don't know if you know about the tale of Alistair Steele and the Infamous Wigpowder. . ."

"Yes, I do – very well," she said quickly. She hated it when people took too long getting to the heart of the story.

"Come in, sir, don't be shy," spat the little old lady.

Alex turned to see a very large gentleman with a big bushy beard, dressed in a three-piece suit complete with bowler hat, enter the room. He seemed intensely uncomfortable around so many breakable objects.

"I heard what you were saying. Keep going," he said gruffly, eyeing a Ming vase and moving as far away from it as possible.

"Well, this is the island where Mr Steele found the Wigpowder treasure," she continued happily. "Of course, it is only an artist's rendering of what it could look like, painted many years after the fact. But it is very romantic to look at, isn't it?"

"So it doesn't tell you where the treasure is?" asked the gentleman, which Alex thought was quite a coincidence, as she was about to ask the same thing.

"Oh, my goodness, no. This is more a picture of what the ideal treasure island might look like. If you want to know what the island really looked like you would have to see Mr Steele's map."

"Do you have the map?" asked Alex. The man started

and looked at her.

"No, no. That was lost years ago."

"Have you looked for the map?" asked the gentleman. Both he and Alex were now standing very close to the little old lady.

"I have no use for a map. Now, I think we have had enough learning for today. There are many other wonderful rooms to visit," she said sharply and gestured for them to leave. The gentleman and Alex looked at each other and then quietly stepped out of the room.

"Excuse me, excuse me, sir," called out the little old lady. The gentleman stopped. "You dropped your monocle."

The gentleman reached out and snatched it from her hand.

"Old bat," he muttered and hurried down the hall.

"No manners!" called the little old lady after the gentleman.

Alex visited some more of the other rooms to no avail. The hour passed quickly and she went downstairs to meet Mr Underwood in the gift shop. He was in a heated struggle over the last copy of *The Glorious History of the Steele Estate* with a man who had strangely decided to bring a hammer sightseeing with him.

"I'm sorry, but I am very certain I did have the book first," Mr Underwood was saying.

"No," said the man, his greasy red hair falling in his eyes.

"Um, actually, yes. I had it in my hands, and you snatched it."

"Mine!" grunted the man and tugged at the book again.

Mr Underwood tugged back. The man tugged again. There was much tugging.

"Mr Underwood?" said Alex, approaching him.

"Hello, Alex." Mr Underwood tugged a final time and flew halfway across the room. The red-haired man had let go suddenly. He was staring at Mr Underwood, wide-eyed.

"Thank you," Mr Underwood said to him, pushing his hair out of his face and readjusting his glasses. He turned to Alex. "Let me just pay for this, and then we can go back to your uncle's shop."

"But, Mr Underwood, I haven't been up to the top floor yet. That's what I was coming to tell you," whined Alex.

"I'm sorry, Alex, but we really have to get back. We promised your uncle we would help him unload his latest shipment of doorknobs." He handed over the cash to the little old lady at the cash, who jumped, clasping her hand to her heart, as the register popped open. He turned and almost walked right into the large gentleman with the monocle.

"Watch it!" the gentleman said.

"Sorry," Mr Underwood replied meekly. "Come on, Alex, let's go."

Alex sighed, and she and Mr Underwood left the house and headed down the hill, both of them feeling disappointed – of course Alex more so than Mr Underwood.

Because Alex had no idea that these two men were to change the course of her rather pleasant little life in only a few hours, she had paid little attention to them in the shop. However, because we do know how important they are, I think it is only right to leave Alex for a brief moment and go back up the hill to watch what happened after she and Mr Underwood left.

"No luck," the gentleman said, joining the greasy red-haired man.

But the greasy red-haired man wasn't listening. "Underwood!" he said, pointing through the window at the pair with his hammer.

"Really?" replied the gentleman, replacing his monocle and squinting after them. "I don't suppose he said where he was staying?"

"Shop!"

"You idiot. Do you know how many shops there are here? It's a bloody tourist town!"

The red-haired man's mouth twitched into a smile. He started to giggle.

There was a great rush of movement, a bit like a tornado, that caused the little old lady at the cash register to scream and duck behind her desk. Suddenly the greasy red-haired man found himself swept off his feet and pressed into the wall of the shop. "You got something to say, eh, Jack old boy?"

Jack giggled.

The gentleman raised him higher into the air. "You moron! Say what you gotta say, you pathetic little weasel!"

"What's going on?"

Released, Jack fell to the floor and lay there, shaking with laughter.

"Oh, ah, hey," said the gentleman, turning to face the man with a black silk scarf tied around his face. "Jack's being an idiot. He's got something to say, but just can't seem to get the word out."

There was a pause. Then slowly the third man's dog guided him to Jack's side. The man knelt down beside him and brought what remained of his ear close.

"Tell me, Jack." The voice was low and smooth.

Jack was so giddy with excitement that the word

came out in barely a whisper. It wasn't a particularly fancy word, I'm sure you or I could have thought of at least a dozen that were far more interesting. But it was exactly the word the third man had wanted to hear. And this is what it was:

"Doorknobs."

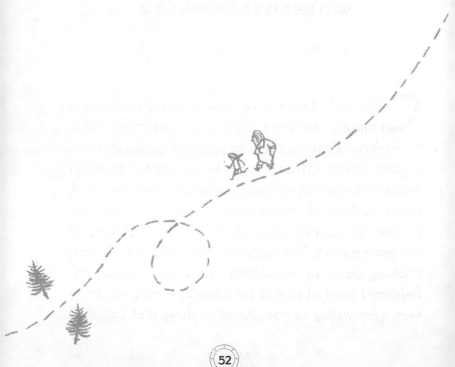

THE SEVENTH CHAPTER

In which we learn the nature of coffee-table books and return to the Steele Estate

Coffee-table books make whatever their content is infinitely attractive. This is because coffee-table books have glorious pictures in them with saturated colours. Often coffee-table books can make the dullest or most disgusting subjects romantic. Like mould. A coffee-table book about mould would have glorious pictures of emerald-green glistening mould shining in the morning sun. You could be convinced that there is nothing quite so wonderful as having a good old-fashioned bowl of mould for a snack. Which would be very, very wrong of you. Another thing that could be made to look romantic in a coffee-table book is a deteriorating old building that sits atop a hill and was once owned by a philanthropist. And that was exactly what *The Glorious History of the Steele Estate* did.

Alex was having a sleepless night. She was wholly dissatisfied with the events of the day. But she had high hopes of the coffee-table book she was now reading by the small lamp on her bedside table. To be more precise, she was looking at the pictures. Now, it isn't that Alex didn't like to read – on the contrary, she quite enjoyed the activity – but her picture-looking was due, once again, to the nature of coffee-table books. Coffee-table books are written to be so extremely dull that you can't do anything but give up and look at the pictures. And you always start by reading the book, you always really, really try, but it is no good. No matter how hard you focus, your eyes will start to glaze over, your mind will begin to wander.

So Alex was looking at the pictures. She had stopped on the chapter about the library where the story about the master's mistress had been told. In the bottom corner of the left-hand page was a picture of the lady of the house's portrait, and taking up the whole of the right was a picture of the secret door, a close-up of the bookshelf. Alex felt certain her hypothesis about the secret door was correct. She had noticed that the titles of the books on the shelf had one common theme. *Mutiny on the Bounty, Kidnapped, Robinson Crusoe* – all involved the sea and ships. What else would one hide behind such a door?

The only problem that remained was sneaking past the little old ladies. They might be small, but they were tough. That thought caused Alex instinctively to rub the bruise she had developed on her shoulder from when the little old lady in the library had gone barging into her side. She stopped. She furrowed her eyebrows. She had an idea. It was absurd, but it just might work. Quickly she turned off the light and curled up under the covers. She had now completely made up her mind that tomorrow, first thing, she would return to the house to investigate.

She sneaked out early the next morning, toothbrush firmly secured in pocket (as, of course, we know, she never went anywhere without it, and it was quite possible she would be out of the house until after lunch, when she would need to use it). Alex knew Mr Underwood wouldn't be keen on going back to the house so soon, and her uncle wouldn't let her go without him, so she had no choice but to sneak out. It would be a perfect day to look for the map. The house on the hill closed early on Sundays, and there would be far fewer people visiting.

She went to pay for her ticket and was greeted by

Poppy again, who eyed her suspiciously. "Where's your adult?" she asked slowly.

"I am supposed to meet him in the library," Alex lied.

Poppy looked at her carefully. There was a tense moment before, "Well, all right, dear," said Poppy, taking her money. "Now, here is your map, and there are guides in each room, so you can ask them anything you want, and remember: don't touch anything, and stay behind the red ropes."

Alex nodded and headed up to the library. She decided that she didn't like Poppy. The old lady definitely gave her the creeps.

Alex entered the library, startling the little old lady sitting in the corner reading *Lady Chatterley's Lover*.

"Oh my," she said, putting aside her book. "Well, aren't we early this morning?"

"I just really like history," said Alex awkwardly.

"I see," replied the little old lady, her tongue grazing the base of her upper teeth to make sure they were still in place. There was a long silence. "Any questions, dear?"

"No, thank you. I just want to look." And Alex moved to the red rope and stood silently staring into the room. The plan was to stay this way until the little old lady forgot she was there, just like the last time when she had bumped into her. She would stand still until she became invisible.

"Well, dear, I'm just going to sit back with my book,

then. You let me know if you do have any questions."
She sat down again and continued with her reading.

At the start, Alex could tell that the little old lady was looking at her occasionally, but as the minutes ticked by, she could sense her settling back into her novel. No one came in. And neither of them left. So the two of them continued in this way for a good hour, standing and reading.

Now standing perfectly still is exhausting and goes completely against the nature of a ten-and-a-half-year-old, but Alex knew it was absolutely necessary. She could feel her neck get stiff and sore and her feet start to hurt. However, she was also the sort of child who, when she put her mind to it, could do anything, and, boy, she wanted to get behind that door. There was a treasure map on the line, as well as Mr Underwood's inheritance at stake! Eventually, and I do mean eventually, her patience paid off. Two hours later, in came another little old lady.

"Tea, Grace?"

"Oh good. I need a little something after reading that last bit." And the two laughed in a way that Alex thought sounded an awful lot like the way she imagined witches would laugh. But they both left, neither of them noticing she was still there.

Maybe their vision is based on movement, thought

Alex as she carefully stepped over the red rope. Because of all their warnings, Alex half expected a cage to fall from the ceiling and trap her. But nothing happened, not even an alarm, and Alex quickly went over to the secret door.

Without waiting – as she knew well enough that, in stories, if you wait or think for too long, you get caught – she pushed the button, and the door opened. Stepping through it, she stopped on the landing. As the door closed automatically behind her, she waited slowly for her eyes to adjust to the dark. Anyone else might have felt slightly nervous at the prospect of heading down those rickety old stairs to the unknown below. But Alex was too excited to consider her situation particularly dangerous.

She went down the stairs and found herself in a small square room with a window way up at the top of the far wall. The room was very plain. To one side there was an old wine rack with a few dusty bottles of wine, the surfaces of which were covered in a thick dust with the odd fingerprint. On the right side was a small door, sealed with a rusty padlock, that Alex assumed was used by Mr Steele's mistress. And in the centre was a table laid out as it might have been back in the olden days. A lead candlestick stood in the middle and two plates were laid with two sets of cutlery. Why it was arranged like this when none of the public would see it, Alex didn't understand, but that thought was put out of her mind when she saw a dusty old book lying on the floor by the table.

Alex bent over and picked it up and smiled. On the cover was printed "*Treasure Island*". She opened it carefully. What she felt next was a mixture of pride and disappointment. The book indeed had been used to hide something, as its centre had been hollowed out, so she was right in that Steele had hidden something behind the secret door. Unfortunately, however, the hollow was just that – hollow. In other words, empty. Alex sighed. She had hit a dead end. And she had been so sure.

Not wanting to waste any more time, Alex turned on her heel and climbed back up the stairs. She put her ear to the door. It sounded quiet, but of course she couldn't be positive no one was there, as Grace had read in virtual silence aside from the odd clicking sound from her dentures. Alex hadn't been down there all that long, and the probability was that the longer she waited, the more likely Grace would return from having tea. So she risked it and opened the door. The room was still empty. Smiling, she quickly stepped through the door, darted across the room and climbed back over the rope. And just in the nick of time, too, because Grace reappeared from around the corner and looked at her.

"You still here?" she asked.

"I guess I can move on now," said Alex happily. She left the room and headed downstairs.

Alex decided she might as well go home. It had been a long morning, and she hadn't had any breakfast yet. Besides, she was keen to help her uncle display the latest doorknobs that had arrived the day before. She was at the door, passing Poppy, when she heard something very strange. It was the sound of her own name. Her own name wasn't that strange, really. In fact there were three Alexes in her year-six class alone, two boys and herself. But hearing it in the manor house on the hill spoken by a Daughter of the Founding Fathers' Preservation Society when she hadn't told it to her in the first place was distinctly odd.

"Alex!" called out Grace. Alex turned to see the little old lady stumbling down the stairs towards her.

"Yes?" answered Alex politely, furrowing her eyebrows in confusion.

"I thought so," said Grace with a wide toothy smile as she approached her. She grabbed Alex by the arm. The grip wasn't strong but it was firm. And it didn't much matter anyway as Alex wasn't struggling, too confused to do anything. "I believe you forgot this," said Grace as she held out Alex's blue toothbrush holder, her name printed clearly in black ink.

"Thank you," said Alex, taking it back from Grace,

but already it was dawning on her what had happened.

Poppy exchanged a knowing look with Grace and then approached Alex, looking her firmly in the eye. "Now aren't you a naughty child," she said, relishing every word. "I thought I had made it perfectly clear that you were not allowed past the red rope."

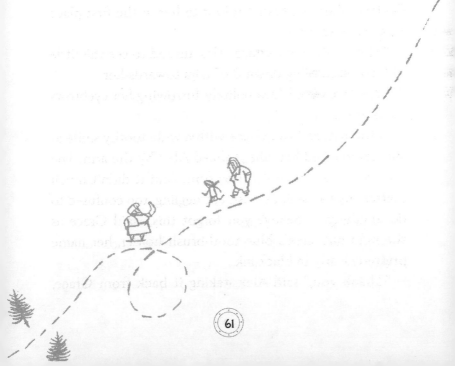

THE EIGHTH CHAPTER

In which Alex suffers a number of Strange and Unusual Punishments

You know those doors in public places that read "Staff Only" or "Restricted, Authorized Personnel Only"? Well, I've always imagined that behind those doors are Joys Beyond Your Wildest Imaginings. Like maybe a table full of cakes and a butler to serve them to you, and silk pyjamas to change into, and your favourite movie playing on a large video screen. Now Alex didn't have exactly the same fantasy as I do, but she had always been just as curious about what was behind those doors. So despite feeling slightly anxious as to what was going to happen to her, Alex couldn't help being kind of excited at the prospect of seeing what was on the other side of the door she and Poppy were facing.

She needn't have been.

Alex was ushered into an average-sized room. The floor was covered by an orange and green abstract design carpet. On the walls were plastered yellowing posters of the Steele Estate and the surrounding tourist attractions. And forming a circle were half a dozen cushy chairs, all of varying sizes and shapes, and all of varying nauseating colours. Like pink and aubergine. In the corner stood a table with a kettle and used mugs and splashes of brown in dusty puddles.

Poppy sat Alex down in a large turquoise, yellow and lilac chair that smelled of cat.

"So what do you have to say for yourself?" she wheezed, leaning down over Alex so that her skin fell forward, hanging off her face.

"Well. . ."

"I'll tell you what I think, shall I? I think you thought you would get away with it. I think you thought, 'Wouldn't it be funny to break the rules? Wouldn't it be exciting?' Well is it? Do you find this exciting?"

Alex looked at Poppy's watery eyes. She noticed there was still sleep in the corners that had accumulated, a sort of brownish grey.

Once more she started, "I. . ."

"What a little adventure, eh? Well, you got caught, ducky. And now you have to be punished." And Poppy stood up, looking around the room. Grace was giggling to herself behind her. She walked over to the kettle and poured a cup of water, filling it up to the brim. "Come here, small person." Alex stood and crossed the room. "I would like you to hold this mug above your head until I come back."

"I'm sorry?" asked Alex. She didn't quite understand.

"It's too late for apologies now, ducky. You just hold this mug over your head, and Grace will stay and make sure you don't put it down. Because if you do. . ." Poppy took her pen out from behind her ear and poked Alex's arm.

"Ow!" Alex rubbed the spot where she had been poked.

"Now, I'll be back once it's closing time."

"Um, I don't think so," said Alex again, putting down the mug and walking towards the door. "Look, I understand what I did was wrong, but my uncle is going to worry if I don't come home soon, and. . ."

"What?! What?!" Poppy wheeled around. She grabbed Alex by her shirt and flung her to the ground. Alex lay there, shocked. "You leave, ducky, and I'll call the police and tell them about your little trespassing jaunt! Perhaps you'd feel more comfortable in a jail cell!"

Alex shook her head.

"What was that?"

"No, ma'am."

"Better. Grace, I leave her to you." She pointed to the mug, and, with a final sneer, swept out of the room.

"You heard her," giggled Grace. Alex looked at her. Didn't she see what Poppy had just done?

"This is wrong!" she stuttered as she rose to her feet.

"Do it!"

Slowly Alex picked up the mug and held it above her head, desperately thinking of what she could do to get herself out of this situation. She didn't want the police to be called – after all she had been doing something wrong – and what would be her defence? "I'm sorry, officer, I was looking for a treasure map," was no excuse for breaking the law. Or, at least, the rules.

As she stood there thinking hard, it suddenly occurred to her that her hands were going numb. Holding that mug above her head had caused the blood to drain from her hands, down her arms, and collect somewhere about her shoulders. The unfairness of the situation burned in Alex's cheeks.

Hours passed before Poppy returned. Now, I forgot to mention that Poppy wore flat brown shoes with a wooden heel. And I am sorry I forgot, because this is important. Wherever she would go there would be this dull click with each step she took. And when Alex heard the click-click of her shoes getting steadily louder down the hall, she couldn't decide if it would be better for Poppy to come back, so she could put down her arms, or worse because of what might yet happen to her. Philosophy is sort of silly like that. We spend all this time wondering why things exist, instead of dealing with the fact that they do. And, in any event, there wasn't much point in Alex questioning her situation because Poppy was coming back whether she liked it or not.

"Did it cheat?" Poppy asked Grace when she stepped into the room carrying the box containing the day's takings.

"Oh it tried, but," and Grace gave a giggle, "I made sure it didn't."

"That's a lie!" said Alex, who, if anything, was always very proud that she did what she was told by authority figures.

"You be quiet, small person," snapped Poppy, sitting down. She opened the box and began to count the money. Which was not a lot since it was Sunday and was even less after she pocketed half of it. "Oh, put your arms down for goodness' sake," she said, glancing up at Alex. "Don't be tiresome."

Alex lowered her arms and felt all the blood rushing back to her fingertips, causing an overwhelming tingling sensation.

Poppy sat back in her chair and sighed luxuriously. "Grace, get a bottle, would you? The others should be finished locking up soon," she said. "And you," she turned to Alex, "give an old lady a foot massage." She propped her feet up on a lime-coloured ottoman and Grace slowly stood and left the room.

Alex walked over and sat on the ground. "Um . . . ma'am. . .?"

"Speak up! Show some respect for your elders!" wheezed Poppy.

"I was wondering . . . you know, why you were keeping me here and stuff?"

Poppy looked down her chin at her and snorted.

Alex sighed inwardly. "Fine, then maybe I should call my uncle. If I'm going to be here a while. He's probably concerned about me."

Poppy snorted again. "I don't think we need to worry about that. Bad children such as you usually result from poor parenting. I doubt he knows you've gone. And even if he knows, I doubt he cares. Now massage my feet before I lose my temper!"

Alex took off Poppy's click-click shoes and pulled off her beige stockings, which had gathered around her ankles. Her feet were very smelly and very wrinkled and very, very moist. Yes, her feet were as disgusting as you could possibly imagine, and since that is the case there is no need to describe the horror of the foot massage that followed. Let's just say it went on for far too long and stopped only when the other four ladies finally joined them.

So let me introduce you formally to all five Daughters of the Founding Fathers' Preservation Society. There was Poppy – we know her well. She was the leader. And Grace with her little book. And then there was Mabel. You might remember her telling Alex about the treasure island painting and that she spat a lot when she talked, and her breath smelled of garlic and she had bright blue hair. And next there was Gladys, who worked in the gift shop. Alex concluded that she must have been rather paranoid because she would jump at the slightest sound, and would nervously examine the door every five minutes. And finally there was Rose, who was quite tall for an old lady and had long white hair and wore overalls, and the reason for this was that she was in charge of fixing things when they broke. Which was very often. And which she wasn't any good at. In fact, she just made things worse. And all Daughters wore the same flat click-click shoes so that when they walked in a group they sounded like a herd of sheep wearing tap shoes.

They all made themselves comfortable in the cushy chairs while Poppy passed out their share of her pocketed takings.

"Ooh, this is lovely," crooned Mabel. "I bet Grace is going to go right out and buy herself a pair of frilly knickers!" And all the little old ladies laughed and then coughed and then laughed some more.

"Well, pour the wine, urchin!" screeched Poppy, remembering Alex and indicating the bottle Grace had brought back with her. Alex, who had never opened a bottle of wine in her life, approached it with trepidation. There was a rusty sharp and twisted corkscrew sitting next to it. The bottle was covered in a thick layer of dust apart from where Grace's firm (but not particularly strong) grip had left fingerprints. Alex suddenly recognized what she was looking at.

"You're stealing Mr Steele's wine," she said indignantly. She had an idea. "And if you don't let me go, when the police come, I'll tell them all about it!"

"How dare you threaten us with such a thing?" said Poppy coldly. "We are responsible for all the items in this house. If we didn't drink the wine, it would go bad."

"That would be awful," squeaked Gladys, who was curled into a tight ball in a brown and white chair, eyeing Alex with deep suspicion.

"But a full bottle of wine doesn't go bad!" insisted Alex.

"Everything goes bad. Even sticky sweet children turn bad, don't they, Alex dear?" said Poppy, the tone of her voice becoming dangerously soft.

To ease her frustration, Alex picked up the rusted corkscrew and jammed it into the bottle. With much effort she managed to free the cork from the bottle. She looked at the dirty mugs with caked-on tea in the bottom and lipstick on the rim sitting on the table in front of her.

"What are you waiting for? We aren't getting any younger, you know!" shouted Rose with a deep voice.

Alex made a face and poured five mugs of wine. She handed one to each of the Daughters, who grabbed it out of her hands greedily, not seeming to notice that the mugs hadn't been cleaned yet. They slurped and chugged and held out their mugs for more, and Alex ran from Daughter to Daughter, pouring mug after mug until the bottle was empty and Grace disappeared to bring back another from the secret room. When she returned the whole thing started again.

Alex had just finished filling Gladys's glass again, which was a tricky task considering her tender nerves caused her to shake constantly, and was heading to fill Mabel's when it happened.

Mabel had been talking about her latest trip to Italy: "There were days I just had to sit around in my birthday suit it was so hot!" A puddle had accumulated at the base of her chair from the spit that flew freely from her mouth as she spoke. But Alex hadn't noticed, and suddenly she found herself skidding, landing on Mabel and spilling the contents of the wine bottle on her lap.

Alex was up in an instant, apologizing profusely. Staggering to a standing position, Mabel slapped Alex hard across the face. "You clumsy oaf!" She looked down at herself. "You've ruined my best blouse!" She collapsed back into her chair and, pulling the base of her shirt up to her mouth, began to suck off the wine. Alex was stunned. She had never been hit before. What sort of grown-up hits a child? Her shock quickly vanished and soon she was shaking with rage. That was it!

Sometimes our bodies do things without our instructing them to. So it was that, in this case, Alex found her body running towards the door to the room, flinging it open and racing down the hall to the grand stairwell. Only when her body reached the front entrance did it decide to relinquish control over Alex and wait patiently for her to tell it what to do next. This was an unfortunate turn of events because, in this brief transition of power, Alex found herself rooted to the spot, giving Poppy and Rose ample time to catch up with her.

Poppy sneered at her as she grabbed Alex by the shoulder. Then Rose pinned Alex's arms roughly behind her, and the two of them dragged Alex back to the staffroom.

"Never do that again, ducky," panted Poppy, "or I swear you will live to regret it." She turned to Rose. "Go solder all those bloody exits shut. Every last one of them!"

Brandishing her soldering iron, Rose gave a small nod and left the room.

"Go sit in the corner and make yourself invisible until we can think of what to do with you next," said Poppy, pointing a bony finger towards a dark corner across the room. "And not a peep or. . ." and she brandished her pen.

Alex nodded numbly, went to where Poppy had directed her, and sat down. In the corner with her were three books and a mousetrap with a dead mouse in it, and the carpet felt damp and smelled of mould (not that sparkling green mould that it would be fun to eat a bowl of, but that real mould that is harmful to your health).

She could feel tears welling up in her eyes. But she knew she mustn't cry, despite all the unfairness. Alex always had worked very hard to do the right thing in her life, and the one time she crossed the line, or the rope as the case may be, she got held hostage and abused horribly! All she wanted now was to go home. Alex couldn't stop thinking about her uncle. Why hadn't he come for her yet? If only she had left a note. He was probably very anxious and would be very angry when she got back. And Mr Underwood would be very disappointed in her as well.

But then when she told them about how she had been treated . . . that she had had to hold a mug of water over her head, and massage Poppy's feet, and serve stolen wine, and above all been slapped in the face! – well, they would be so upset that they would forget about getting angry at her. They would immediately Take Legal Action against the Daughters of the Founding Fathers' Preservation Society. This made Alex smile. Hope has that effect on a person.

As Alex tried to make herself as comfortable as she could in her little corner, she decided that, while she waited, perhaps there was a way to take advantage of her situation. After all, here she was trapped in a building that she knew somewhere housed a treasure map. There must be a way to convince the old ladies to allow her to wander through the house, especially now that the exits had all been soldered shut. She wasn't yet sure how, but she was just going to have to work it out.

However, first she must look nonchalant. Alex reached over the mousetrap and picked up the three books.

And that's when Alex found the map.

THE NINTH CHAPTER

In which Alex finds the map

Of the three books Alex had picked up, she had chosen to look at a worn copy of *The Glorious History of the Steele Estate* because, as we know, she quite enjoyed looking at the pictures in it. She had inadvertently flipped open the book to that same page about the library she had studied only just the night before. And her eyes had hazily scanned down to the portrait of the lady of the house in the bottom-left corner. Everything then had suddenly come into focus. The sharp look behind those bright green eyes, the curls in her long dark hair, and the letter N on the fan she held coyly half open by her ear.

The letter N?

And. . .

A little arrow. . .

Of course! Alex knew from geography class that every map had an N and an arrow to indicate which way was north. Alex thought more. The mere fact that a little old lady said the painting had been put up to keep an eye on the master of the house didn't mean that it was true. What if the painting had been put up after he had died? What if the lady of the house wanted to leave a clue behind, just in case something happened to her? And a lady as selfish as she was would have wanted to keep that map in her sights at every moment. What better way than to put it on her fan, something she would keep with her all the time?

Alex's heart began to race. It was perfectly clear to her where the fan was. She had seen it, but she had been so preoccupied by the painting of the island that she hadn't really focused on it. But she now clearly remembered the fan sitting on the small table directly beneath it.

She glanced up at the Daughters, fearing that somehow they could read her mind, but they were laughing and lolling in their revolting armchairs and didn't seem to remember she was still in the room. Alex wasn't sure what to do. Oh, come on, she begged her brain, how are we going to get that fan? If only she had noticed the picture last night. If only she had gone straight to the lady of the house's bedroom and grabbed the fan. She wouldn't have gone to the library, and she wouldn't have gone behind the door. She wouldn't have been unsure whether or not it was safe to come back into the library, and she wouldn't have rushed to get back to the correct side of the red rope, and then she wouldn't have dropped her toothbrush.

Toothbrush.

She stood up and walked over to Poppy, who, when she saw her, automatically poked her in the arm with her pen.

Alex winced.

"What do you want?" she slurred, her eyes closed.

"I need to brush my teeth," said Alex.

"Tough."

"If you don't let me brush my teeth, when the police come I'll tell them all about how Mabel hit me and stuff and maybe I will even say that you kicked me too," she said.

Grace giggled.

Poppy opened her eyes.

"Look, I just want to brush my teeth. If you want, you could let someone take me. How about Gladys? She's only had two glasses of wine." Alex prepared herself for another poke.

But Poppy just looked at her with a sneer. After a

long look, she relaxed back into her chair, closing her eyes. "Oh, go on, then. Gladys, take her."

Gladys opened her eyes wide. "But, Poppy, it's all dark out there now."

"I said do it, Gladys."

Gladys uncurled herself nervously and stood up.

She and Alex left the room and walked down the dark corridor towards the toilets. With each step they took, the floor creaked, and with each creak Gladys whimpered. They reached the toilets, and Gladys stood over her as Alex opened the blue carrying case and took out her toothbrush and brushed her teeth. Then they turned around and headed back to the room. And when they were halfway down the hall by the grand staircase, Alex stopped suddenly.

"What, what is it?" asked Gladys, jumping.

"I thought I heard a noise from upstairs. It was probably nothing, though." Alex looked up the dark staircase and shuddered.

"What . . . what did it sound like?" whispered Gladys, grabbing on to her arm.

"I don't know. A little like an axe murderer trying to be very quiet, so he could wait for us all to be asleep and then kill us. But I could be wrong," whispered Alex in return.

Gladys began to moan softly to herself. "What are we going to do?"

"Well, I could go up and look, I guess."

"But you could be killed!"

"Or we could wait until tonight. . ."

"Oh, go look! I'll stay here."

Alex nodded and gave Gladys's hand a comforting pat. She took a deep breath and headed up the dark stairs. Everything was going exactly as she had planned, but Alex couldn't help but wonder if maybe there actually was an axe murderer waiting for her in the darkness ahead. She turned down the darkened hallway, and instead of going into the library, which just a few hours ago would have been her first choice, she turned the other way and entered the lady's boudoir.

A stream of moonlight filtered through the window on to the floor. Alex's heart began to race again, and Alex took that as a sign that she was nervous. And when she had crossed the room and picked up the lady of the house's fan, the one that sat beneath the painting of the island, she noticed her hand was shaking as well.

Delicately Alex opened the fan, half afraid it might crumble in her hands as old things have a tendency to do. But it didn't, thank goodness or we wouldn't have much of a story from now on. She opened it. First she saw the N and the arrow, and then some writing and then a drawing that was shaped not entirely unlike, but not entirely like, the painting that was hanging directly above her head. Alex felt giddy, like when you get a perfect grade for your maths test. Here, after generations of Wigpowders and Steeles had fruitlessly searched, a ten-and-a-half-year-old girl had found the Infamous Wigpowder's treasure map!

Alex knew exactly what to do next. She took her toothbrush holder, opened it and took out her damp toothbrush. Looking around the room, Alex decided to hide it under the pillow on the bed. She then carefully folded the fan up again and with fingers crossed placed it in the toothbrush container. It fitted, just barely, but it fitted. Alex sighed with relief. She put the holder back into her pocket and left to go back downstairs.

As she reached the top of the staircase, Alex paused. When she went back down the stairs to rejoin Gladys, she would soon find herself in that room again with all the Daughters. And who knew when they would let her back out? If there was going to be a time for Alex to try to escape, this would be it.

She tiptoed back into the lady's boudoir, and took stock of the room. She was too high up to go through a window. And of course all the exits were soldered shut downstairs by a very vigilant Rose. There must be a way, she thought. Come on, Alex! She needed more time.

"Gladys, you there?" she called out, trying to make her voice shake a bit.

"Oh, my goodness! Yes, are you all right?"

"Well, the boudoir window was open, so I'm going to take a look around up here, just to make sure the axe murderer isn't hiding in a wardrobe or anything."

A sound like "eep" floated up in response.

"Won't be a minute!"

Alex crossed the hall into the dark library. She looked out of the window – again a steep drop down. She could see her town twinkling in the distance. It was infuriating how close she was to escape, and yet so far! There must be a way. There was always a solution to any problem, you just had to find it. Alex turned and shivered. The moonlight lit the portrait of Mr Steele's wife in such a way that the eyes seemed to glow as they stared right at her. Alex held the toothbrush holder tight to her chest.

And then it occurred to her.

There was one exit that possibly Rose had missed.

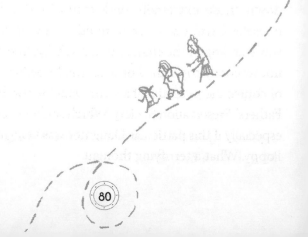

THE TENTH CHAPTER

In which Alex is rather impressive

I think it is rather impressive that in her delicate emotional state, Alex was able to remember the secret door used by Mr Steele's mistress in the secret room. Equally as impressive was the fact that she was able to make her way down those extremely dark stairs hidden behind the bookshelf, without a torch, mind, and that although she was standing in the middle of a pitch-black room she was not remotely frightened of what might be in there. Except of course the potential of a sixth Daughter of the Founding Fathers' Preservation Society. Which seemed quite possible, especially if this particular Daughter was being punished by Poppy. What a terrifying thought.

Alex stuck her arms out ahead of her and felt her way to the door. She felt for the padlock; it was dusty and rough to the touch and not at all like a soldered lock would feel. So far so good, she thought. Alex grabbed and pulled. The rusted padlock made a slight cracking sound, but stayed firmly in place. Trying to stay calm, Alex thought hard. The key thing was not to panic. She remembered a story of a friend of her uncle's who had managed to get his head stuck in between the rungs of a ladder under water, and, instead of panicking, he had thought for a moment and then calmly turned his head to the side and slipped out. She needed to stay just as collected in order to save herself. She had to look at this problem logically.

The lock was old and had given way slightly. This meant she was on the right track with trying to break it. What she needed was something to hit it with. Well, what was in the room that she could use?

In school there are certain games that seem really useless. There is a game, for example, in which you have all these objects on a table, and then you have to close your eyes and try to remember them all. Now when on earth are you ever going to be in a situation where you will need to remember all the objects on a table? Well, let this be proof to you that even the most useless-seeming games can actually be excellent life lessons.

Because Alex remembered a table in the room with objects on it. And now she needed to remember what they were. Her future depended on it.

It was set as if for a dinner party, she thought, with plates and knives and forks. Maybe she could pick the lock with a fork. But that was a silly thought because she hadn't the foggiest idea how to pick a lock. And . . . there . . . was . . . what else was there? There was . . . there were candlesticks! Alex stumbled over to the table and felt around for a bit and grabbed a candlestick. To her joy the candlestick was heavy, really heavy. Now the question was whether she was strong enough to break the lock.

Alex returned to the door and found the lock again. She took the candlestick and hit it. It made a dull thud. She did it again, and again. Her adrenalin was pumping, and if she had to she could keep hitting that lock all night. But fortunately she didn't have to, because after her seventh hit, there was a sudden crack and shatter, and the lock fell, smashing on to the floor. Alex pulled the chain out from the door handle and tugged on the door. And it opened. Slowly and only a crack, but it opened. She pulled again, and she felt a gust of fresh air on her face. Light flooded the room, which is funny because it was dark outside, it being night-time and all, but it was still lighter outside than inside. Being small for her age, Alex didn't need to open the door any further. She slipped outside into the car park, and, without looking back, hurried down the hill away from the house.

It was the best feeling in the world running away from the Steele Estate, seeing the large, grand home get smaller and smaller, and as she found herself back in the familiar deserted streets of her town, a smile crossed her face. She would soon be home in her own bed. She would soon be telling her uncle of the horrible way she had been treated and presenting Mr Underwood with the treasure map. The only thing that disappointed her slightly was that she wouldn't get to see the look on Poppy's face when she realized she was gone. That thought made her laugh out loud and she turned her run into a sprint.

Because Alex wasn't there to see it I thought I'd tell you exactly what Poppy's look looked like. It looked like one of those pug dogs about to bite the postman. Which is a very funny expression, especially on the face of a Daughter of the Founding Fathers' Preservation Society. Of course, none of her fellow Daughters laughed. Especially not Gladys. They were all busy ducking furniture and tea mugs being thrown in their general direction. When she had finally exhausted herself, Poppy sat in her chair and reached for the telephone.

My dear friend, let this be a warning to you. In life, you will find there are certain things you are able to get away with like, for example, not washing your socks for a week, if you have tolerant friends. But there are other things, far more serious things, that I am afraid, no matter how carefully you plan, no matter who is on your side, you simply do not get away with. You do not get away with robbing a bank, that's a good one. Another one is murder, you do not get away with that. You also do not get away with not calling your mother, so just don't try not to. And, my friend, above all things, you most definitely, definitely, do not get away with stepping over the red rope.

THE ELEVENTH CHAPTER

In which a very unpleasant discovery is made

What is a bad sign? Perhaps one that has mud all over it, so you can't read how far it is until the next motorway services. Or perhaps one that is so rebellious that no matter how many times you write "Danger: Falling Rocks Ahead" it insists on saying "Do Come Over Here and Stand Under this Precariously Teetering Boulder". Or maybe one written in a non-existent language, like Flurbit.

I am sure you have seen such a sign, but the bad sign I am about to talk about isn't a piece of cardboard, or metal, or synthetic material with writing or a picture on it. In this case, it was a broken window. And a door. If you just saw a broken window and a door on the side of the road, you probably would think someone was renovating their house, and not take it as anything you needed to think about. But when Alex saw the broken window and the door, she thought, "Something isn't right." Because these bad signs were still very much attached to her house.

You see, when she had left the house that morning, as far as she could recall, the window in the front of her uncle's shop hadn't been broken. And also, while they had always had a door, it usually was on both its hinges and not just dangling off one. And this made Alex suspicious.

The next thing that concerned her was that all the lights were out. Certainly it was the middle of the night, and unless you are scared of the dark or have a great love for the electric company, you turn your lights off in the middle of the night. But Alex knew her uncle would definitely not be able to sleep without knowing she was safe, and thus would probably have had at least one light on.

So this was why Alex had a knot in her stomach as she crossed the bridge and approached the door. Now sometimes, and I don't know how it knows, the weather decides it wants to help with a certain situation by creating Atmosphere. At this moment, it decided to blow a gust of wind that rattled all the non-broken windows and properly attached doors of the buildings along the bridge. This made the knot in Alex's stomach tighten more, because it was scary. It also made her feel extra cold as she passed through the doorway into the shop. Even though it was her home, Alex felt like a stranger.

She heard a sudden creak of a floorboard and she turned abruptly, her heart in her throat. At the window stood a person silhouetted in the moonlight. "Alexandra Morningside?" asked the silhouette.

Alex took a step back. "Yes?"

The silhouette stepped towards her so that Alex could see the face. It was a young woman dressed in a police uniform. Having a police officer waiting for her was another bad sign.

"Alexandra, I'm afraid that there has been an Incident," said the officer.

Alex stood rooted to the spot. The word "Incident" frightened her to the core. This was because she knew that "Incident" didn't mean her uncle was held up at a meeting. She knew that the officer had decided that it would be easier to hear bad news if certain words were used as opposed to others, words like "Incident" for example. Of course it isn't the word itself that causes fear, but that which is being described, so changing a word doesn't actually help that much.

The young officer seemed to realize this and stopped in the middle of her prepared speech.

"I am afraid that . . . your uncle is dead."

"I see," said Alex. Her stomach, which had only moments ago been so tight, now vanished altogether, revealing a bottomless pit deep inside her. She clenched her fists, not out of rage, but because that was how her fists responded to the news.

"It would seem that some burglars visited your house. As far as we could see nothing was taken, but as they left they knocked over a bookshelf of doorknobs, and I am afraid it fell on your uncle." The officer's voice broke. "I am so sorry." She moved towards Alex and hesitantly placed a hand on her shoulder.

"Oh," said Alex. Her mind was a blank. There was nothing there. Nothing. Where was everything?

"If you wouldn't mind coming down to the station, we could take care of you," said the officer carefully.

A bespectacled face floated into Alex's consciousness. "What about Mr Underwood?" asked Alex, looking up at the officer for the first time.

"Who?" asked the young woman.

"Mr Underwood. Is he already at the station?"

The young woman shook her head. "I'm sorry, I don't know who this Mr Underwood is."

"Never mind," said Alex, thinking hard, trying to prod her mind into action. The officer guided Alex to the door. "No, wait!" Alex stopped. "Look, can I get some things and meet you there? I promise I'll come. I know I am only ten and a half, but I am very responsible. I just need some time alone," she said. After saying this, she realized it was true.

The officer looked concerned. "I don't know if I'm allowed to do that."

"You could say that . . . that you waited and waited but I never showed up, so you left me a note," offered Alex.

The young woman bit her lip.

"Please?"

The officer looked at Alex, who in the moonlight appeared even smaller than usual. But she also seemed fiercely determined. "I guess I could," she said hesitantly, "but you promise you'll come?"

"Of course."

The officer nodded and slowly walked out of the house, glancing over her shoulder at Alex as she passed through the door.

Once she was alone, Alex sat down on the floor cross-legged. Her grief was so overwhelming that she herself couldn't take it in. Her uncle. Her lovely, sweet, clever uncle. He was gone. Not to the market or a board meeting.

But gone . . . for ever. How could she even begin to comprehend what to do at a time like this? When her parents died, she had been too little to understand what had happened, so it wasn't as if she was familiar with feeling this way. What was she was supposed to feel then? Alex had no idea. She didn't even know if she should cry. She just felt numb. What she needed . . . what she needed . . . was Mr Underwood.

She stood up. Yes, she would not dwell on the actual horribleness of what had happened. She couldn't afford to think about that at the moment. What she needed to do was figure out where Mr Underwood had got to, find him, and then he would take care of everything else.

With that in mind, the first thing she needed to do was pack her bag. She was heading for the stairs to climb to her room when she tripped on something small and square. Leaning down, she picked up her camera. Alex was puzzled. Her camera, along with all her other photography equipment, was kept in her room. What was it doing downstairs? She hastily ran up the stairs and turned on the light.

Alex unscrewed the top of her film-developing tank and removed the coil inside. She got a jug of fresh developing fluid from her closet. As she had done so often before, she closed her door and switched off her lamp so that her room was pitch-black. Opening the back of the camera, she pulled out the film and wound it on to the coil. She put it back into the developing tank, switched on the light and then poured the developing solution into the tank. After the right amount of agitation and the right amount of time, she poured the developer into her sink and replaced it with stop bath. Finally, she poured in the fixing solution. When the film was no longer sensitive to light, she opened the tank, washed the film, squeegeed off the water and looked at the small images through her magnifying glass.

Many people would have found this a tricky thing to do. The pictures were small and, being negatives, reversed, so that what should have been dark was light and vice versa, but she was good at looking at negatives and scanned them easily. Most of them were shots she had taken recently on a trip around town with her uncle and Mr Underwood. Many of them were silly, but a few had turned out really well, actually.

And then she suddenly came across a photo she didn't recognize at all. She examined it closely. It wasn't a very good picture, taken at a funny angle, and the figures in it were slightly blurred. But she could see that there were four of them. One was very big with a bushy beard and hat and monocle, and another quite small, dwarfed by the coat he was wearing, and behind them, practically a shadow, was the third with what looked like a huge dog.

Though he was barely more than a dark outline, Alex felt a strange wave of terror wash over her as she looked at the third man. The feeling was momentary, only really noticeable after it had passed, like when you touch something hot and only feel it after you've removed your hand. Alex couldn't imagine it had meant much, and so she moved on to the fourth figure.

Which was Mr Underwood. He was being held tightly by the first two men and seemed to be putting up a struggle. What was even stranger was the expression on his face. You would assume that when you were being attacked by three strange men you would have an expression of either fear or anger. But the look on Mr Underwood's face was neither. He was giving a look of warning to the camera, a look that Alex often got when she wanted to be helpful in a social situation but her uncle didn't want her to interfere. Mr Underwood was telling the person taking the picture not to get involved. And the only person who could possibly have been taking the picture was her uncle. He was trying to protect her uncle.

Protect her uncle.

From whom?

From . . . from. . .

Who on earth would be interested in kidnapping a year-six teacher?

Unless. . .

Alex gasped, then covered her mouth. It all made perfect sense. These men weren't kidnapping a year-six teacher, they were kidnapping the heir to a pirate fortune! Mr Underwood had been captured by Steele's men! They had finally succeeded. Well then, there was only one thing she could do. She would just have to rescue him. Somehow, and the task struck her as virtually impossible, she would have to track down the *Ironic Gentleman*.

With her heart pumping wildly, Alex printed and developed the picture. After clamping her hairdryer to the back of a chair, aiming it at the still-wet print, she hastily packed a few things into her rucksack, emptied into it the contents of her piggy bank and carefully hid her toothbrush holder containing the fan between a jumper and change of socks. She then reloaded her camera with film and placed it on top, throwing in a few extra rolls for good measure.

By then the picture was ready, though still quite damp, and Alex examined it more carefully. Two of the men looked strangely familiar. Well, she would think about that on her walk over to the police station. What a nuisance, she thought, but she had promised the nice young officer, and didn't want to get her in trouble by not showing up.

Alex went back downstairs and stepped out of the shop on to the street once more. The wind was still doing its Atmosphere thing and Alex wasn't looking forward to the long walk to the station across town. Then, just as she started out, there was a loud crashing sound that made Alex jump out of her skin. She stood perfectly still for a moment, and when she felt she wasn't going to be attacked, she looked up. Mr Underwood's bicycle lay to one side, the front wheel spinning slowly to a stop. The wind had blown it over. Alex set it upright. Well, she might as well ride it to the station, she reasoned. And, of course, Mr Underwood would be wanting his bike back – he never went anywhere without it.

She teetered slightly when she climbed on to the seat. It was, after all, an adult's bike and she was very small. But she got the hang of it quickly and found herself riding towards the police station at a very respectable speed.

THE TWELFTH CHAPTER

In which Alex has to fill out a form and is interrogated

Alex had concluded that a police station was no place for a kid. The room she was sitting in was pasty grey, with dull lights buzzing overhead. All the windows were covered in heavy bars, and adults, some in uniform, others in handcuffs, rushed by her without a second glance. She was sitting on a hard, grey plastic seat. Next to her sat a very large round man, covered head to toe in tattoos, some expressing his love for his mother, others his appreciation for hawks devouring small rodents. On the other side, a leathery-looking bag lady, who frequently coughed violently into a handkerchief, would gaze at Alex unblinkingly whenever she stopped. Alex sighed softly. She felt tiny and invisible and cold. And very, very much alone.

Finally, two hours after arriving at the station, after she'd had her fingerprints taken, drunk a cup of warm chocolate-flavoured water, and had the young policewoman come to see her three times and apologize for the delay, Alex found herself sitting in the local police department's interrogation room. She was being looked down at by two unpleasant men, one with a body that was virtually a perfect square, the other a hunchback with a shirt that read, "Pay no attention to the man behind the curtain." The young policewoman sat in the corner, nervously taking notes.

The interrogation room they were in was very unpleasant because it was lit by fluorescent lighting, and this kind of lighting makes things look dull and cold. The walls were soundproofed so that, "No one can hear you scream," as the square-shaped man had explained as he sat Alex down at the large metal table in the middle of the room and lit himself a cigar. The whole setting made Alex feel uncomfortably as if she was the criminal and not the victim.

"So you are telling us," growled the square man, "that your uncle was found lying under a pile of doorknobs?"

"Well, I'm not telling you, you told me. I'm just repeating what I heard," replied Alex, looking nervously at the young officer.

"If you read the report, Detective, you will see that Alex didn't discover her uncle herself but. . ." started the officer.

"Officer, I am in the middle of an interrogation!" shouted the detective, turning to face her.

"Sorry, sir."

The detective shook his head fiercely and looked at Alex.

"Did he do this often?"

"What?"

The man exhaled a cloud of smoke and bit down hard on his cigar. "Lie under doorknobs?!"

"No, he didn't."

"I see." The man walked slowly towards the back wall. Then he said, rather slowly and deliberately, "Were you aware that your uncle was the owner and manager of a store that exclusively sold doorknobs?"

"Yes, I lived with him."

"Detective Thickwit," interjected the young policewoman once more, "I believe the girl has already explained to us that she was her uncle's ward and that. . ."

"When I want your opinion, Officer, I'll ask for it!" yelled Detective Thickwit, turning a light shade of maroon.

The officer nodded and buried her nose in her notes. He turned back to Alex.

"I only bring up the issue of your uncle's shop because I wonder. . ." and he brought his face very close to Alex's, " . . . what else you were expecting your uncle to be lying under? Surely not. . ." and he snorted, "oh, I don't know . . . pink slippers!"

"I think, Detectives, perhaps we ought to address the issue of the robbers. . ." insisted the young officer.

Alex gave a quick glance over at the young officer. She really didn't want to talk too much about the "robbers". For some reason she just didn't want the police to figure out who they were. It didn't seem any of their business.

"Robbers? What are you talking about? Honestly, Officer Prudence, can you not think of any possible reason why it is you who are sitting in the corner taking notes and it is I and my colleague here who are very important detectives in this bureau?" asked Detective Thickwit with a smirk on his face.

Officer Prudence frowned. "Because you have more experience in these matters?"

"Yes," agreed Detective Thickwit, and Officer Prudence breathed a sigh of relief. "And also because we are smarter than you. At any rate, what we need to get to this instant, before any more time is lost, is some important documentation." He signalled to the hunchback, who brought over a large brown box filled with papers and dropped it heavily in front of Alex on the table. "I want you to fill out these forms in full, in FULL, do you hear me?! This is very, VERY important. Once she's done, Officer Prudence, you can fetch me. I need a coffee." And he stormed out of the room, followed closely by the hunchback.

Alex and Officer Prudence briefly exchanged a glance and then Alex took up the top page and read, *"The form you are about to fill out is legal documentation. In the event that the form is lost, stolen or accidentally eaten, the department takes no responsibility. Any information that is not in the form is not subject to be treated as real and any information that is not real that is in the form is treated as a subject. Subjects to be treated include information that is real and in the form, but do not exclude subjects that are not. Question one: Is your name Peter? If no, skip to question three, if yes, write the word 'avocado'."*

Alex read the paragraph four times without fully understanding what it was asking her. This was upsetting to her because Alex was quite a good problem solver and hated not understanding things. However, she did know her name wasn't Peter, so she skipped to question three.

"Question three: Why not?"

Alex threw down her pencil in frustration. Officer Prudence looked up from her notes.

"Are you all right?" she asked.

Alex shook her head vigorously. She could sense her eyes welling up with tears, and a great rush of feeling came bursting out of her.

"No, I am not all right," she said, angrily wiping away her tears. "My uncle has been killed, my best friend has been captured, and I don't have any idea why I wasn't named Peter. All I know is that these men. . ." She stopped herself.

"Yes?" asked Officer Prudence.

"I. . ." She looked at Officer Prudence carefully. "If I tell you something, will you promise not to share it with the detectives?"

"It would be my pleasure!" replied Officer Prudence, drawing up her chair next to Alex.

"Well." Alex lowered her voice to a whisper. The two of them looked up at the two-way mirror in the wall. It is typical in most police-station interrogation rooms to have such mirrors, so that from the inside the criminals can only see themselves reflected, but from outside the room the police can watch the criminals as if they are looking through a window. However, at this particular station, they had installed the window the wrong way, so that instead of looking in, you could look out. And in this case, when Alex and Officer Prudence glanced over to the window, they found themselves watching Detective Thickwit making kissing faces at himself in the mirror on the other side.

"Go on, it's safe," said Officer Prudence.

"Well, I happen to know that the robbers . . . well, they're pirates."

"Oh my!"

"And what I really should be doing is finding their ship, but. . ." Alex bit her lip.

"But?"

"But I don't have any idea how to do that." She looked at Officer Prudence, who smiled warmly at her. "Do you know how to get to the sea?"

Officer Prudence seemed genuinely surprised and pleased to be asked her opinion on something. "Well," she said, thinking carefully, "I suppose the first step would be to get to the seaside city of Port Cullis."

Alex hit the table with her hand. "Yes, what a good idea!"

"But that is a bit of a journey," continued Officer Prudence. "You would have to find some kind of transportation that was quite fast. You could take the train!" she suddenly said.

"The train, of course!" said Alex. The two of them laughed. Then they both started when the telephone on the wall began to ring. Officer Prudence looked at Alex with surprise, and Alex returned the look with a shrug. Officer Prudence stood up to answer.

"Yes?" she said. "I see. I see. I see." She glanced over at

Alex. "Of course. I understand. Will do." She hung up the phone. Quickly she darted over to Alex and picked up her rucksack.

"Get up, you have to leave now," she whispered, helping Alex put it on her back. "I don't know if it has anything to do with you, but there's been a report made by some old ladies that a kid who matches your description did some bad things up in the manor house on the hill yesterday."

"But I didn't, I mean, it was me but. . ."

"Shh. . ." Officer Prudence opened the door to the interrogation room. "There's a back exit down the hall and to the right."

Alex turned and looked at Officer Prudence. "Will the police come after me?"

"Unlikely. Detective Thickwit is far too concerned with making forms and having people fill them out. It would be too much of a nuisance to chase after you. But if you are already here, well then, that's different. Just go."

"But you'll get in trouble!"

"No more than usual, and at least this time it will be for something real."

"But . . . I did cross the red rope," said Alex, feeling rather guilty.

"I'll pretend I didn't hear that." She grabbed Alex by

the shoulders and looked at her firmly in the eyes. "Look, I can tell you're a good kid. And anyway, you have more important things to deal with right now than a bunch of old ladies and Detective Thickwit. Just go. Now!"

Alex gave Officer Prudence a quick hug. Then she ran as silently as she could down the hall, out of the back door and into the beginning of a very long day.

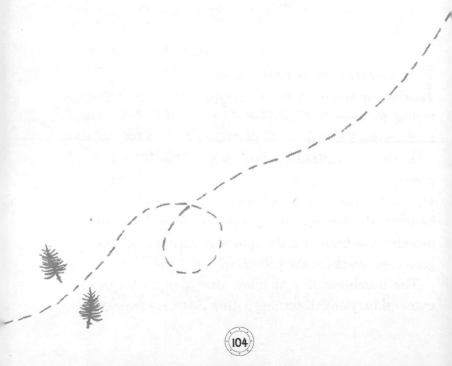

THE THIRTEENTH CHAPTER

In which Alex meets a very old man with a mop

Leaving the police department, Alex hopped on the bicycle and made her way towards the train station, trying to keep her balance as it clacked along the cobblestoned streets.

She hadn't realized just how long she had been in the police station. The sun was already coming up and there was a strange sense that somewhere, buried deep beneath the streets, the manic energy of a Monday morning was bubbling, about to ooze forth out of sewer grates and cracks in the pavement.

The usualness of a Monday, after things of a most extraordinary and disturbing nature that have happened the weekend before, is a really strange feeling. You might have felt it. It's as if you've landed on a different planet, or a planet you know of but have never been to before. When you meet your friends at school again, they seem a bit like strangers, and the idea of doing schoolwork seems foreign and inappropriate. And somewhere deep inside and ever so small, a strange feeling – fear? or maybe dread – well, a strange feeling sits in the bottom of your stomach. It subsides by the afternoon, of course, but a Monday morning can be a very strange time.

However, what is even stranger than going back to school on a Monday morning is not going back to school on a Monday morning (especially if you are a fugitive). Instead of feeling like a stranger, you feel . . . well, you feel . . . invisible. People rush by, doing their usual routine, kids are late and parents yell at them, and parents are late and their bosses yell at them. And everyone has a task and no one pays any attention to you. Then the streets suddenly empty at nine thirty and you are left in the company of deliverymen and nannies with very small children – in other words, the underworld of the weekday, with all the strange creatures who inhabit a place that has nothing to do with school and lessons and PE classes. Creatures like . . . postmen.

But none of this really mattered right now, because it

was still too early for Monday to begin, and so it seethed quietly, unobtrusively, as Alex found her way to the train station on the outskirts of town. The building was painted a faded red, and a sign marked "Train Station", as that was what the building was, swung on rusty chains in the morning breeze. It was an eerily quiet place. Alex supposed that not too many trains came by at this time of day. She pedalled up to the front and climbed off the bike. Then, walking it through the front entrance, she approached the ticket office.

"Ticket office is closed," said a voice from behind her.

Alex turned to see a man, very old and hunched, leaning on a mop at the other end of the waiting area. He was lit by a pale ray of light from the dusty window above him.

"Oh." She looked at him, waiting for an explanation. When none came she asked, "How can I purchase a ticket to Port Cullis?"

The very old man stared at her for a moment and went back to mopping.

Alex turned back to the ticket office and sighed. Leaving the old man inside, she stepped out on to the platform into the morning sunlight. Stretched out in front of her was a vast field of browning grass. To her left the tracks sped out of sight around behind a grey hill and to the right disappeared into the dark of the forest.

There was not a soul to be seen.

Alex walked down the platform and, resting the bicycle by the wall, sat herself down on a dark brown bench, its paint peeling from long exposure to the sun. She swung her small legs idly, looking both up and down the track for any sign of a train. The moment's pause gave her time to think. Which she did not particularly appreciate.

It was easy to put the night's events out of her mind when she had to focus on getting away, but now, waiting, she could only think that her uncle was dead, that Mr Underwood had been kidnapped by Steele's men, and that she was very, very much alone. Her stomach felt empty, and not just because she hadn't eaten in a day, but because she was so sad.

She had really loved her uncle, and she really missed him. However, she also knew that, had she been at home when the pirates had come, then there probably would have been no one to rescue Mr Underwood. Yes, that was the one good thing. She had to focus on rescuing Mr Underwood, and then the two of them could go after the treasure. Once they had done that, then she could feel sad, but right then, being upset wouldn't help anything. She wiped the tears from her face, tears she hadn't even realized she was shedding, and sat a little taller in her seat.

Suddenly she heard a slight rumble from her left. She looked and saw a plume of smoke rising up from behind the grey hill. She got up, grabbed the bicycle, and walked to the centre of the platform, watching as the train snaked around from behind the hill and slowly made its approach.

"That's not your train," said a voice.

Alex jumped and turned to see the very old man, still clutching his mop, standing in the shadow of the doorway.

She didn't really know what to make of that statement.

"Does it not go to Port Cullis?" she asked.

"All trains heading west go to Port Cullis," said the very old man, squinting in the sun.

Alex shook her head and took a step closer to the edge of the platform.

"That's not your train," the very old man repeated.

"I don't know what you mean by that!" said Alex in frustration, turning to him again.

By now the train was approaching the platform, slowing down and coming to a stop.

"That train, that train *there*," said the very old man, putting an extra stress on the word "there" and pointing behind Alex. "That train is not your –" he pointed at Alex – "train." He looked at her closely with sharp brown eyes.

"Yes, fine, thank you," replied Alex slowly. "I think I'll ask the conductor, though, just in case." And she raised her eyebrows at the old man as she turned and walked down to where the conductor was now standing.

"Excuse me," said Alex. "Does this train pass through Port Cullis?"

The conductor smiled a friendly smile. "Well, yes it does. And how did you know that?"

"I didn't. Do you think you could take me on board?"

"Well, now, I don't see why not. That should be a lot of fun, now, shouldn't it? Yes, by all means. Hop on board!" And he extended a hand to her. Alex took it and with a bit of help bringing up the bicycle, hopped on board.

"Don't! That's not your train!"

Alex looked back at the very old man, who was jogging up to join them. "It goes to Port Cullis. It is my train!"

"No! That train is not your train. That train is a bad train," he said, stopping below them.

The train began to pull slowly away from the platform.

"But why?!" Alex called out, but she was now too far away to hear his reply. She shook her head and frowned. She watched as the very old man watched her in return. Then he, too, shook his head and frowned. And disappeared back into the shadows of the station.

THE FOURTEENTH CHAPTER

In which Alex explores the train

OK, so the first thing you now have to understand is that there are two kinds of conductors people can be in the world. There is a train conductor who blows a whistle and calls "all aboard", and there is a symphony conductor who waves a little stick at a hundred or so people holding wooden or brass objects in order that they all make a noise at the same time. I only mention this because seeing as Alex got on a train you may have naturally presumed that the conductor was the first kind. But he wasn't. He was the second kind. So I apologize if I confused you. You see, I automatically assumed, since he was wearing a tuxedo and not a uniform, you would have guessed correctly. But I had forgotten to tell you he was wearing a tuxedo. Sorry.

Anyway, Alex, left her bike by the door, and was led hastily by the conductor down the narrow passage. The train lurched violently, and Alex felt nervous as they rushed along. After all, that very old man had seemed extremely adamant that she should not board the train. What was he frightened of? But she followed obediently, occasionally checking over her shoulder, for what, she wasn't quite sure.

Suddenly the passage opened up on a grand dining carriage. Alex gazed open-mouthed. Plush purple curtains were drawn across its windows, so that not a shard of sunlight filtered into the room. Instead it was lit by a giant chandelier, which hung, swaying with the movement of the train, over a long dark rosewood dinner table laid out for dinner with complete sets of silverware, china and crystal glasses.

Alex immediately relaxed. This train was nothing to worry about. At most you could call it stuffy or pompous, and that didn't seem threatening, at least not to Alex. She smiled and shook her head. And she realized that, while some very old men could be extremely wise due to their advanced years, some were simply senile. Alex concluded that the one with the mop most definitely had no idea what he was talking about.

This train was beautiful. It was elegant. Some would even go as far as to call it grade-A classy.

Alex was so lost in her thoughts that she had to run to catch up with the conductor, who had already sped through the room and was heading into the next carriage. She quickly ran to catch up. They entered the adjoining carriage, which was, if you can believe this, even more spectacular. This room, too, had plush curtains covering the windows, but also a shiny wooden floor, and at the far end was a stage outlined in small fairy lights. On it, in three rows, were seats behind white stands with "Jimmy C and His Orchestra" written across each.

The conductor stopped in the middle of the wooden floor and spun on his heel to face Alex.

"Welcome to our party!" he said, his arms outstretched and a broad smile on his face.

As if on cue, the far door swung open and a young woman entered. She was very pretty, with light-blonde hair, cut, Alex realized with a smile, much like her own. Around it she wore a band with one large peacock feather stuck in the front. A black sequinned dress hung loosely off her slim form, and a long string of white pearls dangled from her neck. She played with it nervously with her fingers.

"Jimmy C, darling, why ever did you step outside? That is so unlike you! And now we are incredibly behind! Why, it's almost time now, and I haven't even changed yet!"

Jimmy C smiled. "Angel, I don't know what possessed me, honestly. I guess the stop just got me rather excited. I'm terribly sorry! But look, look who I met!" And he turned to Alex. "Isn't it wonderful! A new friend!"

Alex smiled shyly at the pretty blonde woman.

"Jimmy C! What a surprise! Well, hello there. My name is Angel." She bent down and kissed Alex hastily on both cheeks.

"Um . . . I'm Alexandra, but people call me Alex," said Alex, unsure how to respond.

"Alex! What a wonderful name! But, darling, I hope you don't mind if I rush things along a bit, time is of the essence, you see. Let's get you a compartment and leave Jimmy C to set up!"

"Um, sure."

With a bright smile Angel grabbed hold of Alex's hand and hurried back through the door from which she had just appeared. Alex was whisked down a narrow aisle with compartments on one side. Nameplates in brass hung on the doors. When they arrived at the one marked "Angel", they stopped.

"Now," said Angel, slightly out of breath, "we have a guest compartment right next to mine. Isn't that exciting?" Alex nodded. Angel pushed open the door.

The compartment was small but luxurious. The walls and furnishings were all made of that same dark wood as the large dining table. Against the far wall was a deep comfy chair with deep red cushions on which lay a variety of sparkly tops and skirts. And above it were those same purple drapes drawn across the window. There was one small bed against the wall with a small reading lamp and storage cabinets above it.

"If you wouldn't mind unpacking your things as quickly as possible, and changing, it would be wonderful!"

Alex nodded.

"Good. I'll meet you in the corridor – shortly, I hope!" And she left, closing the door behind her.

Alex stood silently in the middle of the room. She wasn't sure exactly what to make of everything. She had never been on a train before, true, but she had never heard of one that looked quite like this. And she hadn't even bought a ticket yet. She bit her bottom lip. I hope it isn't that expensive, she thought, reaching into her bag and taking out her camera.

She took a few quick shots of her room and then went to draw back the curtains to take a picture of the view. But she found that to be impossible as the window was painted black. Which seemed kind of a strange thing to do. Especially as the curtains were more than effective at keeping the light out.

Alex drew the curtains again and looked at the clothes on the chair. She had better change. She didn't know why she had better change. She just knew that Angel was anxious that she did, and did so as quickly as possible. Once she was given a moment to get her bearings, she would ask Angel what was going on. Choosing a satin blue camisole that was quite long enough to be a dress for her, Alex hastily changed her clothes and picked up a beaded headband similar to the one Angel was wearing. She shrugged and put it on, adjusting it in the mirror. She joined Angel (now dressed in pale pink) in the corridor and was whisked off back towards the dining room.

Jimmy C and his orchestra had begun to play some discreet dinner music. He waved as they flew past, causing the percussionist to compulsively smash the cymbals together, and then the trumpet section to pick up the coda, resulting in the trombonist missing his solo, which made him run off to his room.

There were already four other people seated at the large wooden table of the dining carriage, dressed just as impeccably as Angel. At the head was a large bear of a man dressed in a tuxedo. He was going bald at the top of his head and had a small pencil moustache. He was fiercely buttering a roll when Angel introduced Alex.

"Everyone, I would like you all to meet Alex," said Angel.

"Is that supposed to be a dress?" asked the man at the head, keeping his focus on his roll.

"Alex, this is Arnold Van Brusen. He produces plays." Angel whispered the last bit.

Alex nodded. "Pleased to meet you, Mr Van Brusen."

He snorted in reply.

Next Angel introduced Fifi and Pudding, fraternal twins dressed in red.

Fraternal?

"Pudding has a mole on her left shoulder and is two centimetres shorter than Fifi," explained Angel. The two small brunettes smiled at Alex, and she smiled back.

"And that is Stuart Nickleman." Angel pointed to a small man in a beige suit nervously tapping a fork on the table. He smiled a weak smile in her direction and then faced front, furrowing his eyebrows deeply.

"When do we eat? We're behind schedule enough as it is!" said Arnold Van Brusen, his mouth full of roll.

"Soon, soon!" replied Angel, giving Alex a gentle but firm push on the back. "Now, Alex, darling, why don't you sit between the twins?"

The twins giggled and pulled out the chair for her. Alex sat down and smiled at them both, wishing she could have sat with Angel instead. She had so many questions. What had the very old man been worried about? What were they all late for? Why hadn't she been asked to buy a ticket? And why on earth were they sitting down to dinner so early in the morning?

"What do you do?" asked Arnold Van Brusen, finally looking Alex in the eye.

"What do I do?"

"Yes, for a living. For example I am a producer, that is what I do. Do you understand now?"

"Um . . . all right. Well, I'm a kid, I guess."

"Well, that isn't much of anything. We've all been kids once, you know. I don't see why you're so proud of that." And he grabbed another roll.

"Honestly, Van Brusen, you are an incorrigible fool, aren't you?" said a voice from behind. Alex looked up to see a young man, arm linked with a young woman in silver, standing in the entranceway. They were shockingly thin – or was it fashionably thin? – with long, angular limbs and prominent cheekbones.

"You must forgive him. Van Brusen had a traumatizing childhood," said the young man, placing a hand on the back of Alex's chair. "Something to do with a pastry shortage in his native village, I believe."

"Oh, Freddy, you're so funny!" laughed the woman in silver, sitting down at the table. Freddy moved to join her.

"What the devil are we waiting for!" bellowed Van Brusen, suddenly standing up. He threw his napkin on the table and stormed off through a pair of swinging doors which led to the kitchen.

"Brusey seems a bit testy tonight," the woman in silver giggled.

"Oh, if only Charles would get here soon, then chef could start serving," said Fifi sadly.

Alex looked at Fifi. "Is that everybody, then?"

"Of course. But Charles is so particular."

"Then why is the table set for so many?"

"That's an excellent question." Angel thought hard. "It does seem silly that we did that."

"And a waste of china," added the woman in silver.

"Good point, Geraldine. Well, we'll just have to remedy that at the next meal. How clever you are, Alex!" And Angel beamed at Alex, which made her feel a bit more relaxed, though really not quite satisfied with the answer.

"Children are notoriously clever. I can never decide if that's a good or a bad thing," a new smooth voice added.

Alex watched as a tall man entered the carriage and sat by Angel. He was probably approaching fifty and had thinning white-blonde hair. He wore a dark blue smoking jacket with a white cravat about his neck and managed to speak flawlessly with a pipe dangling out of

the side of his mouth. And he looked at Alex carefully
with extremely pale blue eyes.

"Charles!" exclaimed Angel. "Good, now quickly
everyone, let's eat!"

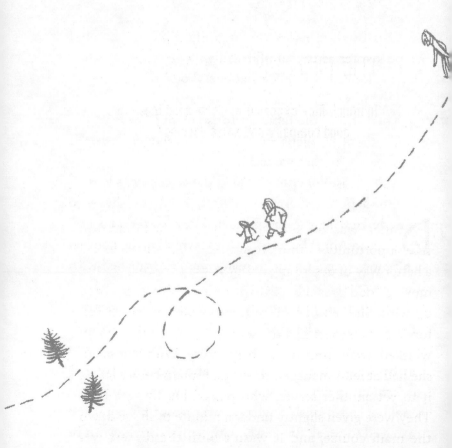

THE FIFTEENTH CHAPTER

In which Alex experiences some good food, good company and some dancing

Dinner was an odd affair. If she had had the opportunity to think it over, she might have found a better way of describing it, but at the pace things were moving, "odd" was the only word Alex had time to come up with. She felt like she was in a movie stuck on fast forward. No sooner had the soup been served than it was whisked away from beneath her nose. With the salad, she had at least managed to snag a tomato before losing it to yet another server, who passed her by in a blur. They were given slightly under a minute to shove down the main course, and it wasn't until the dessert was served, along with a large bottle of champagne, that things suddenly reverted to a more normal speed.

The champagne's arrival seemed to excite the party. Angel pleasantly smiled in Charles's direction. He popped the cork and started to pour. There was a moment where he paused over Alex's glass. Possibly he was unsure of whether a child should be offered alcohol – Alex couldn't quite tell – but he continued and filled her glass as well. Once everyone had some champagne, Charles rose to his feet, gave a quick toast, and downed the drink in one gulp.

Alex took a small sip. The moment she swallowed she felt an incredible sensation. Suddenly she had energy flowing through her veins instead of blood, and though she hadn't slept for two days now, she felt she might never need to sleep again.

Quickly Alex set her glass aside. If one sip affected her that way, she probably shouldn't drink any more. The rest of her party finished their drinks in one gulp like Charles, after which Angel announced, "Let's dance." And they all got up and moved to the other carriage.

Dance? thought Alex as she was dragged along with the rest. She'd only just begun to catch her breath from dinner.

Jimmy C and his Orchestra were playing full force now and everyone began to dance with everyone else, often being tossed by the train to the other end of the carriage. The music was fast, and everyone was doing the charleston – which is a dance that involves kicking and fast footwork and, well, looks rather frenetic. Stuart Nickleman was kind enough to show Alex a few basic steps, and after a few songs, Alex decided to stop fighting it and began to enjoy herself genuinely. After all, there were probably worse ways to travel to Port Cullis than in a crazy, high-speed party. And certainly everyone she had met seemed friendly enough. So they went on dancing away, song after song, dance after dance, until everyone was very tired and sweaty.

At this moment, when things seemed to be winding down a bit, Angel stood up on stage and began to sing a ballad. She had a very beautiful voice and everyone stood to listen to her, except for Freddy and Geraldine who danced together slowly. Alex smiled calmly to herself. She didn't feel tired, exactly, just content, and everything had a dozy sort of feel. Memories of her uncle and Mr Underwood were faded and kind of a pastel-pink colour. She felt as if she could listen to Angel sing for ever. As she hazily scanned the room, she got the impression the others were thinking the same thing too. Except for Charles. Who obviously couldn't have been thinking the same as he was staring right at Alex. Her heart paused for a moment. She came out of her trance-like state and looked away quickly. When she looked back, Charles was looking at Angel like everyone else.

When Angel finished singing she smiled softly. Then she announced into the microphone, "Nap time!"

And the fast-forward button was pushed again. Everyone quickly left the floor and rushed to their separate compartments. Alex found herself standing alone in the middle of the floor, watching the orchestra pack up their instruments and vanish up somewhere in the train. Only Jimmy C remained. He sat himself at the piano and softly began to play.

Alex walked over to Jimmy C and leaned against the piano. "Jimmy C?"

"Yes, beautiful?"

"I've just been wondering. When do you think we will be arriving at Port Cullis?"

"Oh, I wouldn't know something like that, beautiful. You'd have to ask Angel." He smiled and closed his eyes. At which point Alex felt a soft hand on her shoulder.

"Alex, darling. It's time to rest up," said Angel. "No dawdling. Come, come, we don't want to waste any time."

"Angel," asked Alex as they jogged along the aisle back to their compartments.

"Yes?"

"When do you think we'll get to Port Cullis?"

Angel stopped in front of her door. "What time is it now?"

"I don't really know," replied Alex, as for the first time it occurred to her that she didn't. The meal had passed by in a flash, but the dancing had gone on for ever.

"Well, once we figure that out, then we'll know. Don't worry about it now, though. You get some rest. You are quite the little dancer." She beamed at Alex as she went into her room.

Alex felt a great sense of release as she fell back on to her little bed. The pillow was really soft and the sheets were nice and cool. Lying there she took off the headband and watched the beads glint in the light of the bedside lamp. Everything would be just fine, she realized. Soon they would be arriving in Port Cullis, where she would find some way of tracking down Mr Underwood, and when she found him they would track down the treasure. And everything would be wonderful.

Alex closed her eyes and felt herself gently drifting off to sleep. When. . .

"Darling, we've overslept! Quick, you need to change! I'll be waiting for you outside!"

Alex opened her eyes to see Angel smiling down at her.

"Sorry. . ." said Alex, sitting up slowly.

"Don't just sit there, darling, get ready!" Angel left

the room quickly.

Sometimes we have such a deep sleep that we feel as though we've only just shut our eyes before we are woken up again. Alex wondered if maybe that was what had happened. She didn't feel particularly tired any more. Gosh, how long had she been asleep, then, she wondered as she changed into a gold camisole identical to the blue one except that it was . . . gold.

She tentatively poked her head out of her door to find Angel waiting for her.

Once again she took Alex's hand and pulled her back down the aisle, over the dance floor, where Jimmy C and his orchestra were playing some light dinner music. Jimmy C waved to the two of them as they rushed past, causing the snoozephone player to choke on his reed, at which the tambourinist fell on the floor laughing.

And then Alex and Angel were back in the dining car.

Where Arnold Van Brusen sat fiercely buttering a roll.

And Fifi was sitting giggling to herself.

And Stuart Nickleman was tapping a knife on the table.

THE SIXTEENTH CHAPTER

In which Alex experiences some good food, good company and some dancing

Alex stood paralysed in the entranceway as Angel took her seat at the table. "Alex," Angel whispered. "Alex!" she whispered louder. Alex turned to Angel. "Your seat is over there." Angel indicated the seat next to Fifi.

Alex nodded numbly and walked to her seat and sat down.

"What kind of a dress is that?" asked Van Brusen.

Alex turned and looked at him. "It's a camisole," answered Alex. "I wore a blue one last time."

"Like I would remember something like that," snorted

Van Brusen. "I have more important things to think about, you know. I am, after all, a producer." Then he stood up and threw his napkin on the table. "Damn and blast!" he yelled. "Do we have to wait on His Majesty every time?"

"Calm down, Arnold," said Angel softly. "You know it takes Charles about fifteen more minutes. Surely you can wait fifteen more minutes."

Obviously, Van Brusen couldn't wait fifteen more minutes, because he stormed off once again through the swinging doors that still led to the kitchen.

Alex felt very uneasy. Even if she had slept for several hours, and it was indeed time to eat again, why were they sitting down to what seemed like the exact same meal, and having virtually the exact same conversation? There was no reasonable explanation for that.

As Freddy and Geraldine sat down to join them, Alex noticed the table was missing someone. Leaning over to Angel, Alex asked, "What about Pudding?"

Angel laughed heartily and shook her head as if Alex had just told the funniest joke she had heard in a long time. "Oh dear, all you children are the same, aren't you!" she said. "We won't have pudding until we finish the main courses, of course. You are just going to have to be patient."

Alex shook her head and understood the mistake.

"No, no, I meant, shouldn't we also be waiting for Pudding to start our meal."

"What is she going on about?" asked Stuart Nickleman, frantically looking around the table.

"I haven't the foggiest," said Geraldine.

Alex looked around the table. "You must know who I'm talking about. Pudding, Fifi's twin sister, Pudding. Her name is Pudding, remember?"

There was an uncomfortable silence.

"Wasn't her name Pudding?"

The silence continued.

For a long time.

Until Fifi burst into a fit of giggles.

"Oh my!" She wiped the tears from her eyes. "Can you imagine me with a twin!"

Her giggling seemed to relax everyone else in the carriage, and they all began to laugh as well.

"Children and their imaginations!" said Angel, smiling pleasantly at Alex.

"I don't think I like their imaginations much," said Stuart Nickleman, tapping his knife on the table again.

"Oh, Stuart, they're perfectly harmless," said Angel, shaking her head. "Children are perfectly harmless."

"No, no, stop it!" said Alex loudly. Everyone stopped and stared at her. "Stop it! You can't have forgotten who Pudding is! She's Fifi's fraternal twin sister! She's two centimetres shorter. And has a mole on her shoulder." She looked at everyone. "Oh, stop looking at me like that," she said in frustration. "I'm not crazy. Why would I make something like that up?"

"It's not even all that interesting."

"Exactly, it's not even all that. . ." And Alex turned around. Standing looking down at her casually was Charles in a dark brown smoking jacket. She stopped talking and stared into his pale blue eyes and bit her lip.

Charles smiled mildly at her and took his seat, quietly filling his glass with water. Alex's head was spinning, but she didn't dare say anything else. She was beginning to think that maybe she had been mistaken. Though it seemed an awfully strange thing to be mistaken about.

When Van Brusen returned, the meal was served at the same ridiculous pace as before. Alex didn't even bother trying to eat, she was simply too confused and uncomfortable to feel hungry.

All too soon it came time for the dessert, a rich chocolate cake. Once again a full bottle of champagne was placed in the centre of the table. It fizzed and bubbled into Alex's glass, and she eyed it with a sense of dread. Yes, it had made her feel strangely energized. But there was something not quite right about the whole thing.

Charles stood to make his toast again and everyone

except Alex drained their glasses in one gulp, and once the pudding was finished, got up to dance again.

Alex felt too anxious to dance, but she slowly stood up and followed everyone on to the dance floor.

Many times when we dream, we are so certain that this time, this particular time, we are not dreaming. "How could this possibly be a dream when I am dreaming about brushing my teeth? What's the point of dreaming about that?" you think. But then you wake up and feel sheepish because yet again you were wrong. And then you get over it and go about your day. But have you ever had the opposite experience, one where you are awake and are completely certain you are dreaming? You feel all floaty and on the outside of everything, watching what's going on. And you think that any second now you'll wake up and that will explain everything. Well, even if you have never felt like that, imagine how it would be, and that is exactly how Alex was feeling at the moment, watching everyone whirl around her.

"I am certain this is a dream," Alex was thinking as she took to the floor.

"Or maybe the previous dinner was a dream," she continued in her train of thought as she started doing the charleston again.

"Or maybe this is the previous dinner." But that

thought made her brain go kind of loopy and she let it go.

The dancing continued for what seemed like hours, and just as Alex began to feel she would fall over in exhaustion, Angel appeared on stage as she had done the last time (if there had indeed been a last time) and began to sing.

This time Alex kept an eye on Charles and watched as he shifted uncomfortably on the spot. He scratched the back of his neck and then looked at his watch. And finally, just as she had been expecting, he looked up at her. This time it was Charles who looked away quickly. Alex shivered. She wasn't sure what it was about those pale blue eyes, but she didn't quite trust Charles. Not that there was anything particularly untrustworthy in what he was doing.

The song finished and everyone left the carriage. Without waiting for Angel, Alex hurried herself back to her compartment. She closed the door quickly behind her and sat on the bed. With all the thoughts swimming in her brain, one suddenly came to the fore. "But what time is it?" it asked politely. And Alex, shaking her head, had to reply, "I don't know.

"All I know," she said to herself, "is that I am very tired. But that could mean many things. That could mean it is late at night, or it could mean that I've danced too much.

But I'll tell you what," she resolved, "I am not even going to try to nap this time. And then we'll see what happens."

She started to feel a little silly sitting there waiting for something to happen. And it was all she could do to prevent herself from closing her eyes. But she did have good intuition. And her intuition was telling her that. . .

"Darling! What are you doing! Hurry and change or we'll be late!" cried Angel as she burst into Alex's compartment.

Alex nodded, changed and followed Angel swiftly back to the dining car (past Jimmy C and his orchestra. He waved as they darted by, causing the cannon player to light the fuse too early and the entire kazoo section to run off screaming).

"Where's Stuart Nickleman?" asked Alex the moment she found herself sitting at the table next to Fifi and watching Van Brusen buttering a roll. It wasn't a real question because she knew exactly what the answer would be.

"I'm sorry, darling, who?" asked Angel, leaning over towards her.

"Stuart Nickleman."

Suddenly Alex felt something hit her on the head.

"Did you just throw a roll at me?" she asked Van Brusen.

"No." He reached for the bread basket.

"Yes, you did!" She held up the half-eaten roll that had just hit her.

"That's not mine."

"Why did you throw a roll at me?"

"Because you insist on saying stupid things, on making up stupid stories about stupid people. And I find stupid people unbearable!" he yelled at her, turning a dark shade of purple.

But Alex didn't care that he thought she was stupid and unbearable. She knew her experiment had worked. She had not been asleep. No time had passed. She was certain now that something completely wrong was going on, and she was going to have to get to the bottom of it.

She sat quietly through the manic meal, through the dessert and through the toast. She danced during the dancing (though she could barely lift her legs), listened thoughtfully to Angel singing, and quietly returned to her compartment.

And when Angel returned to escort her, Alex went through the whole thing all over again, panicking slightly when she noticed Freddy had now gone missing too. And as the festivities wore on and on, the panic rose steadily in her chest. Suddenly it seemed as if she might never get to Port Cullis. That this train would never reach its destination. And that this party would never end. And that, worst of all, she herself might disappear.

As she once again sat waiting for Angel in her room, and feeling rather nauseous at the thought of another dinner, she felt a rush of energy. She stood up, crossed over to the window and threw open the drapes. She ran her finger over the window. It was rough, painted on the inside. This was a good sign. She looked frantically around the room and spotted the bedside lamp. She prised off the metal shade and took it to the window. She began to scratch. Small flecks of black paint floated into the room. After several moments of frenzied scratching, she had made a small hole about the size of a pea. Alex put down the shade and peeked through the hole. What she saw made any effort in keeping from panicking pointless. She now panicked, and panicked freely.

THE SEVENTEENTH CHAPTER

In which Alex meets Giggles

The first thing she noticed was that despite all the time that had seemed to pass, the light in the sky looked very much the same as the light when she had boarded. But the strangest thing was that, just at the moment she was peeking through the hole, the train was passing through a station. A station that looked very, very familiar. And standing on the platform was a very familiar very old man with a mop. She had the distinct impression he was staring right at her.

Since the train was passing through the same station from which she had boarded, and since the sun seemed not to have moved, Alex reasoned that time was now meaningless. This of course meant two things. One, since time had always had a purpose before she had been on the train, it was the train that had caused this strange shift in the laws of the universe. And two, that she therefore needed to get off the train immediately.

Alex tentatively opened her door and peered out down the hall. She half expected Angel to be waiting for her again, but evidently not enough time had passed for yet another meal. Without waiting, Alex quietly slipped out through her door and made her way silently, but as fast as she could, down the corridor in the opposite direction from the one she usually took. She knew if she went the other way Jimmy C would see her, and although he was nice, he wouldn't let her go by unquestioned.

So she sped down the hall, unsure of where she was going and what she would do when she got there, passing other compartments with other nameplates. She read them as she went along. "Michael Maguire". She looked at the one next to it: "Trudy English". She had never heard of these people. She read name after name: "Joyce Burns, Anthony Brown, Orlando Adams". Her stomach turned. What had happened to them all? Had they gone missing as well? Most likely yes, her brain answered quietly. She continued down the never-ending passage, name after name, in a manic state now, rushing along at a surprising pace so that the nameplates had become nothing but bright brass-coloured blurs passing alongside her.

Suddenly and most unexpectedly, she came to the end of the carriage. Discovering that the carriage was not infinitely long brought Alex back from her panic to cold harsh reality. She was facing a door through which she could see another door leading into the next carriage.

A deep dread now flooded her innards and made its way up her spine. She opened the first door and stood briefly between carriages, holding tightly to the doorknob of the other door to maintain her balance. She could feel fresh air on her face for the first time in who knows how long, and it gave her a sense of purpose as she turned the knob and entered the other carriage.

It took a few moments for her eyes to adjust to the darkness. The carriage was long and relatively empty. In the middle was a large round wooden table. On it stood a tall narrow wooden column on which was resting a large bowl that looked a lot like something you would keep your pet goldfish in. Attached to the bowl, by a rubber tube, was a brass pump. The whole thing was lit from somewhere, giving the apparatus a very ominous glow.

Alex was drawn to the table, mesmerized. The bowl seemed to grow taller as she got closer. Then she jumped into the air. She jumped into the air because a large white bird that was sitting in a cage hanging in the shadows had made a sudden squawk. And the bird had made a sudden squawk because a lithe reddish-brown cat had just made a lunge at it from the dark. The cat clung desperately to the bars of the cage and then came crashing to the floor, hissing as it landed.

"Are you all right?" asked Alex. She bent down to have a look at it. In the glow from the table she saw it would have been a very pretty cat if it hadn't been missing tufts of fur here and there. It was lean and had a stripe of black that ran along its spine, ending in a point at its tail. It looked at her incredulously, raised what would be the closest thing to an eyebrow at her, and sauntered off to a dark corner.

"Very impressive," said a cool voice from behind her.

Alex stood up and turned quickly.

Of all the thoughts that could have come to her – thoughts like, "How irresponsible of me to have walked into this room so brazenly without even considering the ramifications", or, "I probably should have knocked first", or even, "I think I'm in a spot of trouble" – of all these possible thoughts that could have occurred to Alex, the one that came into her head was this:

"Of course."

Standing opposite her and smiling smugly, was Charles. His face seemed even more frightening lit from below.

"You know, Giggles hates just about everyone. Usually anyone who dared get as close as you did would probably have found themselves without an eye at least," he said.

Alex just continued to stare at him.

"OK, OK. Go ahead. Ask what all this is, then," he said with a smile, indicating the contraption on the table.

"What's all this, then?" said Alex softly, because, though she sensed she was probably in considerable danger, she was also genuinely curious.

"I'm glad you asked!" Charles rubbed his hands together. "It's a vacuum. I didn't invent it, in case you were feeling impressed."

"I wasn't."

Charles placed a loving hand on the glass bowl. "It is terribly complicated to explain. Would you like a demonstration?"

Alex, who had never heard Charles sound so enthusiastic, nodded her head slowly. Instantly she wished she hadn't. Charles had removed the big white bird from its cage and placed it into the large glass bowl, covering the top with a lid.

"No!" she cried. "It'll suffocate."

"I always knew you were clever, but no, it won't. Not quite yet. Not until I do this," he said. And he began to turn a handle attached to the brass pump. He turned faster and faster. The look on his face remained etched there, excitement mixed with concentration.

"Please stop!" Alex was watching the bird flying anxiously around in the glass bowl.

"You see, what I am doing is creating a vacuum inside the bowl," Charles explained quickly. "All air, everything, is being sucked out of it. Wait till you see what happens next!"

But what was to happen next, Alex never found out. Just as Charles had finished talking, he let out a rather girlish scream. Giggles, who seemed to be of the same mind as Alex, had jumped on Charles, much the same way as he had jumped on the birdcage. This time, however, his claws were perfectly suited to digging into the man's chest, causing Charles to release the lever and spend a few moments frantically fighting the feline. Climbing up on to the table, Alex took off the lid of the bowl and gingerly lifted out the motionless bird. She held it for a few moments and then said quietly, "It's dead."

"Is it?" asked Charles, having finally unhooked himself from Giggles, who now dangled ungracefully by the scruff of his neck. "Drat, and I so wanted to show you what would happen." He shook his head and then looked down at Giggles. "Well, you heard about curiosity and the cat?" And he took Giggles and shoved him into the glass bowl.

"Oh, please don't. I understand now," said Alex, reaching up for the bowl.

"Now, now!" said Charles, pushing her roughly to the side. "You haven't had the full effect." Giggles was squirming and hissing, his ears flat to his head and his teeth bared. His tail now resembled a fir tree. "Would you like to try?" Charles indicated the handle.

"No, of course not! Please let him go!" begged Alex, struggling against Charles's arm.

"No."

"Please!"

"This is ridiculous, I'm starving! This is what you invited me to see, is it? What a waste of time."

Both Charles and Alex stopped their struggle.

"Van Brusen, I apologize. I was momentarily distracted," said Charles, calmly releasing Alex and walking over to where Van Brusen was standing by the door of the carriage. "Of course, this isn't what I wanted you to see. This is nothing, a model. A game. No, no, what I wanted you to see is far more impressive." And he guided Van Brusen down the carriage.

Alex quickly released Giggles, who struggled against her hold briefly, then looked her firmly in the eye, made some sort of decision, and went limp, purring softly in her arms. She carried him over her shoulder and followed Charles and Van Brusen down the carriage, keeping to the shadows, and hoping to make herself almost invisible, as she had with the Daughters of the Founding Fathers' Preservation Society. She could have left, but she wanted answers and knew that somehow as a result of whatever was going to happen to Van Brusen, he would probably not be joining them for dinner.

THE EIGHTEENTH CHAPTER

In which Alex learns something interesting about champagne

Charles was busy explaining his invention to Van Brusen up ahead of Alex. "It follows the basic idea of a vacuum, but I've modified it so that instead of sucking air, well . . . it would be easier to explain to you with a demonstration, really."

This made Alex uneasy. She wasn't really a fan of Charles's "demonstrations".

They passed beyond a thick black curtain that split the carriage in two, and found themselves standing in front of a huge version of the vacuum, consisting of a human-sized glass bowl with a glass roof, and a large brass pump with an equally large handle.

"That's big," said Van Brusen.

"Yes, it is," said Charles. "Care for a demonstration?"

Van Brusen shrugged. "Then can we go eat?"

"I can guarantee that once I finish my demonstration, we shall have a very enjoyable meal indeed," said Charles.

He walked over to the large glass bowl and pushed gently against it. A previously hidden door opened.

"If you would be so kind."

"I don't think so, Charles. I saw what you did to that bird," said Van Brusen with a laugh. To both his and Alex's surprise, Charles started to laugh as well.

"Van Brusen! I'm not going to kill you. Don't be a fool. I said I modified it. It doesn't suck out the air. How can it when I have made all these little air holes?" He indicated a few holes the size of apples perforating the glass.

"Well, I don't know, it still looks fishy to me," said Van Brusen.

"Only because it's fishbowl-shaped. Trust me, you won't die. And you definitely won't regret it." Again he gestured towards the door. "Please, it will take at most fifteen minutes."

Van Brusen shrugged and, to Alex's complete shock, strode into the glass bowl. Charles closed the door firmly behind him and walked around to the handle.

"Now, I was trying to explain to you exactly what this machine did. As I said, it doesn't suck out air. I have modified it to suck out, what I suppose could be called, energy."

"Energy?" asked Van Brusen. "What, like electricity?"

"Alas, no. It is more . . . spiritual than that, you could say. My original idea was to find an alternate fuel, more cost-efficient, you know – but I found something even more useful." And he pressed a button. The handle began to turn automatically. "What I have managed to create is a device that can suck out . . . well, to be poetic, the soul."

This made Van Brusen visibly uneasy. "The soul?"

"Yes, a very powerful form of energy, it is capable of fuelling this whole train. And while that is all rather interesting, what is most interesting is the effect it has on people." The handle turned faster and faster. "You see, if this energy is consumed by other humans, well, it's like the fountain of youth. Eternal energy of spirit."

"'Consumed' as in 'eaten'?" For the first time the idea of food didn't seem too appealing to Van Brusen.

"Or, more easily, drunk – yes," and Charles nodded towards the corner. Alex looked over to the corner and saw a stack of boxes, one of which was open. Inside she could see bottles. "Never wondered what the bubbles were in champagne? Never wondered why it was such a popular drink?"

"You can't be serious!" said Van Brusen.

"Oh, fine, I'm joking. Most champagne is normal champagne, but our champagne, ours is the elixir of life! Isn't that exciting?"

Van Brusen didn't appear all that excited. In fact he had stopped responding altogether. His skin had begun to turn a grey colour, and his movements were slow and directionless.

"True, there are some kinks in the works. Selective memory loss being one of them. However, once I have perfected my machine, I will be able to mass produce my champagne, sell it at ridiculously high prices, corner the market and become extraordinarily filthy rich. The only problem is that it would seem that one person's spirit can only make one bottle of the stuff. Which is not very cost-effective, as it would mean running out of people at a greater rate and losing profit."

Van Brusen suddenly collapsed. Still conscious, he now lay on his side, quietly blinking. Charles walked over to the other side of the pump, where he picked up a smaller glass jar. There didn't seem to be anything in it, but it vibrated as he held it in his hands.

"Which is where young Alex comes in." He turned to look at her.

Hmm, thought Alex. Obviously he hadn't forgotten about her after all.

"I've been watching you since you came aboard, little Alex. You haven't been drinking the champagne, have you?" he asked.

"Just one sip – once," she whispered.

"And yet you've not tired at all, participating in our little party?"

"Yes, actually, I'm exhausted."

Charles smiled. "Still, you made it. What a spirit you must have!"

And then Alex understood.

"I never stop this train, but I did when I saw you and I knew I was right. Children are the answer. Children will help with my profit margin!"

Alex took a few steps back.

"Why are you explaining all this to me? I mean, why didn't you just trick me like Van Brusen or force me into that . . . that thingy? Why show me?"

"I don't know. I like hearing the sound of my own voice. And I also like scaring the bejeebus out of people. I have scared the bejeebus out of you, haven't I?"

"Yes, yes you have."

"Good. And now, it's time to test my hypothesis." And he made to grab for her.

But Alex was getting quite good at running away from people. With Giggles holding on to her shoulder for dear life, she ducked away and managed to get to the other end of the carriage and wrench open the door. She stood between the two carriages and quickly pulled across a chain on the door she had just come through. She entered the next carriage, grabbed a chair and put it against the door. She turned and gasped.

Stuart Nickleman was staring at her, nose to nose. He was as pale as Van Brusen, and at first she didn't think he had seen her. But then he reached out to touch her face. Giggles made a soft hissing sound.

"You're so warm," Stuart said without expression. There was a sound of muttering, and Alex looked to see the carriage was full of grey expressionless people. She saw Pudding, and Freddy as well. And there were dozens of others, sitting on long benches that ran parallel down the length of the carriage. Some sat quietly staring ahead, while others seemed very interested in their shoelaces. But they all looked up when Stuart spoke. With empty eyes they stared at Alex and then, slowly, they all came up to her and reached out to touch her.

"So warm," they muttered.

Alex found herself turning, throwing aside the chair and passing through the door again, slamming it behind her and ending up yet again between carriages. Suddenly the other door moved as if someone was banging something heavy against it. Oh, for Pete's sake, she thought. Charles, the ever-so-suave mad scientist, on one side, the soulless mob of zombies on the other.

Alex needed to think, to approach the situation coolly. The door moved again, and Giggles let out a small growl. And Alex had an idea. She flung open the door that Charles was behind and threw Giggles at him.

In slow motion, this is what you would have seen. You would have seen Giggles flying through the air. You would have seen the confused expression on his face until he saw Charles's head coming towards him. Then you would have seen his mind set to purpose, his claws ready, and, with fierce aim, his landing on Charles's face.

In fast motion, you would have seen a blur and then Charles's face obscured by a cat. Charles staggered back into the room violently, as Alex watched, momentarily hypnotized by the action in front of her. He thrashed about the room, knocking over boxes and breaking bottles until he found himself against the glass bowl.

Then Alex performed step two of her plan. She opened the other door and hid behind it. Slowly the bodies started to file out of the carriage and into the one where Charles was still contending with the cat. With much effort he pulled off Giggles and threw him across the room. His face was scratched and bloodied, and he stood there panting.

It was Freddy who made contact first. He touched

Charles's bleeding face and said, "Warm." Charles was surprised to be surrounded suddenly by his old dining partners, and much more surprised at the strength with which they pressed against him. He moved sideways along the bowl, occasionally attempting to hit one of the bodies, none of whom seemed to respond to the blow. And then, without warning, he fell.

The door of the bowl opened, and he found himself inside. He struggled to get out, but Van Brusen got between him and his exit and caused the door to shut. Still trying to reach him, the others rammed their arms through the air holes, flailing with all their might.

"No, don't!" Charles gasped. "It will become a real vacuum!"

But of course they didn't stop.

"Stop! I can't breathe!"

Alex stood in the doorway, looking over at the handle of the machine. It was still turning from the "demonstration" with Van Brusen. She edged quietly along the walls towards the on/off button for the machine. When she found herself at the other side of the bowl, she discovered the button completely obscured by the bodies still muttering "Warm" to themselves. She wasn't sure how to approach it without being mobbed herself.

She could just stay hidden and do nothing, but she

had never meant for anyone to be hurt. There must be a way she could distract the bodies without being mobbed herself. Come on, Alex, she thought angrily, think!

While she was desperately wracking her brain for a Part Three to her plan, she noticed that the muttering had stopped. She looked up and saw that the bodies were exploring the room aimlessly and quietly. Quickly Alex darted over to the button and turned the machine off. She opened the door, but Charles and Van Brusen lay motionless.

Suddenly there was a crashing sound. Alex turned. One of the bodies, a small round woman Alex had never seen before, had come across a bottle of champagne. She had picked it up and then smashed it open, its contents spilling everywhere. The woman touched the champagne with her fingers and smelled them. She put her fingers in her mouth. She stopped and looked around.

"Well, now," she said and repeated the action. She looked around and spotted Alex.

"Help me, child, I may have an idea," she said very coherently. "Which is impressive as I haven't had one for a long time." And she knelt on the ground and began to lick the champagne.

Alex stood in surprise as the woman began to regain some of her colour. Her cheeks started to become rosy and her skin peach.

"Yes, I am certain this is a good idea. Quick, dear, let's do the rest," she said as she stood up with a big grin on her face.

Both Alex and the woman picked up bottles, popped the corks and showered the bodies with champagne. As the drops fell in their mouths, the others began to understand and opened bottles of their own and drank. Soon the bodies became people again, chatting excitedly with each other, some even hugging. Pudding was giggling hysterically.

Alex took a bottle and went over to the machine. She first tried Van Brusen, pouring some liquid down his throat. Then Charles. She waited. Nothing happened. She tried again, but still nothing happened.

"Dear?" said the woman. Alex looked up at her round face. "I don't think that will help them," she said quietly.

Alex took a step back. She felt the woman's warm hand on her shoulder, and she suddenly started to cry.

"Oh no, oh no!" said the woman, hugging Alex to her. "Don't be sad! Van Brusen was a fool but a decent person, and it is sad he is gone, of course. But Charles, well, he was a nasty piece of work, now, wasn't he?"

"It's not that," said Alex into the woman's shoulder.

She didn't know what to say. Could she explain about her uncle? And about how selfish she felt that, in the presence of two other people who had lost their lives, her main thought was for him? Missing him hurt so much, and it was very nice to be hugged by someone. When at last she decided the hugging was enough, she said, "It's nothing. Really."

It was a very bizarre reunion in the dining car because, of course, the guests who had not been turned into zombies had forgotten of the existence of the ones who had. It was as if a haze had lifted as the old guests all took their own chairs again, and slowly Angel and the others started to recognize them. It was confusing and strange, and so they all did what all normal people do when something extraordinary like that happens. Pretended it hadn't.

And then halfway through dessert Alex felt a strange sensation. It was sort of an anti-feeling. Like something that had been there wasn't any more. It took her a few minutes to realize that what was missing was the movement of the train. When she understood what had happened she quickly rose from her seat. This was her chance finally. She didn't care if things had returned to relative normality, she needed to get off this train. Alex made her way to her compartment, slipped inside and found that she had company.

"Um, hey there, Giggles," she said. He acknowledged her existence with a nod and a flick of his tail. Working around him Alex packed up her rucksack, while he watched her suspiciously. Just as she finished, he jumped into her bag.

"No, Giggles, you're far too heavy." But Giggles wouldn't budge. "All right, fine. But if we're going to leave quickly, you are not allowed to attack anyone."

He scoffed, and closed his eyes.

Alex returned to the dining room and said her farewells. Then Angel and Jimmy C escorted her to the door.

Angel peered out into the darkness. "I don't know how I feel about all this," she said, smiling nervously. "The train stopping, you leaving. I don't think I like change very much."

"I don't think anyone really likes change that much," reassured Alex. "But it happens, and we just have to make do. Don't worry, you'll all be fine."

Angel nodded, though she didn't seem entirely convinced.

"Take care of yourself, beautiful," said Jimmy C.

Alex hugged them both tightly. "Well," she said, grabbing Mr Underwood's bicycle and hoisting her bag over her shoulder. She looked at the two of them smiling pleasantly at her. "Goodbye."

And she stepped down out of the train into the dark.

Yes, just like that.

THE NINETEENTH CHAPTER

In which Alex stumbles upon *The Emperor and the Necklace*

Alex stood for a moment taking stock of her surroundings. She was on the edge of the forest, and she could see in the distance behind her the lights of her town in the background. She had no idea how long she had been on that train, but it seemed obvious she hadn't got very far. What a waste of time! From now on she was going to travel by her own means, rely on no one but herself. First, though, she needed to find a place to sleep for the night.

She decided to follow the train tracks. She felt this was probably a good plan, as they would most likely at some point take her to Port Cullis, and the light of the train would guide her way.

After an hour or so, it seemed quite obvious that she wouldn't be getting out of the woods any time soon. The light from the train had faded to darkness, and she was so tired that she could barely lift her legs. She decided it was time to settle down for the night. Alex stepped off the track and made herself as comfortable as she could at the base of a large tree.

She opened up her rucksack and had a look inside. Giggles was curled up snugly on top of her jumper. "Sorry 'bout this," she said and pulled the jumper out from underneath him. He looked up at her. "Hey, I'm going to sleep now, so . . . well, just so you know."

Giggles nodded and jumped out of the bag.

"What are you doing?" asked Alex, as she laid out her jumper to lie on. But he simply looked at her, and she gave a little shrug. Cats, she thought.

He sat and watched as she got comfortable. Once she had found a position that wasn't too hard on the back, he sat by her and faced out towards the night.

"I don't think there is anything to watch out for," said Alex with a yawn. "And we both could use some sleep after all that excitement."

Giggles gave her a look as if to say, "That's what you think. Now go to sleep already, I know what I'm doing." And faced out again.

Alex thought this was wholly unnecessary, but it was a nice gesture all the same, and soon she was asleep.

The sleep was delightful. It was a truly pleasant thing, not the sort of sleep imposed on you when you are in the middle of a good book, or a TV show, or a game and you are suddenly told rather unceremoniously, "Time for bed!" That sort of resentful sleep is not that pleasant, despite the fact that when morning comes all you want to do is stay under the covers. No, I mean the sort of sleep that comes when you finish a good book, or TV show, or game, stand up and with a stretch and yawn say, "Well, I do believe it's time for bed!" And you skip upstairs of your own free will and curl up under the covers. This was the sort of sleep Alex had that night and would have continued to have had late into the afternoon had some very strange noises not woken her up.

She sat up, stretched and looked for Giggles. Who was exactly as she had left him, and so she didn't need to look for him that hard.

"Did you hear that, Giggles?"

Giggles indicated in his cat-like way that he had heard and that it did not please him one bit.

"Oh, you're suspicious of everything. Honestly, Giggles, lighten up." Alex stood and took stock of her surroundings.

You know the old saying, "can't see the forest for the

trees"? Well that's sort of what it was like looking about. She was in a forest. And there were lots of trees. And other than the train tracks, which wound their way out of sight, there was no other sign of humans. Oh, except the sudden loud yelling which came from somewhere deeper within the brush. A loud yelling of a word which it would just not do to repeat in this particular kind of novel. But it was very shocking to hear, I don't mind telling you.

"Goodness," said Alex. Giggles agreed, and they decided to investigate.

They found the going tricky (goings are often tricky, especially with bicycles), having to step over things and under things and around things and through things, and the sun being rather hot and all. But they kept following the offensive word, which punctuated the silence of the forest every few minutes, until finally, drawing aside a giant branch with giant leaves on it, they discovered its source.

The source was a chubby man with long black hair and stubble on his chin. He was wearing hiking boots and a hooded jumper that had "*The Emperor and the Necklace*" written on the front and "*The journey goes on and on and on. . .*" on the back.

"Dang and blast!" he cursed more tamely. "What are we going to do, then? We were supposed to start an hour ago!"

He was standing in a clearing surrounded by technical-looking equipment, so that the trees and shrubbery of the forest gave way to tall metal stands with giant lights rising overhead, and, instead of vines, cables snaked across the floor of the forest. Large silver metal boxes with large metal clasps stood in place of rocks and boulders, and instead of cute little squirrels and chipmunks and things, there were men and women of various heights and ages in baggy T-shirts and jeans and white running shoes, as well as baseball caps that all read *The Emperor and the Necklace*.

Alex stood quietly at the edge of the clearing, her jaw open wide. Now she understood. She had happened upon a film shooting on location. Giggles shook his head disapprovingly, and his tail turned into a fern tree again. It seemed it wasn't just mad scientists on trains that Giggles didn't like. Except for Alex, it appeared Giggles didn't like anybody. She thought it might be wise to put him back in the bag, and did so, much to his resentment.

Alex then wandered into the clearing, trying to stay out of the way, and especially trying to avoid the expensive-looking film equipment that was strewn everywhere.

"Wait! Wait, wait, wait!" erupted the man with long hair loudly. "What's that?" And he pointed right at Alex.

A sudden silence fell over the clearing as everyone stopped what they were doing and stared at her.

"No, no, no, no. This is the last straw! Could someone remove the kid? Please?" he shouted, his voice cracking.

Instantly Alex was whisked off her feet. She flew through the clearing to a group of chairs and a table with bagels and a coffee urn sitting on it. She was placed roughly in a seat by a woman with a ponytail, who kneeled down and asked, "Who are you and where are your parents?"

Alex was reminded of the paperwork at the police station. "Um, I'm Alexandra Morningside, but most people call me Alex, and my parents are gone, but that's OK, it happened a long time ago," she said obligingly. She didn't add anything about her uncle and Mr Underwood because she hadn't been asked, and it wasn't anyone else's business anyway.

"So why are you here?"

"Oh," said Alex slowly, "well that is a very long story that involves Pirate Captain Steele and his men, and you seem very busy, and it would take a while to explain it to you."

The woman with the ponytail nodded in agreement. "Well, what do you want, then?" she asked.

"Well. . ." Alex thought. She knew it wasn't a literal question. There was no point in telling the woman she wanted to find Mr Underwood, or the Infamous Wigpowder's treasure. And that deep, deep down she would give up either to have her uncle back. But there was one thing that right now she wanted more than anything and that was. . . "To get to Port Cullis."

The woman looked at Alex for a second and then smiled. "I think we can manage that. I'm sure once we're done here, we could give you a lift."

And without realizing she had been carrying it around with her, Alex felt a large weight lift off her shoulders.

"Oh, thank you so much!" she said.

The woman smiled. "Right, then. My name is Holly, and for the time being it is really important you stay out from under our feet. You can have some food if you want." She gestured towards the table. "And please try to stay away from Steve, he's . . . he's in a mood."

Steve, she explained, was the pudgy man with long hair and stubble, and was also the director for *The Emperor and the Necklace*. She added that he was really stressed out because a certain star performer was proving difficult.

"Which explains the state of his appearance," she said, pouring herself a cup of coffee. Alex nodded. Though, judging by the length of his greasy hair, she thought, that would have meant he had been stressed for a decade or so.

"Who's the star?" asked Alex.

"Oh, it's not who, it's what."

"I'm sorry." Alex rephrased the question. "What is the star?"

"The Extremely Ginormous Octopus," replied Holly, shaking her head sadly and taking a gulp of coffee. "And he's gone missing."

THE TWENTIETH CHAPTER

In which we learn about motion capture and visit the Duke's Elbow

Alex blinked twice. "I'm sorry . . . pardon?"

"The Extremely Ginormous Octopus."

"Would that be an octopus, then?"

"One that is very, very big, yes." Holly sighed heavily and turned to Alex to explain. "We had arranged to work with the Extremely Ginormous Octopus in pre-production, but now he has vanished and we have no clue where he is."

"But why do you need him? I mean, don't you use,

you know, special effects for that sort of thing?"

"Oh, gosh, it's more complicated than that," sighed the woman, refilling her cup of coffee and adding three sugars.

"It is?"

"OK. Well, have you heard of motion capture?" she asked Alex.

"Sort of."

"OK. Imagine you take a piece of paper and you draw a picture on it of a flower in glue. Then you throw sand on the glue and when it dries the glue disappears, but the sand stays shaped like a flower. You following me?"

"Yes, of course," said Alex, trying to give the impression of an intelligent child who picked things up more quickly than most, which was, in fact, what she was.

"Well, that's the same with motion capture. Imagine that you have a person in a bodysuit – the shape of the person is like the shape of the flower and the bodysuit is like the glue. Then you cover the person with these things that look like ping-pong balls. That's like the sand."

"Right, right."

"And those ping-pong balls send information back to a computer. So that what you see on the computer is the form of the person because of the ping-pong balls, but not the person himself. And the form moves when the person does and so on. So then you can 'capture' movement on the computer and use it later. For example, if the person hopped, then the image would hop. If the person sat down, the image would sit down. Hmm . . .what else?" And she pondered what else could be captured by motion. "Tap dancing?"

Alex, who was keen to get back to the topic at hand asked, "What does that have to do with the octopus?"

"Sorry? Oh, yes, so we took pictures of him and now have his stills in the animation software. And he agreed that for one day only we could capture his movement and then we would leave him be. Well, today is the day, and now he has vanished! And that's what Steve is stressed about," finished Holly as she drained her coffee cup for the second time.

"OK, people, listen up!" Steve called out, holding up his mobile phone. Everyone stopped running about once more. "Right! We have a tip. We have word that the Extremely Ginormous Octopus has been terrorizing a small village pub just half a mile down the road. So let's get our things together and get a move on."

Everyone got very busy packing up lights and cables. Alex began to feel a little antsy.

"Holly," she asked, "when will we be heading for Port Cullis?"

"Oh, don't worry! Once we've finished with the Extremely Ginormous Octopus, we can give you a ride. Port Cullis is about an hour from the pub. Just stick with me."

So that's just what Alex did. She helped the crew haul some equipment over to several parked trucks just beyond the edge of the clearing. And before you could say, "Don't forget the gaffer tape," they were all trundling down the bumpy road. In around twenty minutes, they turned a corner and came upon a tiny pub standing in a semicircular clearing just off to the side. It was white, with windows trimmed in dark brown, and had a slanty roof that looked like it might slip off at any moment. In front hung a sign that read "The Duke's Elbow". Standing huddled together in the street was a small group of people looking worried. A sturdy-looking woman in coveralls and an apron approached them right away.

"Thank goodness! We just don't know what to do! He's already insulted my cooking, drunk three bottles of Jeff's best whisky and told young Martha she looks fat in her new dress. He then started to trash the place, and what with them eight arms of his, it looks like a war zone in there. We all just had to get out before he did some serious damage and injured someone. Can't you control him?" she asked pleadingly.

"Don't worry, Mrs Windsor, we'll take care of him," said Steve, and he made a signal.

Two big men in black wearing sunglasses stepped forward with large rifles.

"You aren't going to shoot him, are you?" said Mrs

Windsor nervously.

"They're just tranquillizer guns, ma'am, don't worry," replied Steve, and he had a quiet word with the two men, who then turned and marched into the pub.

Holly went up to join Steve, and Alex followed close at her heels. The three of them waited.

. . .

. . .

. . .

It was very quiet.

. . .

. . .

. . .

A bird turned to its friend and went to say something but then changed its mind.

. . .

. . .

. . .

And then. . .

There was the unmistakable sound of smashing glass, which went along with the unmistakable sight of two men in black flying backwards through the ground floor windows of the Duke's Elbow and landing on the road in front of them.

"That worked, then," said Holly to Steve.

Steve rushed up to the two men in black and gave

them some new instructions and pushed them back into the pub.

And the same thing happened again.

And he sent them in again.

And the same thing happened again.

"Those guys are pretty tough," said Alex.

"He'll kill them if he keeps sending them in like that," said Holly, shaking her head.

She and Alex watched in dismay as Steve signalled yet again to the men in black. Who looked at him in disbelief. And then slowly, with their heads hanging down, they dragged their feet into the pub.

And were once more flat on their backs in front of Steve, Holly and Alex.

"That does it!" said Steve. "I'm calling back-up!" And he took out his mobile.

Alex looked at him. "Holly?"

"Yes?"

"How long will we have to wait for back-up?"

"At least an hour. Probably more."

For Alex it was the last straw. Without a word, because she knew they would try to stop her, Alex headed towards the entrance of the Duke's Elbow.

THE TWENTY-FIRST CHAPTER

In which Alex reasons with the
Extremely Ginormous Octopus

Alex approached the door to the pub and went to open it. Then she had a thought. She bent down and opened her rucksack. "Giggles," she said. He gave her a look that it is best not to describe as it was so vile. "Do you think you could maybe just keep an eye out for me? I mean, don't do anything rash or anything . . . just, well, you know. . ."

Giggles looked at her resentfully. He did know. But he

didn't much like being kept confined in a rucksack like that.

"Please?"

And with a look that said, "Let's get on with it," Giggles and Alex entered the Duke's Elbow quietly.

You know how sometimes a place can look really small on the outside, but can turn out to be much larger on the inside? Well, this was not one of those times. The inside of the pub was tiny, made all the more so by all the broken tables and chairs strewn about the place. It was made even tinier because there was an Extremely Ginormous Octopus at the bar. But it probably would have looked equally tiny on a regular day as well.

The Extremely Ginormous Octopus was indeed extremely ginormous. There was no question about that. He stood (or rather would have stood had he not been sitting) three metres tall and each of his eight arms stretched to around six metres. In three of his tentacles he held snifters of whisky, in the fourth, a handkerchief that he waved back and forth wildly. Two others were occupied randomly picking up and throwing pieces of furniture across the room. And the last two hung loosely by his side.

"'For God's sake, let us sit upon the ground and tell sad stories of the death of kings,'" he was saying to himself in a large, booming, throaty voice. He then began to weep. "'How some have been depos'd, some slain in war, some haunted by the ghosts they have depos'd, some poison'd by their wives, some sleeping kill'd – all murder'd.'" And with that he put his head on the bar and sobbed wildly.

Alex took another step forward. Unfortunately, her step happened to land on a broken bottle of Jeff's best whisky and a small but distinctive cracking sound pierced the room.

For a drunken Extremely Ginormous Octopus he had incredible reflexes. The two arms lying limp at his side suddenly swept towards Alex and Giggles, picked them up and held them in the air.

"That's strange," said the Octopus, not turning around, "you are much lighter than you were the last time." He squeezed tighter. "And you seem to have forgotten your guns. How unfortunate for you."

"Please, sir, we don't have any guns," wheezed Alex.

Hearing her voice, the Extremely Ginormous Octopus turned his head slowly. His eyes were red from crying and he blinked heavily.

"Who are you?" he asked, the words slurring slightly.

"Alex."

"I see. And this?" he asked, holding up Giggles, who was trying fiercely to bite the octopus.

"Giggles."

"I see. So they decided a little boy and a cat would be

better at bringing me down than two large armed gunmen. How strange." He brought Alex and Giggles up next to him at the bar. "Ah, if only they knew! They can't bring me down. They can't bring me any lower than I already am!" And a large tear ran down his cheek.

"Please, Mr Extremely Ginormous Octopus, sir, we aren't here to 'bring you down'," said Alex as calmly as she could.

"No?" roared the octopus suddenly. "No!? Tell that to the two oafs who attacked me just a moment ago!"

"I'm serious, Mr Extremely Ginormous Octopus. I don't have anything to do with those other men. I was just interested . . . that is, I just . . . wanted to know why you were hiding from the film crew, that's all. I mean everyone wants to act in a movie, don't they?" continued Alex.

"Don't talk to me about acting, my son," said the octopus coldly.

"I'm a girl."

"Are you? Well, don't you talk to me about acting either," he said, squinting at her.

"Why not?"

"You all laugh at me! All you see is a brute of a monster. Some sort of stupid animal. But in my glory days . . . no, that is the past." He dabbed his eyes with his handkerchief. For a moment it looked as if he was finished and Alex was about to speak when the Extremely Ginormous Octopus erupted again. "The past! Let us not talk about the late hours in the pub regaling each other with stories – ah, the stories! Such wonderful stories. But who is left to tell them now? The giant squid is dead, yes, he is dead. And Nessie has become a recluse. You talk of acting, my child. You think these animated screen creations can act? These computer-generated image monstrosities? They have no passion, they have no motivations! Where is the art? I have been in twenty-one films. I have played the Old Vic! I have worked with all the great ones, Sir Larry, Sir Alec, Sir Massive Kimono Lizard!"

"I don't understand what this has to do with this movie," said Alex quietly.

"No, how could you? How could you know what it feels like to have been someone who spent his days and nights with the most creative of beasts, only to watch their roles be usurped by animated drawings. Oh, the shame! I shall never forget the day Godzilla announced that, after years of heartache and struggle, they were going to bring him back to the silver screen. How we celebrated – we drank so much that night! It was not until a week later that he discovered all they wanted was to watch him storm about so that they could recreate his movement and construct their own monster on a computer!"

"That must have been sad." Alex was beginning to feel sorry for the creature.

"Sad doesn't begin to describe it! Sad, she says! Sad!! Imagine your heart being ripped out of your chest, cut into tiny pieces, burned till black, then glued back together again, shoved back into your chest and ripped out all over again!"

Alex tried to imagine it.

"And now it is happening to me. Just as it happened to him. Oh, the pain, the anguish!" And he started to sob again.

Alex looked at the poor creature. It did seem really unfair that he was being replaced by a computer, and she could quite understand why he would feel so upset about it.

"That is really awful," she said. "To have been a star and now to be reduced to this. It isn't fair! Have you told anyone this? Steve or anyone?"

The Extremely Ginormous Octopus looked at her hard again. Then he gently sat her down on top of the bar and released her. "If I let go of the cat, will he bite me?" he asked, looking at Giggles.

"He might," admitted Alex.

"Then I won't let go of the cat," he said and kept a firm hold of Giggles, who by now was mad with rage.

With the arm he had just freed he grabbed a glass and poured some whisky. "Drink?" he offered.

"No, thank you," replied Alex. The octopus nodded and swallowed the whisky in one gulp.

"You asked me if I had spoken to Steve. Would it matter if I had? Would he listen?" he sighed. "Would he care?"

"How could he not care? You are one of the greatest monsters of your generation!" insisted Alex. "In fact," she reached into her bag for her camera, "I would love to have my picture taken with such a famous celebrity!"

The octopus exhaled slowly and shook his head. Alex thought for sure he was about to say no, but then he quickly placed a tentacle around Alex's shoulder. With her arm outstretched, she took a picture of the two of them smiling, heads leaning together.

"If you send it to my agent once you develop it, I can sign it for you!" said the Extremely Ginormous Octopus.

"That would be great!"

The octopus thought carefully for a moment. "Well, maybe you are right, that Steve would listen to me. I am, after all, pretty terrific."

At which point the two men in black suddenly burst through the door again. With one fell swoop of a tentacle they were sent soaring back out through the window. Instantly the Extremely Ginormous Octopus returned to his enraged self.

"You see! He only sees me as some stupid animal!" The Extremely Ginormous Octopus turned and glanced out of one of the windows. "Look at them all, watching to see if the great director can tame the wild beast. None of them see the true artist inside. I shall not be paraded like some sort of circus monstrosity!"

Alex sighed. She had been so close. There was a silence as she stared out of the window at the large crowd. "OK, if I can convince the rest of them to leave, and ask only Steve to stay and talk with you, would that be OK?"

There was no response.

"Look, let me talk to him," said Alex. "I'm pretty sure I can persuade him."

The Extremely Ginormous Octopus gave an extremely ginormous shrug. "You'll come right back?"

"I'll come right back," Alex assured him, hopping off the bar. "Um . . . I guess you can keep a hold of Giggles for now." And she gave Giggles a look of apology. Which he did not accept.

"He wants what?!"

"He wants to act. He wants to be in the movie. I'm sure that if you let him, then all your problems will be solved," said Alex.

"No, I can't. I just can't. I mean, what about all that expensive motion capture equipment we've bought? What about our advertising campaign: 'The Greatest Special Effects Movie of All Time'? No, it's impossible," said Steve, putting a plaster on the big toe of one of the men in black.

"Look, special effects aren't that special any more anyway," insisted Alex. "I mean, how much more original would you be if you used a genuine monster? Think of that publicity!"

"She makes a good point," said Holly. "He could actually be the face of *The Emperor and the Necklace* – we could get him on talk shows! People would certainly be interested in seeing that!"

Steve thought about it, scratching the stubble on his face.

"Would we have to pay him?" he asked.

"I think it has more to do with pride than money," said Alex.

"Are you sure he can be trusted, though? I mean he is a monster."

"Well, first you have to send everyone away. He only wants to talk to you. But that means. . ." Alex looked at Holly. "Steve, will you be able to drive me to Port Cullis afterwards?"

Steve looked at Holly, who raised her eyebrows at him.

He gave a short nod. Holly then quickly set about dismissing everyone for the day, which really wasn't all that difficult to do as everyone was pretty ready to call it quits anyway. And Alex escorted Steve towards the pub, explaining softly, "I think that if you ask him nicely, and really, you know, compliment him and stuff, he'll like that a lot."

Steve shook his head. "I don't know about this."

"Wait here a minute," she instructed and she re-entered the pub.

"Well?" asked the Extremely Ginormous Octopus as Alex climbed back on top of the bar.

"They are very interested in having you act in the movie. They want to make you the face of *The Emperor and the Necklace*. They want to put you on talk shows!" said Alex with a big smile.

"Talk shows!!" roared the octopus. "Do they want me to sell my soul as well? Perhaps they would like me to tap dance and juggle twelve poodles while I'm at it!" He slammed a tentacled fist on the bar.

"Um. . ."

"I am an actor. I am an artist!" He stopped, panting heavily. After a few moments of charged silence he asked, "Did they say which talk shows?"

"Look, I'll go get him, and he can explain everything to you."

Now if Steve was normally pasty white it was nothing

compared to how he looked approaching the Extremely Ginormous Octopus. He picked up a bar stool and tentatively drew it up beside the octopus, who all the while was glaring at him intensely.

"Hey . . . Ginormous Octopus," he said nervously.

"Hey? Hey?! That's all you have to say after trying to kill me," said the octopus in a very low voice.

"No, not kill you, no just . . . you know . . . stun . . . you. . ."

"And that's better?!!" exploded the octopus. "That's better, is it? You ask for my help and then treat me like some sort of . . . animal!"

"Now, to be fair," said Steve, gaining some nerve, "you did sort of leave us in the lurch there. I mean, we did make a deal."

"Oh, I'm sorry. I am so sorry. Do forgive me for leaving the very important director man in the lurch," sneered the octopus.

"And you know what else? You are an animal! How else do you want me to treat you?" retorted Steve, bringing himself nose to nose with the octopus (or rather nose to where an octopus's nose would be, if it had one).

"That's enough!" interrupted Alex. "Steve, didn't you have something you wanted to say to the Extremely Ginormous Octopus?"

Steve backed off and shifted uncomfortably in his

seat. Alex waited for him to say something. But he didn't.

"Well, he was thinking," started Alex instead, "that it might be nice to have an actual monster in the movie and not a CGI one."

The Extremely Ginormous Octopus turned his back to them.

"Um . . . and that normally they would never make this offer, but you are one of the greatest movie monsters of your generation. . ."

To which the Extremely Ginormous Octopus made a sound like, "Harrumph."

"Oh yes!" joined in Steve, finally clueing in. "When I was a boy, I remember seeing you in . . . that big movie of yours . . . and being frightened to tears."

"Was he that frightening?" asked Alex.

"Yes, he was that frightening," replied Steve.

The Extremely Ginormous Octopus said quietly, "I have always been famous for frightening people to tears."

"And for obvious reason!" continued Steve with more confidence. "And you make a good point, I mean why animate pictures when you can have the real thing? I mean . . . can animations feel?"

"Can they cry on cue? Do they understand the arc of a story? Do they study the poetry in the text? I think not!" added the Extremely Ginormous Octopus.

"Now, of course, we don't exactly know what you would take in payment. . ."

"Twenty cases of whisky would be sufficient," the octopus said quickly.

"Done!" And Steve extended his hand. The octopus grasped it with four of his and they shook.

"Excellent!" exclaimed Alex. "Well, now that that is taken care of," she said, clasping both of them on their backs, "don't you think we'd better get going?"

Steve nodded and smiled. It was only when he did that that Alex realized she had never seen him do it before. He suddenly seemed like a normal person. And she smiled back. And then the Extremely Ginormous Octopus smiled too.

And then the door of the pub exploded off its hinges in the most violent and destructive way possible.

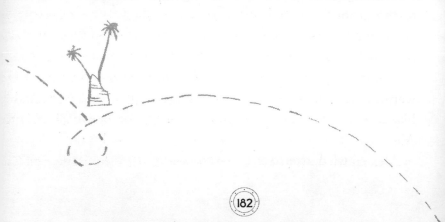

THE TWENTY-SECOND CHAPTER

In which Alex finds herself trapped

Alex, Steve and the Extremely Ginormous Octopus turned and blankly stared at the gaping hole that had recently been the entrance of the pub.

"Oh!" exclaimed Alex. Without pause she dived low to the ground and hid behind the bulk that was the octopus, her mind racing. It wasn't possible, it just wasn't possible.

"Good afternoon," said a voice, with an attempt at warmth, but failing miserably. "I hate to barge in on you like this. But, you see, I am looking for my grandchild. Alex."

Alex crawled over so that she could peer between two

of the octopus's tentacles. There, in the doorway, stood the leader of the Daughters of the Founding Fathers' Preservation Society, Poppy. Behind her stood the other four, arms crossed and grinning sweetly. All except the tall long-haired Rose, who spat the pin of the just detonated grenade on to the floor with a resounding clink.

"I'm afraid Alex is," continued Poppy, "how can I put it delicately . . . mentally disturbed, which is why he has run away from home."

"Isn't Alex a girl?" asked the octopus.

Without batting an eyelash Poppy said, "Yes, that was merely a test. Isn't that her crouching down behind you?"

Alex whimpered as the octopus turned to look down at her.

"We don't want to take up any more of your time, dearie. Please, she needs to be with her family."

But Steve and the octopus didn't move. Alex could understand their hesitation. There was something deeply troubling about the way Poppy spoke. Though every word she uttered made perfect sense, she somehow still came across slightly as a crazy lady who'd been locked in an attic one too many days.

Poppy edged closer to the octopus.

"If you don't mind," she said, trying to manoeuvre herself around him. Alex was merely centimetres away from those click-click shoes of hers.

"She seems quite scared of you," said the octopus, taking another glance at Alex. "But at the same time . . . I mean, family is a great thing." Alex shook her head at him, but he had turned back to Poppy. "I have always felt that very strongly because . . . well . . . because I never knew my father, you see. Though I have been told he was a great actor in his day. . ."

"Yes, yes, how sad for you, dear." Alex watched the click-click shoes shuffle to the left and then the right.

"The greatest, I would imagine. I remember once, ha! This you might find amusing. He wasn't around when I was growing up, you see, and one day I decided to find him. Oh my, yes, how silly of me . . . how old was I then . . . oh, I can't remember. . ."

"Dear, is this really the time?"

"I know I had just been in a youth production of *The Tempest* – I played Caliban. Do you know *The Tempest*? Well, it is quite popular, I should imagine. . ."

"Look, to be frank. . ."

"I mean the question is more like, who hasn't seen *The Tempest*? Though interestingly. . ."

"I insist you desist with this blathering. . ."

". . .I knew an abominable snowman who hadn't. Now that, I told him, is abominable!"

"Will you shut up, you degenerate beast!!"

There was a stillness that seemed oh so wrong.

"What did you call me?" asked the Extremely Ginormous Octopus softly.

"You heard me. Now out of my way, before I get Rose to do something very unpleasant to you, you filthy animal! What . . . stop that, put me down this instant!"

Alex watched Poppy's feet lift off the ground until they vanished from her line of vision. Revealed to her, like a curtain rising on a play, was Rose, by the doorway of the pub, reaching for a crossbow. Suddenly Giggles plummeted from on high, landing in front of her with a thud, and Rose was whisked off her feet in his stead, followed closely by the other three.

"How dare you?" the octopus said in a low voice that vibrated through the pub. "Who are you, you old hag, to call me such despicable names? What plays have you ever been in? What stars have you worked with? Are you the face of *The Emperor and the Necklace*?"

Steve made a small noise that indicated he would rather his film were left out of this particular confrontation at the moment, but that he still thought the octopus was an excellent actor and he hoped he wouldn't be offended by his making that small noise.

"I don't think so!" boomed the octopus, oblivious to Steve. "I am not some creature that lives only by its baser instincts! I am not some monster for you to gawk at! I am not, as you so delicately put it, a degenerate beast!! I am . . ." He rose to his full height, which was sincerely impressive, ". . . an actor!!"

Alex stood and looked at Steve, who had been cornered accidentally by the octopus in his fury. The octopus had begun to swing his captives around slowly, while the Daughters were screaming and blaming each other for this predicament. All except Poppy, who pointed at Alex.

"You can't hide from me, urchin! Wherever you go, whatever you do, I'll find you!!" She swooped over Alex's head and back, and then again.

Alex bolted through the doorway of the pub, grabbing Giggles as she did so and stuffing him back into her bag. She hopped on Mr Underwood's bicycle and began to pedal down the dirt road in what she hoped was the direction towards Port Cullis. As she went, she passed a parked tan car with the bumper sticker "Driving slower than the speed limit is legal for your information", which she presumed belonged to the Daughters.

The road was long and narrow and there seemed to be no turn-off in sight. Pedalling as quickly as she could, Alex realized that, eventually, once they were released, the Daughters would overtake her in their car. She slowed to a stop and took stock of her situation. There were no two ways about it. She looked mournfully towards the thick brush of the forest. And then, with a resigned determination, she climbed off her bike and, pulling it behind her, pushed her way through the trees.

She plodded along for a while, and then, when the foliage had thinned somewhat, she started to run. She ran. And she ran. She ran as fast as it was possible to run dragging a bike with you. She did not dare stop. Every time she slowed down she thought she heard the dreaded click-click of their shoes, anticipated feeling a bony hand grab her shoulder, and she would jump as if she had been electrocuted and speed up again.

She continued to run until she could run no further, and for the first time she looked behind her. No one. Nobody was following her. She stood quietly, and aside from her heartbeat, there wasn't a sound. Alex collapsed on to the ground and sat, stunned. She wanted to cry. She wanted to cry because she was both relieved and angry. She had managed to elude the Daughters of the Founding Fathers' Preservation Society once again, but she was also back in the forest. Not only that, she was still no closer to reaching Port Cullis, to finding Mr Underwood, or the treasure. And just to add insult to injury, it appeared that maybe . . . Alex looked around . . . no, not maybe, she was quite certain of it . . . she was also completely and utterly lost.

THE TWENTY-THIRD CHAPTER

In which we come across a very Illustrious Hotel

Now Alex was a determined person. When she set her mind to something, she stuck to it. This meant that when she set a goal for herself, like, for example, rescuing a year-six teacher and seeking out his fortune, anything that hampered the end result was very, very upsetting to her. And what upset her even more was how nothing seemed to be going as she planned it. All she wanted was to get to Port Cullis, and that simple goal had somehow become impossible. She couldn't take the train. And now the road was off limits as well because of those little old ladies.

Rage filled her gut. What were those little old ladies doing there anyway? Alex wondered furiously. How had they found her? Would they plague her for the rest of her life? Didn't they have better things to do than to chase a ten-and-a-half-year-old girl across the countryside? Alex leaned her head against a tree.

Suddenly her rucksack launched itself into the air.

"Oh, Giggles!" she exclaimed and opened the bag for him. He leapt out and looked at her resentfully. "Sorry." She picked him up. With a shake of his head, he curled up in her lap and she scratched him behind his ears. "So, Giggles," she said with a sigh, "what do we do now? Do we just keep going and hope that we'll just stumble into Port Cullis? Do we turn around? Do we just move into the forest and live here for ever?" Giggles looked up at her. "Not really, don't worry." She sighed. "I just don't know what to do. I don't know which way to go, I can hardly tell up from down. It all seems so pointless, it all seems so . . . is that a lawn mower?"

Giggles jumped off her lap and slowly she stood up. They walked through the trees towards the sound and suddenly found themselves standing in a beautifully manicured garden. This was surprising. What was even more surprising was the large white hotel that stood just beyond it.

It was a particularly odd hotel, though at first glance

you wouldn't have thought so. It was very grand with a veranda that wound all the way around the ground-floor level. And, yes, you are right that the gardener pushing the little mower around the front room was not particularly strange. In fact, he was downright friendly. This would be even clearer to you if you knew that his name was Tom Friend, but you don't know that, because he never introduced himself to Alex and plays little to no role in this particular chapter. But I still insist that this hotel was a strange thing. And now I will explain why.

There are lots of different factors that contribute to owning a successful hotel, but the most important thing to know about is location, location, location. For example, if you have a hotel in the heart of the theatre district, then that is good because then all the people who like to see plays will stay in your hotel. But if you have a hotel deep in the heart of a big, thick forest, a hotel to which no road goes and that everyone has forgotten exists, well, dear reader, I can confidently say that no one will stay in your hotel. And this was why this hotel was so strange. It was completely out of place.

"What a strange hotel," said Alex. She looked at Giggles and Giggles looked at her, and they silently agreed to investigate.

They approached the hotel, walking up the gravel drive, and climbed up the pristine white stairs to the entrance. Next to the door was a sign that read, "On the Edge Hotel". Inside they found themselves facing a wide white staircase, which led up to the upper floor, where three large windows filled the room with light. The floor was done in pine wood, and two well-tended orange trees framed a desk where a young lady in a crisp grey suit was busy writing in a book. She glanced up momentarily as Alex and Giggles wandered past her out of the foyer, through to, what appeared to be, the dining room.

It was huge, with round tables topped with perfect place settings and mini-orange trees. It was also completely empty, aside from two men standing at the far end. Alex wandered into the brightly lit room to look out of the huge windows that revealed the well-tended front garden and gravel drive. As she approached the two men she caught some of their conversation. One of them was dressed in a tuxedo and the other – well, the other was quite impressive. He stood nearly two metres tall and wore a tweed jacket with matching beige trousers and shiny brown shoes. Under the jacket he had on a crisp white shirt, and around his neck he wore an impressive purple bow tie. His hair was a golden colour and curled at his forehead.

"Where is my pen?!" he was demanding of the frightened-looking maître d'.

"I'm sorry, I haven't found it. When did you last see it?"

"What sort of question is that? When I was using it of course! This is completely unacceptable!"

"I'm sorry! I'll gather the staff together, and we'll search the hotel."

"Don't tell me what you are going to do, do what you are going to do!" said the man loudly.

"Of course, right away, sir," said the maître d', practically running out of the room. The man in the bow tie watched him go and shook his head sadly.

"Come on, sweetums," he then said and he headed in the direction towards Alex.

Alex was trying to figure out who "sweetums" could be, when she felt a sudden mad scrabbling at her back. Giggles was trying desperately to get into her rucksack. Alex slipped it off, and he scrambled inside, quietly hissing to himself.

"Giggles, what is wrong with you?" she asked, but she soon understood.

As the man approached, she noticed a small dog with a bow in its hair following close at his heels. It trotted along quite as if it owned the place, but it was so tiny that it was less than half the size of Giggles. "Why, Giggles, you old coward," laughed Alex into the bag, but he wouldn't look at her, so she closed it up and put it on her back again.

She turned around and found herself face to face with

the man. Or rather nose to navel. She looked up as he looked down at her.

"You're late," he said.

"Am I?" asked Alex.

"Lord Poppinjay does not tolerate lateness."

"He doesn't?"

"And the Baron of East Westcliff has more important things to do than wait on personal assistants."

"I would imagine so."

"I am a very busy man, running such an illustrious hotel as this."

"Oh, gosh, yes I would expect that takes a lot of work," agreed Alex quickly. She continued to stare blankly at the man, and then suddenly she understood. "You're Lord Poppinjay!"

"Of course I am!"

"And also the Baron of East Westcliff?"

"Look, what is the matter with you? Of course that's who I am. I just said that, didn't I? Oh, enough of this. I need someone with excellent typing skills, good filing technique and superb dog-walking abilities. I assume you have your CV with you?"

Alex shook her head no. Now it was all making sense. Lord Poppinjay obviously had her confused with someone else. Someone who was meant to be applying as his personal assistant or something! Well, she just didn't have the time now for such mistakes.

"Lord Poppinjay, I'm sorry, there has been some mix-up. I just happened upon your hotel by accident. I am in a fight against time to rescue my year-six teacher, and unless you can take me to Port Cullis, or at least show me the way, I'm afraid I will have to leave immediately."

"Oh no, you can't go to Port Cullis. That part of the forest is particularly dangerous to travel, especially on your own. No, no. You'd best stay and be my personal assistant. Now since you don't have your CV with you, I suppose what we could do is give you a little test, then. I assume you are familiar with dictation?"

"I am familiar with the concept, yes, but I really don't have the time for a test. You see I'm not. . ."

"Well," he interrupted, "I have come up with my own variation on the theme, which I think you will find very exciting. Here," he handed Alex a pad of paper and a pen and leaned against one of the dining tables. "Now the concept of dictation, as I know you are well aware, is for you to write down everything that I am saying, right?"

"Of course." Alex resigned herself to taking his test. It would probably be quickest to do so and then leave, as opposed to standing there arguing with him for who knew how long.

"Well, one day I was sitting thinking of all the useful things that I could be doing when I had the brilliant epiphany – what the world needed was Mental Dictation!"

"Mental Dictation?"

"Yes! Think of those precious moments wasted translating thoughts into speech when you could simply have someone copy down your thoughts in the first place! I couldn't believe no one had ever come up with this before! In fact I called my friend Evans Bore, a CEO of a very important company, and asked if anyone else had ever thought of such a thing. He said he had never heard of anything quite like it before and admitted that if anyone could come up with something like that, it would be me. He is a dear friend of mine, Evans Bore. Have you met him?"

"No."

"Well, I have, because he is a great friend of mine. Since then, I have been running this hotel based on the premise of the staff being able to read my thoughts. So let's test you out, then," said Lord Poppinjay, and he placed the first two fingers of each hand on the side of each of his temples. "When I say 'go', I want you to write down everything I am thinking . . . ready? And . . . GO!" And he stood there, his fingers pressed to his temples and eyes shut tight, one could only assume thinking hard. Alex just stared at him in disbelief for a good few seconds. The dog whimpered quietly.

"There!" said Lord Poppinjay, opening his eyes suddenly. "Let's have a look."

Alex handed over the blank pad tentatively.

Lord Poppinjay gave it a once-over, nodding. "Good, good, excellent. You passed the test. I wasn't thinking about anything!" Alex bit her bottom lip to keep from laughing. "You're hired!" he said, clapping a hand on her shoulder. "Here, let me show you to my office."

"Lord Poppinjay, while I am terribly flattered that you would hire me, I think it is about time I was on my way," said Alex as she was pushed back towards the foyer.

"Nonsense, I thought we already went through this. Unless of course you don't want to be my personal assistant!"

"Actually, that's exactly what I don't want."

Lord Poppinjay laughed loudly and then suddenly stopped, looking at her through squinted eyes. "That was very funny, but you should know that from now on I make all the jokes. Got it?"

"Yes," said Alex meekly.

"Good," said Lord Poppinjay, smiling again. "Now the position is unpaid, but you do get free room and board – and the privilege of working for me, of course!" When he mentioned the free room and board, Alex looked up at him sharply. "Now, I think what we need is some tea to celebrate. How does that sound?"

Alex had to admit to herself that she was quite hungry. Also, if she was going to get a free room, she might as well spend the night. The sun was already setting, and it would be nice to sleep in a proper bed after having slept on the hard ground the night before. It was also possible that someone here would be able to direct her towards Port Cullis, maybe even provide her with a map! So she decided to humour Lord Poppinjay for the time being until the next day. And if this meant pretending to be his personal assistant, then, well, that would be what she would do.

"I'd love some tea," she said with a smile.

"Great, go get us some!" Lord Poppinjay pointed through to the other side of the dining room towards which Alex imagined must be the kitchen.

"Uh . . . OK. . ." And after a slight pause, she started in that direction.

"Oh, and make up a batch of scones too!" Lord Poppinjay called out to her. "I'll see you back up in my office!" And he sauntered off, humming a happy tune, his little dog scurrying along behind him.

THE TWENTY-FOURTH CHAPTER

In which Alex meets the MakeCold 6000

Alex made her way through the dining room and eventually found herself inside the kitchen. She was shocked at how big it was. I mean, it was really big. Really, really big. And everything was made of stainless steel. I'm not just talking about the appliances here, but the walls, the floor, the ceiling, the shelves, even the cookbooks. It was all Alex could do not to run into the edge of the counter as it was completely indistinguishable from the wall. The place was also entirely empty and not a spot of food could be seen anywhere.

How the devil was she going to make tea and scones

in here? Forget that, how the devil was she going to make scones at all? She had never made a scone in her life, and this was for two reasons. One, she had never really learned to cook anything yet, and two, she hated scones, and why on earth, if she had learned how to cook anything yet, would she have learned to cook scones if she didn't even like them?

Alex thought that her best place to start would be by looking through the cupboards, but this proved problematic as the cupboards were arduously difficult to locate. She did open a freezer and an oven, however. So at least she knew where they were.

"Can I help you?"

"Well I don't know," replied Alex, looking up. She said it in all pleasantness, assuming she hadn't noticed whoever was speaking to her before that moment, because of the sheer size of the kitchen. But when she stood and turned to where the voice was coming from she found herself facing a wall.

"Well, what seems to be the problem?" it asked helpfully.

"Um. . ." said Alex.

"Don't be frightened," it said. "Ask me anything."

"Are you a wall?" asked Alex, eyeing the wall up and down.

"Oh, goodness me, no!" it laughed. "I can see why you

are confused. But that would be very silly, wouldn't it? A talking wall!" The voice continued to laugh merrily. When it finished it added, "I'm a fridge."

"Are you?" asked Alex, astonished.

"Yes. I am the MakeCold 6000. 'The helpful friend in the kitchen.' I am programmed with over eight thousand recipes, can tell you if the milk's gone off and can water the plants while you're away, providing they are within a seven-metre radius." A sudden squirt of water passed over Alex's head and landed in a little puddle on the other side of the room.

"Cool."

"Yes, I am. I can be programmed at five different temperature settings, from 'Refreshing' to 'Unnecessary'. I can also speak in twenty different languages and perform calculations up to and including the number 13,459,820,647,189,203,926,970.24."

"Can you help me make tea and scones?"

"Not only can I help you make tea and scones, but it would be my pleasure to do so!" And with that it popped open the door. Like everything else in the kitchen, the fridge was huge, which is why it could be so easily confused with a wall. So huge, in fact, that Alex could walk right into it. The fridge easily guided her around inside, lighting up the ingredients she needed, all the while giving useful tips like, "If you leave the pit in the avocado after you've cut it, it won't go brown!"

Then, step by step, it instructed Alex how to make the scones.

"Do I have to put raisins in?" she asked.

"Raisins, though popular, are not necessary. What makes a good scone is timing, patience and, of course, love," it replied.

"So I don't have to put in the raisins, then?"

"No."

When Alex had finally finished mixing all the ingredients and laid out the little doughy globs on the baking tray, she popped them into the oven and stood back to admire her work.

"Not bad," she said.

"For a first try," agreed the fridge happily.

Alex jumped up and seated herself on the counter.

"So how long have you been working for this hotel?"

"Ten years," it said proudly.

"Wow. So you must know a lot about the place. I mean, why is it in the middle of the forest and everything? They can't get many guests here, surely?"

"You are quite right. The On the Edge Hotel hasn't seen a guest in five years. But that doesn't stop Lord Poppinjay from keeping everything pristine just in case. It used to be a very illustrious hotel, and it was very popular, being just outside Port Cullis on the edge of the forest. And everyone agreed that Lord Poppinjay was the best hotelier in the business. Then he had an idea which affected the most fundamental operations of the hotel."

"Does it have something to do with Mental Dictation?"

"Exactly. Lord Poppinjay decided to run the hotel by thought. It was a disastrous decision. No one could read his mind and they had to guess what he wanted. And when the forest started to encroach on the hotel, the staff would get yelled at if they raised the issue with Lord Poppinjay instead of reading his mind. Slowly, the forest eventually encircled the hotel. Lord Poppinjay refuses to believe anything is wrong, and the staff are too frightened to say anything."

"Like 'The Emperor's New Clothes', " said Alex.

"Like who?"

"There is a story about an emperor who gets these special clothes made that supposedly only are seen by very special people. So everyone claims they can see them, even though in reality there is nothing there. It's only when a little kid points out that the emperor is actually naked that he realizes the truth."

"Good story," replied the fridge. "I guess it is something like that, then." Alex watched the scones start to rise in the oven. "You know, you're a kid," it realized slowly.

"It's true," replied Alex.

"Maybe you could say something to Lord Poppinjay."

Alex laughed. "What could I do? If the staff he's had for years can't convince him, how could I?"

"I don't know. It was just an idea," said the fridge sadly.

Alex hopped off the counter and opened the oven. The scones were steaming hot and actually smelled really good for scones. She took them out of the oven to cool.

"Look, I'll see what I can do." Alex hated to disappoint an appliance, especially one that had been so helpful.

"Thank you so much," it said happily. "I know I am only a fridge, but I have been here long enough to become quite fond of the place. It would be nice if there were people to cook for."

"I suppose it would be," replied Alex. She started to arrange the tea on a tray, and then put the scones, still hot, on a plate. "I guess I'd better get these back to him," she said. "Thanks for all the help."

"It was my pleasure!"

Alex found her way to Lord Poppinjay's office, made him a cup of tea, and poured out some milk into a bowl for his dog. She then sat back in the seat opposite his large oak desk and thought hard about how she was to help the fridge.

Lord Poppinjay seemed to be thoroughly enjoying himself. "I love these scones!" he was saying. "You are the first person to have correctly read in my mind how much I despise raisins."

"Thank you," said Alex, taking a bite of one herself, admiring her handiwork.

"In fact you are the best mind reader I have on my staff. I think you will go far," he added.

"Yes, I already knew you would say that," said Alex, who didn't, but had found that every time His Lordship used the word "think" and she admitted to prior knowledge of the fact, he was very impressed.

"Of course you did! Of course you did!"

Alex finished her scone, brushed her hands together and reached for another. But just then she had a brainwave and sat up straight again. It was as clear as daylight. She knew exactly how she could help Lord Poppinjay and the fridge, while at the same time helping herself. All of a sudden her goal of reaching Port Cullis was just within her grasp! Alex calmed herself down before she spoke again.

"Lord Poppinjay," she said, "may I ask you a question?"

"If you feel you need to."

"Well, I was wondering exactly how you felt about not having had a guest in five years," she asked, avoiding his eye contact.

"Who told you that!" cried Lord Poppinjay, standing up abruptly, glowering at her.

"The fridge," she said softly.

Lord Poppinjay stared at her for a moment, then he bowed his head and sat back down. "Yes," he said and sighed heavily. He stroked his dog for a few silent moments. Then carefully, without looking up at her, he asked, "What do you think I feel about it?"

Alex looked at him and pretended to read his thoughts. Then she nodded slowly and said, "I think it makes you feel sad. And that you wish your staff would realize your plans to improve the situation. But of course they are too simple to understand you and so make a mess of it every time."

Lord Poppinjay looked up at her, wide-eyed. "You're amazing! That is exactly what I was thinking."

"Of course it was what you were thinking. It was very easy to understand really," added Alex, smiling inwardly to herself. "For example, I know that for years you have been aware that the reason you have no guests is that you have no road that leads to your hotel. For years you have known the simple solution. You must build such a road. For years all you have wanted to do is lead an expedition into Port Cullis to meet with the people in charge of urban planning so that you could finally get a road built. And then, once you got the road, you could have a big festival and party and invite very important people, because you know many important people. . ."

"I do, I do," he said, nodding so enthusiastically it looked as if his head might fall off.

"And these important people, of course, are just dying to come and see you and stay in your hotel. If only your simple staff could understand you. If only they weren't that . . . simple." Alex didn't much like calling his staff simple, because she really didn't think they were, and she hadn't really met them anyway, but every time she called them simple, Lord Poppinjay would nod emphatically.

"That does it. You're getting a raise. How much are you being paid?" he asked her.

"Nothing."

"Double it."

"The only thing is, sir, I just don't know if we can prepare the expedition in time for tomorrow, as I know you are planning. I mean, it is so last minute, and after all, the forest is quite dangerous," finished Alex, hoping that the suggestion would work.

Lord Poppinjay stood up again and slammed a fist on the table. "Oh, so it is too hard, is it? Can't handle the challenge, can you? Well, too bad. We will leave first thing tomorrow, even if that means we have to work through the night. Do I make myself clear?" he asked loudly.

"Yes, sir, of course, sir. I'm sorry, sir," said Alex, cowering slightly, though inside her heart was jumping for joy. But then, of course, she had been hopeful several times before with everything going wrong instead. So she asked, "But what if it is raining tomorrow?"

"Rain? Are you scared of a little rain? Even if it snows, even if there is a tornado, nothing will put off this expedition. Stop being so cowardly and be a man!"

"I'm a girl."

"Then be a girl!"

"Yes, sir!"

THE TWENTY-FIFTH CHAPTER

In which we watch a spontaneous musical number and the expedition prepares to depart

There here was a festive spirit in the air that evening. Often a festive spirit isn't easy to pinpoint. Because after all a spirit is invisible, so usually the only people who know it is around are the people who are experiencing it. Usually. However, on occasion it is possible to witness a physical display of a festive spirit. This is a rare occurrence. Rarer still is the particular manifestation that Alex witnessed shortly after the staff meeting had finished and everyone began their particular duties.

What she witnessed was a Big Musical Number. That
went something like this:

(Lord Poppinjay's Recitative)

"I think this plan of mine is so stupendous.
What other could arrive at such a plan?
My brain must be entirely tremendous.
Does anywhere exist a smarter man?

I think I am the perfect hotelier!
Most giving – dare I say most handsome too?
And while some may disagree
And shake their heads at me
I have no doubt it's absolutely true.

For. . .

(Lord Poppinjay's Song)

That's what I think, yes, what I think,
And what I think is what I know!
And what I know, yes what I know,
And what I know must needs be so!

And till little Alex found us here
Our situation was quite drear!

But Alex knows just what I think,
And what I think is what I know!"

(STAFF)

"She knows just what he thinks,
And what he thinks is what he knows
And thanks to her we all do too
And thanks to her our future grows!

And we're feeling mighty happy
And the reason we feel happy
Is we rarely feel this happy
'Cause we typically feel quite down.

For tomorrow for the first time,
For the first time in a long time,
Yes, tomorrow is the first time that tomorrow's
*   not the worst time*
'Cause tomorrow we're going to town!"

(DANCE BREAK involving much tap dancing and
the occasional lift. And jazz hands. Then:)

[AT THE SAME TIME:]

(LORD POPPINJAY)

"That's what I think, that's
  what I think,
And what I think is what
  I know!
And what I know, and
  what I know,
And what I know must
  needs be so!

And till little Alex found
  us here
Our situation was quite
  drear!
Because she knows just
  what I think
And what I think is what
  I know!"

(STAFF)

"We don't care what he thinks
  so long
As Alex thinks we ought to do

Something that would benefit
  the
State of this hotel and staff
  too.

And if that means we must
  pretend
To read his mind like she's
  taught us
Well we're willing to do that
  un-
Til there comes a time he's
  caught us."

(STAFF)

"And we're feeling mighty happy
And the reason we feel happy
Is we rarely feel this happy
'Cause we typically feel quite down."

"For tomorrow for the first time,
For the first time in a long time,
Yes, tomorrow is the first time that
 tomorrow's not the worst time,
'Cause tomorrow we're going to town!

Yes, tomorrow is the first time that
 tomorrow's not the worst time,
'Cause tomorrow we're going to town!"

The whole thing finished with Lord Poppinjay lifting Alex up into the air on his shoulders and the rest of the staff posing around them, smiling toothy grins towards the entrance of the hotel. There were a few brief moments of silence. And then Alex said, "All right, everyone, Lord Poppinjay thinks we should all get back to work!"

It wasn't until two in the morning that plans were finalized for the trip the next day. After five years of isolation, it seemed that everyone who worked at the hotel felt they had reasons that they would be indispensable on the trip. Even the boy who cleared tables made the very sound argument that without his presence there would be no one to offer to pepper the dinners. So it was eventually decided that everyone would go. Then they all had to get their things together. And this was why it was as late as it was when Alex finally got to go to bed.

*

The next day dawned bright and cheerful. Alex felt wonderful, having slept soundly, if briefly. She woke up Giggles, who had finally felt safe enough to climb out of the rucksack and curl up under the covers with her. He yawned and stretched his paws. He looked at her and stood up.

"Your fur is all messed up," laughed Alex, patting the fur flat. Giggles hopped out of the bed and wandered over to the window. Alex followed him and opened the curtains. She looked over the front lawn and saw that everyone was already awake and bustling. The woman in grey was directing all the activity, reading off instructions from a clipboard and pointing in various directions. In the middle of all the chaos stood Lord Poppinjay in a khaki shirt and trousers and brown boots. He also wore a pith helmet.

Alex got changed quickly, held the bag open for Giggles to jump into and tore through the hall, down the stairs and out of the front door, grabbing her bicycle on the way.

"Alex! I was just thinking about you! Wonderful, wonderful!" said Lord Poppinjay, approaching her through the hustle and bustle.

"We are leaving soon, right?" she asked, dodging out of the way of six waiters carrying six large silver trays piled high with truffles.

"Within mere moments!" he announced with a wave of his hand. There was an added bustle to the hustle, and suddenly the entire staff of the On the Edge Hotel were standing in a perfect queue. Alex quickly reached into her bag and took a picture of them all. It was quite an impressive sight. Leading the way was the woman in grey holding a fierce-looking machete. Behind her was an army of waiters loaded down with bags. There followed four burly-looking men, who were normally dishwashers, carrying on their shoulders a magnificent white sedan chair for Lord Poppinjay. They were followed by the chambermaids, who had been put in charge of tents. The chef and his assistants came up behind them, toting wheelbarrows full of food, and last but not least sauntered Tom Friend, happily chewing on a piece of grass.

Alex climbed on to her bike.

"Are we ready?" called out Lord Poppinjay. His staff let out a loud cheer. "Then . . ." He climbed up into his sedan chair. It teetered dangerously, and the dishwashers tried desperately to counter Lord Poppinjay's weight. He lay back on its white cushions, ". . .off we go!"

There was a lurch forward that was immediately stopped by the woman in grey, who called out, "Wait! What's that?"

A distinct crunching sound was coming from the forest in front of them. It was difficult to figure out exactly what it was. It could have been a bear. It could have been a mouse wearing large shoes. There was no real way to tell.

Lord Poppinjay picked up a pair of silver-plated binoculars and squinted through them. "It's hard to see through the undergrowth." He looked down at Alex.

"Shall I take a look, then?" she asked, knowing the answer full well. Perhaps she actually could read his mind. Well, it didn't matter. She wanted to get this show on the road!

"Precisely what I was thinking! You are amazing! When you get back you can ride next to me!"

Alex nodded, taking off her rucksack. She passed her bike to the maître d', who took it in his white-gloved hands, and went to investigate. The crunching noises got louder as she approached the edge of the forest. She turned around to look at the queue waiting impatiently behind her. The khaki blur of Lord Poppinjay gestured for her to go on.

Alex pushed her way into the brush. She felt something rub up against her foot and she let out a small scream. She looked down.

"Giggles! Don't do that! You scared the living daylights out of me!" she said. Giggles shook his head and ran off deeper into the forest to scout out. He came charging back almost instantly, a look of panic on his face.

"What? What is it?" asked Alex.

Suddenly there was a loud roaring, but not of any animal. It sounded like a machine. It sounded like a . . .

"Chainsaw?" asked Alex. She took a step backwards. The tree in front of her began to sway from side to side, gathering momentum as it went.

"Giggles, jump!" The two of them leapt to the side as the tree came crashing down. Alex looked up. Through the debris and dust floating in the air she could see the silhouette of a tall figure holding a chainsaw.

"No," said Alex. The dust began to settle. A group of figures behind the tall one materialized. Alex looked at Giggles, who looked back at her with disbelief. "How are they doing this?" Slowly Alex got to her feet, and dusted herself off.

One of the group broke free and moved into the foreground.

"Hey, Poppy," muttered Alex.

"Hello, deary!" replied Poppy with a satisfied, if yellowing, smile. "Come now, let's have a little chit-chat." She gestured to the rest of the Daughters of the Founding Fathers' Preservation Society, who moved towards her menacingly. Rose revved her rusted chainsaw. It sparked dangerously. If Rose had wanted to, she could have made a rubber band spark.

"Well, obviously I'm going to run away now," said Alex. She sighed and turned around. Then she ran as if her life depended on it, which, Alex strongly suspected, might actually be the case.

She burst into the clearing and charged up the steps of the hotel, followed closely at her heels by Giggles.

"What's going on?" asked Lord Poppinjay as she flew past. Actually to Alex it sounded more like, ". . .t's goi. . ." but she got the gist.

She looked over her shoulder and could see the Daughters following apace. They moved quite fast for little old ladies. Alex wondered if they kept in such good shape by chasing small children. The staff gave them puzzled looks as they passed.

Alex stood paralysed in the lobby, not sure where to go. She suddenly realized she had cornered herself in the hotel. She should have run deeper into the forest and not into the only building for miles. But she couldn't have kept running for ever. She needed to stop the Daughters, otherwise this would never end. Right now, however, she needed a place to hide. She looked out of the window at the people in the expedition queue, who were all standing, quietly minding their own business.

Wasn't there anyone who would be willing to help her?

"Of course!" Alex exclaimed and ran into the dining room. She had forgotten that there was at least one someone, or rather something, that had been more than willing to help her once. She had to hope it would be up to the challenge again.

"MakeCold 6000!" she called out as she skidded along the stainless-steel floor of the kitchen.

"Did I hear someone call out my name?" asked a friendly voice.

"Hey, it's me, Alex!"

"Alex! How nice to meet you again! Say, how did Lord Poppinjay like the scones we made?"

"He loved them. And he's actually outside right now waiting for me so that we can go into Port Cullis and get this hotel into shape!"

"Oh, Alex, you are amazing! Thank you so much. I wish there was something I could do to thank you. Ooh! Do you like soufflé?" It popped open its door.

"Actually," said Alex, looking inside, "there is something that you could do for me. I need someplace to hide."

"Hide?"

"Please?" begged Alex.

"Well, why not? It could be fun!"

THE TWENTY-SIXTH CHAPTER

In which Alex is trapped. Again

Moments later the Daughters of the Founding Fathers' Preservation Society burst into the kitchen. Alex could hear their click-click shoes crossing the room, amplified by the stainless steel. The sound made Alex shudder, and she prayed they wouldn't find her in her very obliging appliance.

"Alex, dear!" called out Poppy. "We know you're in here. There's no way out. You're trapped!" Her voice got louder as she moved closer to the fridge. "Come on, Alex, darling, help us out!"

Alex took a deep breath.

And then something happened that made her insides

tighten to the compactest of knots. The fridge, upon hearing the word "help", jumped into action. "Well, hello there. Did I hear someone ask for help?"

There was a pause and Alex silently tried to communicate with the fridge.

"Actually," replied Poppy slowly, "I'm looking for a small child. I don't suppose you've seen it anywhere?"

"Indeed I have. I assume you are talking about Alex?" asked the fridge.

"Please, please," whispered Alex to herself.

"Yes, Alex. That's the one."

"I happen to know that she is hiding inside me. Isn't it fun? Behind the large jar of mayonnaise. But don't tell anyone. It's a secret!" The fridge popped open its door. Alex could sense Poppy looking inside it. She tried to make herself as small as she could.

"Oh, I won't tell anyone," sneered Poppy. "Come on, girls."

Alex could hear the click-clicking as all the Daughters entered the enormous fridge. Was it necessary for all of them to corner her like this? Well, it was a silly tactic, and one that Alex was incredibly grateful for.

She jumped out of the oven and cried, "Now!" The fridge instantly swung its door shut, but not before Alex got a glimpse of Poppy's expression, that pug-dog one that she had missed the morning she had been discovered gone from the house on the hill. Alex gave a little wave as the door slammed in Poppy's face.

"Oh, MakeCold, you were amazing!" laughed Alex.

"I always thought that if I hadn't been a fridge, I could have been an actor," it said happily. "Oh my!"

"What is it?"

"They're banging against the door," it said.

"Is there any way they can get out?" asked Alex nervously.

"Oh no. The only way they can open the door is if I choose to let them. And I just won't!" The fridge laughed merrily.

"Thank you very much!"

Giggles meowed gently from the doorway.

Alex turned to look at him and understood. She walked over to the fridge. "I'm sorry, MakeCold, but I have to go now."

"OK, well, I'll see you when you all get back, then!"

Alex looked at Giggles, then back at the fridge. "I don't know if I will be coming back," she said slowly.

"Oh. Oh, well, then . . . I guess this is goodbye?"

"Yes, I guess it is."

"Well . . . goodbye, I suppose. I'll. . ." It sounded as though it was choking back tears, if it had been capable of producing them. " . . .I'll miss you!"

"I'll miss you, too," replied Alex, spreading her arms and leaning up against the fridge. "Maybe we will meet again. You never know! In the meantime, take care of yourself, and thank you so much." She let go of the fridge.

"No, thank you," it replied. Alex smiled and went to join Giggles. She turned for one last look at the fridge. It didn't wave because it didn't have arms. And it didn't smile because it didn't have a mouth. But Alex knew it would have if it could have, and so she smiled and waved in return.

It took two days and two nights until the staff of the On the Edge Hotel found their way out of the forest. But then, almost unexpectedly, they were free of it. And they found themselves standing in a farmer's field next to a rather startled cow.

"That road there," announced the woman in grey, "should get us to Port Cullis in a little over half an hour."

All the staff cheered loudly. Loudest of all was Alex, who could hardly believe she was finally free of that forest. She looked back at it, the trees extending in either direction for what appeared infinity. Had she known just how vast it had been, she quite possibly might have decided to give up.

"Well," said Lord Poppinjay, "let's stop for lunch, then,

before we make our grand entrance."

Instantly everyone set to work. Alex, who was feeling anxious at being so close to the city, sat up and watched the activity for a few charged moments. She leaned back and looked over at Lord Poppinjay, who was whistling happily to himself and filing his nails.

"Um . . . Lord Poppinjay. . ." said Alex slowly. "I've . . . been meaning to talk to you about my job. I think it's time I offered up my resignation."

"No, you must stay!" Lord Poppinjay insisted, examining his pinkie carefully.

Alex sighed. Plan B, then. "Don't pretend, Lord Poppinjay, you have to remember that I know what you're thinking. You like me well enough, but I know you don't think I am, well, classy enough for such an illustrious hotel."

Lord Poppinjay paused picking at his pinkie and peered at Alex pensively. "I can't hide a thing from you, can I!" he laughed, throwing his hands in the air. "Would you like me to write you a reference letter?"

"No, that's all right," she replied. And then she thought for a moment. "Although, I don't suppose you know anything about going to sea?"

Lord Poppinjay laughed and he gave his dog a scratch on its belly. "No, but I do know a lovely young lady who may be able to help. Her father is my personal dentist, or at least was years ago when I went to Port Cullis regularly." He smiled, revealing his flawless teeth.

He went on to explain that this young lady owned an inn in the heart of Port Cullis called the Gangrene, which was frequented by all sorts including sailors, and he wrote down a set of directions for her. He also very generously instructed her to put any expenses on his tab.

And then with a hearty handshake, Alex slipped off the sedan chair.

She grabbed Mr Underwood's bicycle and readjusted her rucksack, which was currently purring. Then, climbing on to the bike, she called out a goodbye to the rest of the staff, who returned it heartily.

"Alex!" called out Lord Poppinjay, peering around the edge of the chair. He looked at Alex intently and then pressed his fingers to his temples and thought hard. When he removed his fingers from the side of his head, she waved. She had no idea what he had thought of course. But she could make a guess at it.

"You're welcome!" she called back. Lord Poppinjay clapped his hands together in amazement.

Alex carefully biked her way through the field and on to the road. There was a sign shaped like an arrow that read, "If you're heading to Port Cullis, then you're almost there!" Alex laughed. It was a very perfect sign.

She felt very relaxed looking down the road ahead, sort of like she would if she was staring out at an expanse of dark blue still water. She took a deep refreshing breath and smiled.

"Here we go, Giggles," she said to her rucksack. And then, because it was the only reasonable thing to do, she turned the bike in the direction the arrow was pointing and started to pedal.

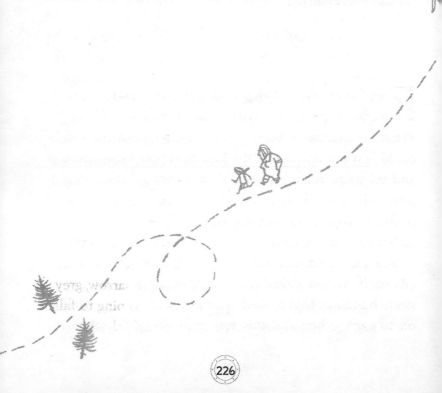

THE TWENTY-SEVENTH CHAPTER

In which we finally get to Port Cullis and visit the Gangrene

Port Cullis! Wonderful Port Cullis! Yes, dear reader, we have finally reached the wonderful seaside city. What an exciting place it was, too! Now, I suppose I could first share with you the long history of Port Cullis, and its trade relations with France, but that is all so infinitely dull that, if I told it to you, you would probably give up on the rest of this book, and we still haven't got to the stuff about Steele and the pirates yet.

You see, what made Port Cullis interesting was the city itself. At first glance you would see tall, narrow, grey stone buildings that looked as if they were going to fall on to each other, and this was really helpful when it rained because it meant that most of the streets were practically covered. There was a big square marketplace within the ruins of a medieval cathedral and a total of a hundred and thirty-two pubs, ranging from the big and brassy to the small and seedy. There were also some really big beautiful houses with complete gardens that over the years had hidden themselves down dark narrow alleys to avoid prying eyes. And some truly lovely squares with gurgling fountains.

The neat thing was that all of this – the tall buildings, the pubs, the fine houses and squares, even the old medieval castle – was built on the ruins of an ancient Roman city. It had been a gleaming white place, with bathhouses and a large forum and also an amphitheatre. But the most impressive thing of all was the huge wall that had been built to separate the fishy-smelling port from the town itself, as well as protect the city from a naval attack.

The wall was sixty metres tall and twenty kilometres long, a stunning feat of architecture in itself. And, bridging the gap that provided access to the city, was a giant triumphal arch. Its pediment bore a large statue of Neptune brandishing his trident, and, intricately carved in bas-relief, the frieze told the famous tale of Roman General Cullis and the banana peel. While both the wall and arch had lost the lustre of their youth, which happens to the best of us, there still was nothing quite so impressive as approaching the city from the sea and seeing the wall loom up before you, managing in its strange way to extend a hand of friendship, while at the same time punching you hard in the face.

So there you see why the whole place was rather magnificent in its dirty way. And why it had become so overpopulated that people flowed through the streets like muddy water. And why also, perhaps, it had become a wee bit of a den for sin and corruption, but was also where Her Majesty's Navy made berth, dwarfing all the common fishing boats with the slightly faded glory of her tall ships.

And you would have thought it all would have been a bit much for Alex, having grown up in a small town as she had. But it wasn't. In fact, Alex thought it was all very marvellous, made doubly so by how much effort she had put into getting there in the first place.

The best thing, though, at least for the moment, was that her bike was perfect here, being a quick form of transportation that was also small enough to negotiate the dark, narrow streets. She immensely enjoyed riding, though she had to admit she was a little shocked by how much faster everything around her moved, especially the little scooters that would suddenly turn a corner and whizz past her at truly unsafe speeds.

Alex did her best to follow Lord Poppinjay's directions until she finally came across a narrow alley labelled "Lantern Place". She hopped off her bike and walked it down the alley to the end and found a sign that read, "The Gangrene Inn". Alex shook her head. The name did not inspire confidence. Nonetheless, she pushed open the door and found herself surrounded by a warmth and friendly chatter that seemed completely at odds with the inn's exterior.

It was an entirely cosy place, buzzing with activity. Composed of several small rooms that led into one another around a central serving bar, it reminded Alex of the puzzles she used to play with when she was really little. Not realizing that specific pieces went with other pieces, she would simply put them together at random and bash them hard with her hand so that they'd stick. It looked as if someone had done the same thing with the Gangrene. None of the rooms quite matched up, so that when you reached the edge of one you had either to go up a few steps, or to go down a few steps, or to veer slightly to the left. And some places where you might hit your head on a low-hanging beam would then suddenly open up to a loft with a skylight above.

The place was also almost bursting with Interesting Clientele. As Alex wandered through, she found one corner that had a pool table surrounded by angular young people. Another was occupied by retired sailors and their various synthetic body parts, including a number of wooden legs and one hook. The larger lofty room was devoted to several games tables, where the concentrated silence would be burst by the occasional explosion of laughter. In dark corners sat dark figures watching everyone else, occasionally making notes in suspicious-looking books with suspicious-looking pens. And at the far end, Alex could just make out a raging fire with deep chairs of various shapes drawn close to it. She could just imagine Lord Poppinjay sitting there, laughing merrily, and could see why he liked the place so much.

A small young woman with strong features marched over to Alex, efficiently weaving her way through a thick crowd of bankers all vying for attention at the bar.

"Can I help you?" she asked, drying her hands on her apron.

"Yes, I was recommended your inn by a friend," replied Alex.

"Were you?" said the young woman, looking at her carefully. "And who exactly recommended us to you?"

"Lord Poppinjay," said Alex.

The young woman burst into hearty laughter. Her eyes, though still sharp, twinkled and her posture seemed to relax slightly. "That's all right, then," she said.

"Gosh, it's been ages since I've seen him. He's quite a character, isn't he?"

"Yes," replied Alex, smiling a bit.

"So then, were you looking for a meal or for a room? Or maybe both," she asked, walking over to a small desk in the corner and opening a notebook.

"Both actually."

"Heather!" a strained voice called from the crowd of bankers.

"Can't you see I'm with a customer, Howard? The world doesn't revolve around you, you know!" she yelled back. She turned back and flipped though the book. "Right. It looks like we have one room available tonight."

"That would be great, thanks! Um. . ." added Alex.

"Yes?"

"Well, Lord Poppinjay said to put it on his tab. But you don't have to if you don't want to," said Alex quickly.

"That's pretty typical of him. He's a nice guy. Only problem is, when is he ever going to come back to pay his bill. . ."

"Oh, he's back now," interrupted Alex.

"Really? Wow." Heather looked around the room as if she expected to see Lord Poppinjay hiding in the corner. "Hey, you! You break it, you buy it!" she yelled when she caught sight of a man turning over a porcelain candlestick with deep interest. She turned back to Alex.

"Right. You can have a seat over there, and how about I bring you over a nice plate of roast dinner?"

"Thank you very much," replied Alex.

Heather nodded once and turned around to push her way back towards the bankers, explaining loudly and slowly as she went, "OK, so when you see someone coming in your direction, you have a choice. You could move to the side, or you could stand there like some sort of gormless troll and wait for me to walk around you. But, unless you want to lose both your legs, I personally would advise that you choose the first option!"

Alex headed over to the fire to sit down. She threw herself into a deep comfy chair of soft leather, her feet just sticking out over the edge. Heather brought over a lemonade for her to drink while she waited for her dinner. The fire crackled happily. And sitting there feeling the warmth spread deep inside her, and her aching muscles relaxing into the soft cushions, Alex did too.

THE TWENTY-EIGHTH CHAPTER

In which Alex meets Coriander the Conjuror

"You look comfortable!" said a pleasant voice. Alex looked up. Sitting opposite her, taking a sip from a pint, was a cheerful-looking man with dark messy hair.

"I guess that's 'cause I am," replied Alex.

"And that would explain it!" he said with a laugh. "That was a fine answer."

"Thanks," said Alex, smiling happily to herself.

"My name is Coriander," he said, leaning forward and offering his hand to shake.

Alex took it. "Alex," she said, shaking. She was getting quite good at handshakes.

"Do you like magic, then, Alex?"

"I suppose so, yes."

"Excellent! Watch this," he said, bringing himself to the edge of his seat. He waved his hands in front of him, there was a puff of pink smoke, and a little bird appeared caged between his fingers.

"Amazing!" said Alex, leaning forward. Out of the corner of her eye she saw her bag, which she had placed on the ground by the fire, move slightly. "But you better put it away," she added.

Coriander looked at Alex, then at the bag. He leaned over. "What's in the bag?"

"Giggles."

"What's Giggles?"

"A cat," replied Alex. "A really temperamental cat."

"Ah! In that case." Coriander clapped his hands together, there was a puff of blue smoke and the bird was gone. "Now can I meet Giggles?"

Alex nodded and untied the bag. Giggles climbed out, warily looking around him. He noticed Coriander. Alex wasn't sure what to expect, and she was ready to grab him and put him back in the bag if necessary. But Giggles appraised Coriander carefully, and then, shock upon shock, jumped into his lap.

Coriander laughed. "This is temperamental?"

Alex shook her head and smiled. "He must like you."

"It's about mutual respect," explained Coriander,

petting Giggles, who began to purr. "Say, do I look like some movie villain like this? Sitting in my leather chair with the cat?" He raised an eyebrow and looked down his nose at her.

Alex laughed. "Sort of," she said, "but you're too nice."

"You're too kind," he said, putting on an accent that sounded a lot like Lord Poppinjay's.

They sat chatting, and Heather came over with Alex's dinner.

"Heather! Join us!" Coriander beamed at her as she passed him another pint.

"Yeah, like I've got time to sit around. Some of us have work, Coriander!" She sounded frustrated, but there was a softness around her sharp eyes that suggested she found Coriander only about half as annoying as the rest of her customers. She disappeared again into the crowd, but they could hear her voice cut through the noise, "Last call, everyone!"

When Alex and Coriander were alone again, he looked at her seriously and asked, "So, Alex, what's a kid like you doing alone in a city like this?"

"Well," she said, "it's a really long story. But I came to Port Cullis because I am looking for my year-six teacher, who has been kidnapped by pirates."

Coriander looked at her, his face unreadable. "That's a very serious business. Which pirates?"

Alex started. "What do you mean 'which pirates'?"

"There be a lot of pirates out there," he said. "I myself. . ." and he stopped and looked around. When he was certain no one was looking he lowered his voice and said, "I myself served on the privateer ship, the *Ill Repute*."

"Is a privateer a pirate?"

"A privateer is a pirate who's been hired by the government to fight their enemies. But essentially, yes," he replied, taking a sip of beer. "The difference between piracy and privateering is a matter of whose ships are being attacked, really."

This gave Alex something to think about.

"So . . ." Coriander asked, "which pirates?"

"Oh. Well, Pirate Captain Steele? Of the *Ironic Gentleman*?"

Coriander choked on his beer. He sputtered for a few moments and wiped his mouth.

"Dear me," he said, shaking his head. "Dear me."

"Do you know the *Ironic Gentleman*?"

Coriander gave a laugh, but instead of feeling warm as she had when he had laughed earlier, Alex felt her insides go cold. "Yes. I've heard of the *Ironic Gentleman*. It's only the most infamous pirate ship of our time."

"Ah. Why's that?" Alex asked lightly, her heart pounding fast.

"I suppose it would be down to Pirate Captain Steele," he replied. "He has a very particular reputation, you might say."

"Particular?"

"The thing about Steele is, he just . . . never lets up."

Alex looked at Coriander.

"Let me explain. Many pirates seize a ship and all the treasure in it and then take some time spending the fortune, having a laugh, you know. I mean why be a pirate if all it's gonna be is work, right? But Steele never stops. It's got to the point where he's been nicknamed 'The Inevitable'. He attacks so many ships that every sailor expects it to happen to him sometime or other. They say his relentless behaviour has to do with his life-long quest to find the Wigpowder treasure. He's become obsessive and bitter, and keeps hoping the next ship he comes upon will have some clue as to its whereabouts. And when it doesn't, his rage is terrible. Do you know the tale of the Wigpowder treasure?"

Alex nodded yes.

"Of course you do. Who doesn't? Well, you could say Steele has accumulated quite a bit of rage because of his failure, and he takes it out on anyone who crosses his path. Many are killed, aye, that they are. But those that survive, well they wish that they too were among the dead. Steele's crew is ruthless. And if they let you live, it's only 'cause you're no longer a threat to them. You may still be a man, but you don't have a soul. And most importantly, they only let you go, so long as you've never seen the great Captain in person. He likes his, oh, what do you call it . . . anonymity, as it were. There is no surer a death sentence than to be brought into his presence. And because no one but his crew knows what he looks like, the navy has a devil of a time tracking him down. Some claim his body has been burned by acid, others that he is three metres tall, but these are ridiculous rumours. Nobody knows for sure, and that's that. He could be here in the pub and we wouldn't know it. He could be me." He looked at Alex meaningfully. "But he isn't."

Alex was speechless.

"And that crew of his," Coriander went on, oblivious of Alex, who had started to shrink into her chair. "There's Dr Brunswick, the surgeon, though he rarely operates on the sick. And Jack Scratch, the ship's carpenter and certifiably insane . . . and a whole host of others, Dude Hector, Sir Geoffrey, The Wall, No-Kneecaps Calvin. And. . ." He stopped.

Alex looked at him. His face had grown pale.

"Am I going to regret asking you what comes after 'and'?" she said.

Coriander blinked and looked at her with a smile.

"Senslesky."

"Bless you."

"No, I wasn't sneezing. Though thank you. I said Senslesky."

"What's Senslesky?"

"The son of the Russian Baron Senslesky the Second. If there was anyone who could make my blood turn to ice other than Pirate Captain Steele, it would be him."

"Who is he?"

"He's Steele's first mate."

"And he's . . . scary?"

"Aye, you could say 'scary'. The thing about the Baron is, well, to put it bluntly, he is rather fond of random acts of violence. It's one of the reasons he's also known as Senseless. You never know how he'll behave, and I don't think that there is anything quite so 'scary' as that. And not to mention he has that big grey dog of his, with the long sharp teeth, which is rather scary as well. And, of course, there's also. . ." He stopped again.

Alex didn't want to ask further. She didn't need to. After a brief pause Coriander started up again. "His appearance."

But what that appearance was Alex never found out as they were cheerfully interrupted by Heather again. "Well, looks like the crowd is thinning finally, I should be able to lock up in a few minutes," she said, presenting

Coriander with another pint and settling herself on the arm of his chair. He looked at her and beamed, wrapping his arm around her waist.

"You two seem to be getting along!" Heather said, smiling at Coriander.

"Yes, we are! Hey, Heather, meet Giggles!" said Coriander.

Heather leaned down to pet Giggles, who begrudgingly let her. "Hey, Giggles," she said. "I really like cats," she told Alex.

"Me too," replied Alex.

"I don't suppose you've found out exactly what a kid is doing alone in the big city?" she asked Coriander.

Coriander nodded as he swallowed a mouthful of beer. "She's on a rescue mission. Her year-six teacher, is that right?" he asked Alex.

"That's right," she replied. "Mr Underwood. He was captured by pirates from the *Ironic Gentleman*," she said and was disheartened to see Heather's face fall.

"Dear me." Heather looked thoughtful for a moment. And then she turned to Alex and asked, "Why was he kidnapped?"

"Oh . . . well. . ." Alex thought carefully. She knew she would be in this situation eventually. So far the map had been a deep secret that had been hers alone, and it took a huge leap of faith to share it with anyone. It was a very difficult decision to make. Could she really trust two people she had only just met? On the other hand, she would have to share the secret with someone sometime. Alex didn't imagine anyone would be willing to help her find Mr Underwood without knowing the specifics. Besides, Coriander and Heather did seem to be two of the more normal people she had met so far. Heather certainly seemed to be a sort of no-nonsense, what-you-see-is-what-you-get, kind of person. And Alex really did need some help. She decided to take the risk.

"Is it OK to wait until everyone else has left before I answer that question?" she asked.

Heather looked at her with curiosity. She nodded and soon she had ushered the last few stray punters out of the pub and locked the front door. When she returned, Alex smiled. When she felt she had Heather and Coriander's full attention she said, "You asked why he was kidnapped." She took a deep breath and pulled out her toothbrush holder from her bag. "I think it had something to with . . . this."

"You think so, do you?" said Coriander with a smirk when he saw it.

"Not the toothbrush holder! This. . ." said Alex, and she took out the map.

THE TWENTY-NINTH CHAPTER

In which the map is analysed and Alex has a strange dream

"Looks like a fan," said Heather.

Alex nodded and slipped out of her chair. She knelt in front of the low table by the fire and carefully unfolded it. It was the first time since she had left the house on the hill that she had looked at it. Heather and Coriander joined her and they all silently examined it. Giggles, who didn't like being tossed out of Coriander's lap, walked around sulkily and sat by Alex.

It was a very typical-looking map, with a drawing of an island, even an X marking the spot. The strange thing was a short poem scrawled to one side:

When the earth makes its peace,

And the elements catch fire,
With a primarily high feeling
Shall you find your desire.

Alex read it over a few times ("Obviously written by a pirate, not a poet," Heather had commented), completely flummoxed as to what it could possibly mean.

The silence was finally broken by Coriander, who had suddenly realized what he was looking at. "That isn't what I think it is?" he asked, eyes wide.

"It's the map for the Wigpowder treasure, yes," replied Alex. "Mr Underwood is his great-great-great-grandson, on his mother's side. That's why they kidnapped him. They thought he had the map, or at least knew where the treasure was. But he didn't, and doesn't. They captured him before I was able to get this to him."

Coriander continued to stare in disbelief.

"So do you have a plan?" asked Heather.

"Not really. I'm sort of improvising as I go. I just know that I have to find Mr Underwood. Once I do that, then he will know what to do, how to find the treasure."

"You know, you ought to copy it out again. The original is so delicate," Heather suggested. "I could do it, I'm pretty good at drawing." She blushed slightly.

"That's a good idea!" said Alex.

"Let's do that now," said Coriander, "I love arts and crafts!"

Heather laughed and went to get some supplies to copy the map.

She was indeed good at drawing, and when she had finished, Alex folded up the original and placed it back in its holder. She took the new map and folded it up carefully and put it in her pocket.

"The thing is," she said once they'd tidied up, "I don't really know how I find Mr Underwood now."

Coriander downed his pint and squinted at her. He pointed. He pointed again. On his third point he said loudly, "I know what you should do!"

"No need to shout, Coriander," said Heather softly.

Coriander waved her off. "You need to get on a ship. If Mr Underwood is on the *Ironic Gentleman*, if he is still alive. . ."

"Coriander, please, you're drunk," said Heather.

"That's beside the point," he said to her with a pout. "The point is, if he is on the ship, all you need is a ship. And then Steele'll find you!"

"Oh, that's a great idea, Coriander. Your master plan is for Alex to wait for some ruthless pirates to kidnap her too? Nice one."

"No need to shout, Heather," mocked Coriander.

Heather sighed. "Alex," Heather turned to her, "you need to give this map to the authorities and then have them find Mr Underwood."

"I can't do that," replied Alex. The idea of giving over the map just didn't sit well with her. Possibly this was because most adults she had encountered recently had not proved themselves very reliable, and the others were downright silly. But it was more to do with the fact that the map wasn't hers to give away anyway. It was Mr Underwood's.

Heather sighed. "I guess you could do a bit of both our ideas, then. You know," she leaned forward and thought carefully, "there is one captain I know. . ."

"Oh, the Captain!" laughed Coriander loudly. "'Ooh, Captain, tell me all about your adventures! Ooh, Captain have a free drink! Ooh, Captain how about a kiss. . .'"

"Coriander, you're behaving like a drunken fool!"

"What are you talking about? I *am* a drunken fool! I am. . ." He stood up, teetering dangerously, and Giggles darted behind Alex nervously. "Coriander the Conjuror! I can make a little bird appear in a cloud of pink smoke!" He waved his hands together and the bird appeared again. "Whoops!" he said as it flew out from between his fingers and began flying around the pub.

"Great. Thanks a lot, Coriander," said Heather,

watching the bird knock over several glasses. Coriander just giggled to himself and sat down again. "Now keep quiet and behave yourself!" Coriander nodded and placed a finger to his lips.

"Alex, I know a captain in the navy. He's a really good guy, and he is not due to resume service for another few months. I don't know if he could help you personally, but he may be able to offer a few suggestions. How does that sound?"

"That sounds wonderful!" said Alex. It was great having someone willing to go out of their way to help her.

"I'll give him a call tonight, and maybe we could go round in the morning," said Heather. "But I really think now you should get some sleep. It might be a long day tomorrow."

Alex nodded. The two stood up.

"I'll show you to your room," said Heather.

"Thanks. Goodnight, Coriander," said Alex.

Coriander shook his head vigorously. "I'm not supposed to talk," he whispered.

"Oh, sorry," replied Alex.

In a matter of moments, she was in her little room, curled up under the covers of a very cosy bed.

She had a strange dream that night. She was lying in bed in a pool of light and then two men approached her all dressed in black, and wearing white surgical masks. They stood next to her, and one man took out a camera, held it at arm's length and took a picture of the three of them. Then a third man approached her. He too was dressed in black and wearing a mask, except that his was on wrong. Instead of covering his nose and mouth, he was wearing it so it was covering his nose and eyes. He reached out and placed a hand on her shoulder. He was wearing dark brown gloves and his hand was very cold. Alex felt a cold surge of terror rush through her.

"There has been an incident," he told Alex. He then reached up and undid the string holding the mask on to his face. He was pulling it away from his face when Alex was jolted awake by a loud crashing noise.

She sat up and listened. She heard another crash and realized the sound was coming from downstairs.

Alex got out of bed. It was still dark out as she walked out of her room, down the hall and stood at the top of the stairs looking into the pub.

"Coriander, please stop it!" said Heather, exasperated.

"No, watch! If I throw it, I can make it freeze in the air!" He picked up a chair and threw it across the room. It landed with a crash on the far side. Alex was reminded of the Extremely Ginormous Octopus. "Why won't it work!?" he said, picking up another chair. "I can do it! I swear!" he said, trying again. Heather came over and grabbed his arm.

"Let go of me!" he said, flinging her away. "You're always laughing at me. Well, I can do it, I can!" He went to pick up one of the chairs by the fire, but it was far too big for him, and he slipped and fell on to the floor.

"Come on, Coriander, time to get some sleep," said Heather, reaching down for his hand.

"I'm staying right here," he said with one of his pouts.

"Fine," said Heather, giving up. "I'm going to bed."

Heather climbed up the stairs. When she met Alex, she looked at her and said, "Hey, so, I called my captain friend, and he said he would be happy to meet us tomorrow. Oh, and Coriander really wants to come along." Alex looked at Coriander sitting on the floor by the fire. He looked like a little kid who had just broken his favourite toy.

"Will he be OK?" Alex was still quite shocked at how hard he had pushed Heather trying to get the chair to float. She had never really been in the company of someone who drank so much (aside from the Extremely Ginormous Octopus, and, well, he was an octopus) so she was unused to such behaviour. What surprised her most, though, was how such a nice, funny person like Coriander could suddenly turn into a rather unpleasant character after a few drinks. He seemed like two entirely different people. It didn't exactly frighten her, but she couldn't help but have this small, nagging feeling of concern.

"Oh, don't worry about him. He'll be fine. He really frustrates me so much sometimes. Coriander's such a great guy. He really is. It's just when he gets drunk, he doesn't realize that what he's doing could hurt someone. But please don't worry about it." She smiled at Alex. "Anyway, it's OK, he'll be fine by morning."

Alex nodded.

"Good. I'll see you in a few hours, then." She headed down the narrow hall, then turned around again. "You all right?"

"Oh yes, the crash just woke me up, that's all," said Alex.

"Yes, well, sorry about that." Heather shook her head sadly. "Goodnight," she said, and passed on down to the room at the far end of the hall.

Alex realized she was cold and went back to bed. She lay there thinking about her dream. She felt a little disappointed that the crash had distracted her from seeing what was behind the mask of that third man. She closed her eyes. Maybe I'll see it this time, she hoped, and presently fell asleep. But it was not to be. I don't know what she dreamed of this time, but it was of no significance, and she forgot it the moment she woke up.

THE THIRTIETH CHAPTER

In which we meet Captain Magnanimous and a plan is hatched

Do you want to be a captain of one of Her Majesty's ships. How do you go about doing this, then? Possibly you do it by being a member of the aristocracy and knowing all the right people. Another way is being really rich and paying off all the right people. But there is also the last way, which is being really good at your job and a decent person and impressing all the right people. Captain Magnanimous had chosen the last method. The only son of a tailor, he had worked his way up as high in the ranks as a commoner could go, until one fateful day when, while serving on the *Seaworthy*, he saved his captain's life. He was then promoted to fourth lieutenant over many objections, and then there was no stopping his climb to the top. He could have become an admiral had he so desired, but all he'd ever wanted was his own ship. For this reason, Captain Magnanimous was a terribly contented individual.

It was a lovely fresh morning when Alex, Heather and a bleary-eyed Coriander were welcomed warmly by the Captain and ushered out into a lovely messy garden. They were seated at a little table that had lemonade in a crystal pitcher waiting for them. They were each poured a glass, though Coriander eyed his with suspicion.

Alex had liked the Captain instantly. She had always assumed that captains would be old with big beards or something. But Magnanimous wasn't. And while he was not typically handsome or anything, he had a very pleasant quality about him and wore a crisp white shirt and blue trousers tucked into black boots. He also had a really nice smile.

"Right, then, I think, instead of talking about the weather, which, let's be honest, is surprisingly wonderful today and deserves a bit of a mention, or your health, which I hope is fine, we should get right down to business," said Magnanimous after joining them. "Alex, Heather told me that you had something that was very important and needed to be discussed immediately."

"Yes," said Alex, looking at Heather, who smiled encouragingly. "Well, this is what it is." She took out the copy of the map and unfolded it. Magnanimous took a pair of glasses from his pocket and examined it closely.

And as he did so, Alex explained to him about Mr Underwood and that she wasn't sure exactly what she should do, and that any advice he could provide would be extremely welcome.

"Well, I don't think it should be that hard finding Mr Underwood. The *Ironic Gentleman* can't be too far out to sea just yet," said Magnanimous, passing the map back to Alex, and folding his glasses.

"What do you mean?" asked Heather.

"Your teacher was kidnapped around a week ago. They'd have to have got him to Port Sherry, I would assume. That's at least two days' journey. Then setting out to sea – well, Steele has only a few days' head start, really."

"But, Magnanimous, you can't possibly be suggesting that Alex go to sea!" Heather placed a protective hand on Alex's shoulder.

"Why not? How else is she going to find him?" asked Magnanimous, leaning back in his chair and looking at Heather.

"I don't know, but it seems so dangerous."

Magnanimous laughed. "I think a child who is able to

find her way to Port Cullis without so much as a hair out of place is more than capable of going to sea. You don't mind, do you, Alex?"

"Well, no," she replied, suddenly feeling very worried. "But the thing is, I've never gone sailing before. I don't know how to use a boat or anything, and even if I could sail, I haven't the first idea of how to go about getting a boat anyway."

Magnanimous smiled that wonderful smile of his. "Oh, Alex, how very brave of you, but of course I was going to help you with that. The *Valiant* has just come out of hibernation and finished her spring cleaning. The crew are all in town with nothing to do. And what could be more fun than a little adventure? Besides, the way I see it, it won't be half as dangerous as you imagine."

"I don't see how not," said Heather.

"We have an advantage on Steele. He doesn't know we're after him. From what I understand of the story you just told me, Mr Underwood was kidnapped for his map – which he didn't have. It is unlikely the pirates know about Alex, and even if they do, very unlikely that they think she has it, as, of course, adults, even pirates, tend to underestimate children. All we need to do is catch them when they typically anchor for supplies, at the port of Lawless."

"But it's the *Ironic Gentleman*! The deadliest ship this

side of the equator!" Heather exclaimed. Coriander moaned. It wasn't quite clear if it was the thought of the *Ironic Gentleman* that made him do so, or simply because his head hurt so much.

"We don't want to attack them, we don't want to arrest them. We just want to rescue Mr Underwood. A covert operation under the cover of night should do the trick, I would think. And, of course, Alex wouldn't be involved in that."

Heather still did not appear convinced, and though Alex thought everything the Captain was saying made a lot of sense, she still wasn't used to such generosity.

"But why would your crew agree to this?" she asked.

"Well, Alex, you need to understand the nature of the sailor. He is never so content as when he is riding the waves. I never understood why we were made to stay ashore for so long when the sea is tempting us, calling out to us. No, did you think I would turn down this opportunity? Alex, the HMS *Valiant* is at your command."

"Really?" asked Alex.

"Yes, of course."

Heather shook her head in disapproval.

"Uh . . . great!" said Alex. "When can we leave?"

"Well, we'll have to gather the crew together, but I think we could get going at first tide tomorrow. Is that soon enough?" asked Magnanimous.

Alex nodded vigorously.

"Excellent!"

"Shhhh!" said Coriander, cupping his forehead in his hands.

So OK, what happened next? Well, Alex spent the day trailing Captain Magnanimous all around Port Cullis, rounding up supplies and filling in paperwork. And eventually when everything was finished and done, Alex returned to the Gangrene.

Her final evening on land was a lively one. Heather had prepared a small feast for Alex, Magnanimous and Coriander (and even a nice steak for Giggles, who was feeling a bit nervous about going to sea). Coriander was looking far more lively than he had in the morning, and, after some cajoling, was persuaded to perform the odd magic trick.

The Odd Magic Trick is a very famous magic trick that has been passed down through generations of magicians. Basically, it has the magician asking an audience member for a watch, putting a cloth over it and, after a few hand movements, removing the cloth and revealing a completely different watch that looks exactly like the original, but one on which the time reads nine fifty-two. To which the audience member usually responds, "That was odd."

Then there was some singing. And then it was time for bed. (Or the floor for Coriander, who had passed out after having been bought several rounds of drinks after his Odd Trick by a pretty young woman in a tweed skirt.)

Alex was lying under her covers, Giggles curled up in the small of her back as usual, when there was a light tap on the door.

"Come in!" she said.

Heather entered the room and sat on the edge of her bed. Giggles looked up and squinted at her sleepily.

"I just wanted to wish you luck with everything. I'm not going to pretend I'm not seriously worried for you, but you will be with Captain Magnanimous, and I don't know anyone better to take you to sea. Anyway, I wanted to give you this," she said, handing over a brown paper bag.

Alex opened it. Inside was a brand-new toothbrush and a tube of toothpaste and even a spool of floss.

"I remembered what you said today, when we passed the dentist's on the way to the admiral's office, about your braces and everything and how you'd sacrificed your toothbrush for the sake of the treasure map. I know it's a strange gift, but, well, my dad's a dentist and I get the stuff for free," she said with a shrug.

Alex smiled brightly. "Thank you, Heather, so much!" she said, sitting up and giving Heather a big hug. "It's absolutely perfect, exactly what I've been needing!"

"Well, you're welcome, then," said Heather, returning her hug.

"Please don't worry about me. I'll be just fine," said Alex, looking at her. "I know what I'm doing." She reached over for her bag and pulled out her camera. "May I take your picture?"

Heather laughed. "Oh dear, I guess so. I never know what to do for pictures," she said.

"Just smile, that's all," said Alex and she took one.

"I think now you should sleep. You've got a long day ahead of you. And I'd better go down and keep an eye on Coriander. He's asleep now, but I don't want him waking up thinking he can fly or anything," she said, shaking her head.

Heather kissed Alex on the forehead, tucked her in and left quietly with a final smile.

Alex fell asleep almost instantly.

And had another strange dream in which, despite having her eyes closed, she knew a burglar was sneaking around in her room. What was even weirder was that somehow she was completely aware of what he looked like. He was all in black, wearing a ski mask over his face. But the holes for the eyes and nose had been filled in. She then dreamed that Giggles woke up and jumped and attacked the burglar. She dreamed this because in real life Giggles had woken up and was attacking Coriander, who was standing in the doorway. This made Alex wake up in real life.

"Sorry, sorry!" slurred Coriander, falling back out through the door, Giggles attached to his ankles.

"Coriander?" asked Alex sleepily.

"I just wanted to say goodbye!" he called from out in the hall. "I won't be here when you get up! Stop that!" he said to Giggles.

"Oh. Well, bye, then," said Alex, rubbing her eyes. Her focus was a bit fuzzy, but she called to Giggles, who released his grip.

"Good luck!" called Coriander, and he staggered out of view.

"That was weird," said Alex. Giggles jumped on to the bed and climbed protectively into her lap. If he had been capable of speech, he would probably have agreed. But as it was, it was neither here nor there that they thought it was weird, as there was nothing that needed to be done about it.

So they both went to sleep. Again.

THE THIRTY-FIRST CHAPTER

In which Alex boards the HMS *Valiant*

There is something unique about early mornings when you have to travel somewhere. First of all, for some reason they always seem to dawn bright but with a crispness in the air, a cold nip to the nose, no matter what the season. And they always have a slight haze about them, like a fog has just recently lifted. Secondly, it seems as if on that particular morning when you are going somewhere, everyone else has decided that they will in fact stay tucked up in bed, as if going somewhere is quite possibly the silliest thing to do this morning. Thirdly, and this I find extremely odd personally, is that, for some reason, suddenly you are obliged to take along snacks of healthy things, things you would never really take with you as snacks on any other occasion, like toasted almonds and apple slices. And the morning Alex left the Gangrene to begin her adventure on the high seas dawned precisely in this way.

Alex shivered slightly on the wagon that Heather had arranged to take her to the ship, and rubbed her nose, pulling her jumper tighter around her. Giggles sat by her side looking around, torn between feeling miserable riding the wagon and wanting to get off, and wanting the ride to continue for as long as possible so that he could avoid boarding the ship.

"Oh, come on, Giggles," said Alex, noticing his expression, "this is the best bit."

Giggles pretended not to hear her.

"This is the bit where we finally rescue Mr Underwood. You'll really like him. He is a really good teacher. And really nice. And anyway, even if you don't like him, once we rescue him, it means we can finally go after the treasure. And that is sure to be a wonderful adventure." She was reminded briefly of her uncle and how much he would have agreed. Alex shook her head and replaced the thought with all the positive things that had happened since her arrival at Port Cullis.

She really was feeling as if things were coming

together. Having Captain Magnanimous on her side was a great advantage and gave her great confidence. It wasn't every ten-and-a-half-year-old in search of buried treasure that had one of Her Majesty's Finest helming the voyage.

It was an incredibly impressive sight passing from the city through the triumphal arch on to the narrow docks. The sky was filled with a forest of masts dripping with nets and rigging. Even though it was still very early in the morning, sailors and carpenters were shouting at each other, and the captains of two rusty fishing trawlers were arguing about who had the right of way.

Then, suddenly, all the other ships seemed to melt away, and Alex's wagon came across a much more organized chaos at the docks belonging to the navy. There were five large ships moored and one on land in dry dock undergoing repairs. With help from the driver unloading Mr Underwood's bicycle, Alex found herself standing on the pier, feeling even smaller than usual. The ships were huge, immaculately kept and painted a stunning combination of gold and blue. She walked slowly down the pier reading the names of the ships as she passed, *Intrepid, Champion, Glory, Dependable.* . .

And *Valiant.* The HMS *Valiant* stood at the end of the queue. Smaller than the others, she was a three-masted frigate. She was also the only one on which there was any sign of life. Sailors were up in the rigging calling out orders to each other, and well-dressed officers stood on the deck yelling out orders to them. Alex approached the gangplank with trepidation.

Two heads poked over the edge of the ship and looked down at Alex. They stared at her for a moment. And disappeared.

Then they reappeared at the foot of the gangplank. The head with dark hair waved and called out, "Hello there! My name is Daniel O'Connell. I'm quartermaster. You must be Alex. The kid."

Alex nodded silently.

"Well, Shakespeare, don't just stand there. Let's help her get her things on board," said O'Connell to the fair-haired man next to him.

"Couldn't you get one of the larger, burlier, and, I may add, stronger members of your crew to do that?"

"My crew are getting ready for the voyage, and as far as I know, there isn't much a ship's surgeon has to do before we set sail."

"Not true, not true. Why already this morning I've had to deal with two splinters and a stubbed toe."

"Which of my men would have the gall to stop work for something as small as that?"

"Your crew? I was talking about myself," replied Shakespeare.

Alex just stood silently watching them argue. They were tall and slim and almost indistinguishable from each other, aside from their hair colour and different accents. And their clothes were different (O'Connell wore the uniform of the navy, whereas Shakespeare was dressed in grey trousers and a shirt and brown boots). But other than that, they could have been twins, and secretly were, though neither of them knew it.

Their mother had died giving birth to them, and their father was a horribly lazy man who insisted that he could not take care of two babies, and so he took Shakespeare (which wasn't his real name but his nickname) abroad and raised him, and put O'Connell into the care of the local government.

When Shakespeare turned twelve he was sent to a very posh boarding school and when O'Connell turned twelve he was sent off to be a cabin boy aboard the _Seaworthy_ where he served with Magnanimous. Shakespeare eventually decided to pursue medicine and O'Connell found himself very adept at sailing. Eventually, when Magnanimous became a captain, he placed an ad for a ship's surgeon, and Shakespeare applied, always having longed for adventure. And this was where he and O'Connell met for the first time. They instantly hated each other.

O'Connell hated anyone from the upper classes, and

Shakespeare hated anyone who hated him because he was from the upper classes. There was serious friction until one night, when some of the crew were playing a secret game of poker in the hatches, and Shakespeare stumbled on their game. O'Connell stood to meet him. Everything went very silent. Gambling was strictly forbidden in the navy.

"What do you think you're doing?"

"What do you think we're doing?"

"I think you're playing poker."

"You got a problem with that?"

"Yes."

"Yes?" said O'Connell, taking a step forward.

"Yes," replied Shakespeare, taking his own. "What kind of chips are those?"

The two looked at the table, where they were using marked pieces of kindling.

O'Connell looked at Shakespeare once more. "What's wrong with them?" He furrowed his eyebrows.

Shakespeare raised his. "Let me get mine."

From that night on, he and O'Connell became fast friends. They discovered that they actually had a lot in common, in fact almost everything. And that what was even weirder was that sometimes it seemed as if they could practically read each other's minds. This probably had something to do with the fact that they were twins.

But they didn't know this. And never would. Which is just the way things happen sometimes.

Anyway, Alex marvelled at how alike the two of them looked as they helped her bring her small rucksack (which Shakespeare carried) and bike (which O'Connell hoisted over one shoulder) on to the ship. Once aboard, Alex felt the butterflies in her stomach start to flutter about, and she picked up the nervous Giggles, holding him close to her.

Alex watched O'Connell and Shakespeare weave their way over to where a tall slender woman with glasses and short strawberry-blonde hair was standing. She was wearing a very striking uniform including a hat and boots with a gold buckle. She looked at Alex and strode over, her arms extended wide.

"*Buongiorno!* Alexandra, it is a most pleasure to meet you finally!" she said richly. "My name is Francesca Giminiano, but please call me Francesca. I am second lieutenant and the ship's inventor."

"Oh, I didn't know ships had inventors," said Alex, following Francesca's lead by kissing the air by both her cheeks. Giggles growled softly as he was squished between them.

"They don't," muttered Shakespeare under his breath so that only Alex heard.

"Ah well, Magnanimous is most encouraging, and he finds my inventions most useful," said Francesca. "For example, I have invented an automatic sail unfurler that works with a single push of a button."

"Wow!" said Alex. "If that's the case, then what are the crew doing?" she asked, looking up at them working intensely.

"Ah, sometimes there is a, how you say, a glitch? So today the button is not working but tomorrow the button will work. I will fix it."

"She's been saying that since last season," said Shakespeare quietly. This time Francesca heard him.

"It will work! It does work! Inventions take much attempts," she explained to Alex. "Many of my other inventions work with perfection."

"I'm sure," replied Alex.

Suddenly a striking young man landed in front of them.

"Tanaka!" said Shakespeare, clutching at his chest. "Was that really necessary?"

Tanaka flashed the most perfect set of white teeth Alex had seen since Lord Poppinjay.

"My apologies, old chap, but I say, look!" And he pointed towards the pier. Just as he did so, there was a sudden eruption of noise, as a cheer filled the air.

"Thank heavens," sighed Shakespeare. "The Captain, finally."

Captain Magnanimous was marching towards the ship

surrounded by well-wishers. Occasionally he would step out of the crowd and shake hands with a fisherman aboard his boat and chat for a moment or so, smiling and waving his arms energetically. It seemed as if everyone in the vicinity had come to see Captain Magnanimous set sail, and Alex felt a glow of pride that she was about to go adventuring with him.

Tanaka launched himself into the air again, did two flips and landed in front of the Captain on the dock with a salute.

"That was Takeo Tanaka, third lieutenant, and ridiculous," said Shakespeare to Alex.

"Not ridiculous!" said Francesca. "I would like to see you try to do what he can do."

"I wouldn't want to do what he can do!"

"Then why are you taking private lessons in gymnastics from him?"

"I'm . . . I'm . . . not!" stuttered Shakespeare.

"He is," said Francesca with a smile. Alex smiled back.

"Captain on board!" called O'Connell.

There was another loud cheer from up in the rigging, and the Captain waved. Shaking his head, he joined O'Connell.

"Looks like a perfect day to set sail, eh, O'Connell?" said Magnanimous.

"Indeed, Captain," replied O'Connell.

"All crew accounted for, then?"

"Aye."

"Well then, Francesca." Francesca stepped forward. "No point in delay. Why don't you take her out for us."

"Aye, sir," said Francesca with a salute. And she took her place at the helm.

"Hullo, Alex," said Magnanimous, approaching her.

"Hey, Captain," said Alex.

"You ready for this?"

"Aye, aye, Captain!" she replied with a salute.

"Ha! I like that!" He saluted her back. "Come on, let's get you a good seat!"

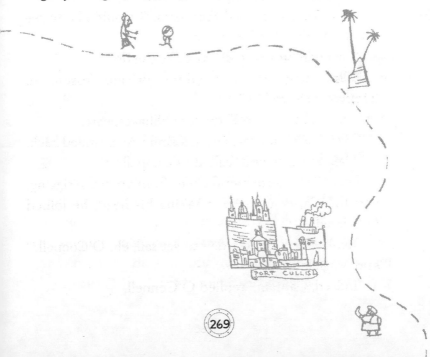

THE THIRTY-SECOND CHAPTER

In which Alex experiences life at sea

As the HMS *Valiant* passed the breakwater and the ship's sails caught the wind, Alex could easily see why Magnanimous was happy to return to sea so soon. It was a truly wonderful feeling standing on deck in the bright sunshine with the deep blue of the sea stretching out in front of them like infinity. In fact, it was a strange thought that it wasn't infinity – that somewhere beyond what her eyes could see was land, and lots of it. Out there was an island with buried treasure, or maybe a few islands, and somewhere lurking in the shadow of a distant port, or menacing some unsuspecting aristocrat aboard his private yacht, was the legendary figure of the *Ironic Gentleman*.

The fishing trawlers and pleasure cruisers around them became fewer and fewer until the ship was travelling in complete isolation. Lunch time passed joyfully, and after Alex had finished the peanut butter and jam sandwich packed for her by Heather, she shared her toasted almonds and apple slices with the crew. Then she took some down the hatches to Giggles, who was feeling very seasick and had found himself a dark corner to mope in. Dinner followed strikingly soon, and she ate with the officers and captain in his cabin. And before she knew it, Alex found herself leaning on the deck rail, taking some pictures with her camera, while watching the sun make some final stretches before crossing the last length of sky.

"Hello there, Alex!" said a friendly, yet unfamiliar voice. Alex turned to see a pleasant-looking man who reminded her a little of Coriander when he was in good spirits.

"Hello," she replied.

"My name is Julian De Wit, and I am first lieutenant. I understand you've never been to sea before," he said. He wasn't terribly good at small talk and rushed the words together slightly.

"Never," replied Alex. "It's wonderful." She looked up at the sails, shielding her eyes with her hand. "I imagine it must feel a bit like flying when you're up there," she added, indicating the crow's nest.

De Wit followed her gaze. "Oh yes, a bit. Except of course your feet are on something solid, and if you were flying they wouldn't be. But the views are quite something else." He looked back at Alex. "Would you like to see?"

Alex looked at him, startled. "Really?" she asked.

"Is that a yes?"

"Yes, yes, it is!"

To climb up to a crow's nest is more difficult than you would imagine, unless you imagine it would be like climbing up a ladder made of fire and sharp spikes, and then it would be less difficult than you imagine. For one thing, the ropes move, so you feel incredibly unstable. For another, the wind grows fiercer the higher you climb. But when it came to heights and climbing (both up and down), Alex was fearless, and where you and I would force ourselves not to look down only to do just that and see the deck swimming dangerously far beneath us, Alex just climbed steadily upwards, with an occasional glance below to see just how high up she had gone. She easily jumped into the crow's nest, surprising the skinny Frenchman who was on lookout ("*Sacré bleu!*" he said). And she and De Wit stared out over the horizon.

Being in the crow's nest indeed felt nothing like flying, for, as De Wit had pointed out, they were standing securely. But it did feel like being on a futuristic moving pavement in the sky, which was just as much fun. The view was spectacular and the sun was just setting, and the wind blew their hair wildly about, and it was all completely perfect.

"You know what?" said De Wit. "We really should have a meeting to discuss our plan of attack."

"That's a really good idea. The sooner the better," replied Alex, taking a snapshot with her camera of the sun sinking low into the water.

"I just think it's terrible what's happened to Mr Underwood. Is he really the great-great-great-grandson of the Infamous Wigpowder?" asked De Wit.

"Yes."

"That's incredible. You know I seem to recall an old sea shanty about him. . ." De Wit paused for a moment. And then unexpectedly, but much to Alex's delight, he began to sing.

THE BALLAD OF THE INFAMOUS WIGPOWDER

"There once was a pirate so feared
Sailors hid at his mere mention,
With a name some admitted was weird,

But it certainly got your attention.

Yes. . .
Wigpowder was what they did call him,
And for this he never felt shame,
He didn't mind simply because,
Of course, that always had been his name.

He was also referred to as 'infamous',
And this made much sense, you see, 'cause
It was easy to gather from all that he'd done
That that's what he most clearly was.

He amassed quite a staggering treasure
That was buried 'way far out to sea,
That became (for its size beyond measure)
More infamous even than he.

There were jewels and gold coins a-plenty
All tucked away safe for his son –
His scion, his heir, who, when twenty
Would inherit the wealth he had won.

Yes. . .
Wigpowder was what they did call him
And for this he never felt shame,

He didn't mind simply because,
Of course, that always had been his name.

He was also referred to as 'infamous',
And this made much sense, you see, 'cause
It was easy to gather from all that he'd done
That that's what he most clearly was.

Now these plans went somewhat awry,
The treasure, left buried, unfound.
And somewhere out there it must lie
Buried still deep underground.

You can try all you want to to find it,
And many a man has done so.
But the map where directions are writ
Has vanished a long time ago.

Plus on cold windy nights you can hear
Him yelling his curse to the air,
His warning to those who seek treasure's clear:
'If you're not a Wigpowder, beware.'

And. . .
Wigpowder was what they did call him,
And for this he never felt shame,

He didn't mind simply because,
Of course, that always had been his name.

He was also referred to as 'infamous',
And this made much sense, you see, 'cause
It was easy to gather from all that he'd done
That that's what he most clearly was.

Yes, he was considered most infamous,
'Cause that's what he obviously was."

"I think that was how it went," said De Wit uncertainly.

"Wow," said Alex, turning to him. "You are a very good singer."

De Wit blushed and looked around. "It's getting dark. We'd better head back."

The climb down was slightly slower because, well, climbs down are usually slower, unless of course you lose your grip, and then they are much faster. But more painful.

When they eventually reached the bottom, De Wit said, "I think I'll gather everyone together for that meeting, then. Shall we say half an hour unless you hear differently?"

"Sounds perfect," replied Alex, and she watched De Wit walk away cheerfully. Which made her all the more cheerful. She was having a really wonderful time. Maybe after all this was done she could be a sailor. She imagined that could be a really fun job, having adventures every day and yet never having to leave your own home. She'd have to talk to Mr Underwood about it. Maybe he would be interested in becoming a sailor as well. She laughed to herself. Although Mr Underwood was the descendant of a pirate, the image of him on a ship seemed to conflict with the usual image of him standing at the front of a classroom. But maybe it was time for a change for him too.

Moments later, with the ship rocking more fiercely than seemed necessary, Alex found herself sitting snug at the Captain's table with De Wit, Francesca, Shakespeare, Tanaka and, of course, Magnanimous.

"Now then," began Magnanimous. "Whereas the action itself is very basic, that is the rescue of Mr Underwood, the task is just not that simple. Our main hindrance is of course. . ."

"The murderous pirates?" asked Shakespeare.

"I wasn't going to put it exactly like that, but yes, yes, I suppose they would be, wouldn't they?"

"Yes."

"I've got word from a man at Lawless that indeed the *Ironic Gentleman* has made berth there, as anticipated.

We sail there, but anchor north along the coastline at the Cave of the Dislocated Thumb, so as not to draw attention, and then send out a small rescue team. I would like this to be led by Tanaka. You may choose your men. Once you have secured Mr Underwood, you will return to the ship, where we will then plan the next course of action," finished Magnanimous.

"And this next plan, of course, would be the finding of treasure," said Francesca.

"Well, I don't think that is our decision to make," replied Magnanimous, looking at Alex over his glasses.

Alex sat quietly thoughtful for a moment. She did very much want to go in search of the treasure, but she had always considered the adventure to be hers and Mr Underwood's, and not the crew of the HMS *Valiant*'s. She was of course being illogical, she pointed out to herself. After all, she and Mr Underwood could not very well go after the Wigpowder treasure in a small rowing boat or anything. Still the idea of so many people being involved in what had begun as a very private affair, known only to three very special people, was frustrating.

"I don't think it is my decision either," concluded Alex. "We'll just have to wait and see what Mr Underwood thinks."

The others seemed satisfied with this answer and set about their business. De Wit and Francesca stayed behind with Magnanimous to plot their course, Tanaka cartwheeled towards the hatches to speak with O'Connell, and Alex decided she should probably get some rest.

As she curled under the covers of her cot, listening to the waves lap against the side of the ship, she felt at home. She really did love living at sea. And she wondered, for the briefest of moments, what would happen when this whole adventure was behind her. Could she really go back to being a schoolgirl on dry land?

"Never mind that now, Alex," she said to herself. Giggles opened an eye and looked at her. Alex laughed. "Oh, just go back to being seasick." And she gave the cat a friendly shove.

THE THIRTY-THIRD CHAPTER

In which we anchor at the Cave of the Dislocated Thumb and something unexpected happens

The next few days were quite thrilling. During the day, Alex learned to do nautical things like how to tie a series of exciting knots, and Giggles even ventured forth on the deck, only to be chased downstairs by the ship's dog, a very friendly mongrel belonging to the gunner. In the evenings, O'Connell would play his violin, and they would dance and sing, showing off for one another. De Wit, who had already proven himself a surprisingly good singer, knew many musical-theatre songs off by heart.

Sometimes after the music, Alex would join

O'Connell and Shakespeare at poker. She never really played. The stakes were too high for her. But O'Connell had decided that Alex was a lucky charm, and she enjoyed watching. Then she would go to bed in her comfy cot, with Giggles curled in the small of her back.

Then, one very foggy day, the Frenchman in the crow's nest let out the call, "Land ho!" (actually, it was more like "Lond 'o", but never mind). Alex rushed to the side of the deck. It was difficult to see through the fog, but suddenly a dark shadow appeared and then disappeared.

"Easy now!" called the Captain, approaching O'Connell from behind. "Take her north by north-east, thirty degrees." O'Connell nodded and spun the wheel. For anyone else it might have been a daunting task in such fog, but Magnanimous anchored the *Valiant* with ease, after which he gathered his officers and Alex together once again in his cabin.

It was agreed that Tanaka and O'Connell would go scout out the exact location of the *Ironic Gentleman* and report back before they all set the plan into motion. There was a nervous hour while they waited for their return, each crew member trying to do their assigned tasks, distracted by their worry over what news Tanaka might bring. Alex watched Magnanimous himself look out of the cabin half a dozen times to ask after the scouts, only to pull his head back inside with a sigh.

Feeling anxious and not knowing what to do with herself, Alex approached Francesca, who was occasionally peering out through a spyglass into the fog.

"I can't believe that this is it," said Alex, nervously feeling her pocket to see if the toothbrush holder was resting securely.

"Yes, I know," replied Francesca, collapsing the spyglass and hanging it at her hip. "I do hope everything goes well. The Captain, he is not fond of complications. That is why he prepares everything so carefully."

"Yes. Although I have to say that, in my experience, things rarely go as you expect them to," said Alex. Francesca nodded. Alex looked down near her hands and saw a large, cheerful orange button. Knowing it would please Francesca to be asked about it she said, "What does this button do?"

Francesca looked at the button excitedly and then frowned. "Hmm, I am not sure. I invent so many things that require a button. But this one is big and orange, and I think it is important."

With amusement, Alex watched Francesca think. Over the course of their trip Alex had encountered several of Francesca's buttons. There was the one that was meant to work the machine that made tea, and it did, but it only made Ginger Zest, which was strange as the machine had been stocked with Earl Grey. Then there was the one that worked the swab machine which was meant to swab the decks for the crew, but it would always be found chatting to the machine in charge of dusting.

"Oh, I think I remember," she said, snapping her fingers. "The orange button, it's. . ."

"Zey're back!" called the Frenchman.

Alex and Francesca looked over the side. Tanaka and O'Connell indeed were back, and they were gesturing for a rope. Magnanimous raced over to help them on deck.

"Well?" he asked.

"Captain, we have a problem," said Tanaka, taking deep breaths.

"Problem? Did they see you?" asked Magnanimous.

"No," replied Tanaka. "There was no one to see me."

"I don't understand."

"I think he means that the *Ironic Gentleman* wasn't there," interjected Alex. She was getting so used to disappointment that she could interpret the problem instantaneously.

"Exactly," said Tanaka, nodding at Alex. "The ship was nowhere to be seen. We went ashore, talked to a waitress of the Disreputable Landlord. She said the *Ironic Gentleman* had left early this morning. We missed her,

Captain. We just missed her."

Captain Magnanimous hit the deck rail with his fist. "So close!" he said. "This changes everything." He sat next to Tanaka. "Did the waitress have any idea where they were headed?"

"She didn't."

"Well," said Magnanimous. He seemed shaken. "Well. We need to revise our plan completely, then." He stood up and looked around. "Yes, well. Right now, I need to think. I need to be alone." And he turned and went to his cabin, waving aside De Wit, who had placed a hand on his shoulder.

"Will he be OK?" asked Alex.

"Don't you worry now," said O'Connell. "He's a smart man. He'll figure something out."

Alex nodded.

"Well, we'd better get back to work," said Francesca, and she and the men wandered off in their separate directions.

Alex turned and stared out into the fog, which had lifted somewhat around the ship. It was a little unnerving seeing Magnanimous upset. She hadn't realized how much faith she had put in him until she saw him so unsure. The Captain had seemed more than a mere man, but now was all too human. Alex wondered if there was any conceivable way of tracking down the

Ironic Gentleman. Where could it possibly have been headed? She had no idea, and it seemed the navy had no idea either. It was a very rare thing for someone to seek out the *Ironic Gentleman* intentionally. Steele was the one who typically did the seeking. So then, how to hunt the hunters? Perhaps . . . she leaned against the rail. Perhaps . . . and she thought back to something Coriander had once suggested.

Alex raced across the deck and burst into the Captain's cabin. Magnanimous was sitting at his desk, his head in his hands. He looked up, startled. "Alex? Can I help you?"

"Captain, what if instead of trying to find them, we get them to find us!"

"Sorry?" replied Magnanimous.

Alex drew up a chair to the other side of his desk. "We let it slip to someone that we have the Wigpowder treasure map and we're looking for the treasure, find ourselves a good spot – that would be your job, of course – and then wait for them to find us!" she said triumphantly.

Captain Magnanimous looked at Alex for a moment. "That might work," he said slowly.

"I think it would."

Magnanimous smiled his fabulous smile. "Alex, you are amazing! Not only is this a good idea, it is a fantastic idea."

Alex blushed slightly. "Thank you."

Magnanimous hit the table with his hand, but this time it was positive sign.

"OK, so we'll send Tanaka back to the Disreputable Landlord and get him to slip the news. But first we've got to figure out where we should make anchor that would suit us best. Excellent! Alex, fetch the officers immediately," instructed Magnanimous.

Alex smiled broadly and quickly went to obey his orders. She found De Wit first, starboard side. He turned and smiled when he saw her.

"The Captain is. . ." Alex stopped suddenly.

"The Captain is. . .?" asked De Wit. "Is this a game? Oh, let's see. The Captain is . . . nice? The Captain is . . . brave? The Captain is. . ."

"No, no," said Alex, holding up a hand. She was looking out into the fog. "I thought I saw something."

De Wit looked over her shoulder. "Where?"

"There." Alex pointed.

"I don't see any. . . Wait. Did you hear that?"

"What?"

De Wit stepped forward and squinted into the fog. Suddenly he spun back to Alex, "Get down, now!" he shouted and pushed her to the deck. A cannonball crashed through the deck rail and dropped into the hatch. A blur of motion, and De Wit was back on his feet. Alex jumped up to join him and nearly collapsed again from shock. Charging them from the cover of the fog like a bull with a toreador's cape impaled on its horns, was a large brig painted black, her deep red sails filling with wind.

"That i-isn't," she stuttered.

"That is," replied De Wit. "All men on deck!!" he cried loudly and ran to the Captain's cabin.

Alex stood staring at the ship, rigid with distress. It was coming for them at an impossible speed, and it didn't seem all that bothered that it was about to crash into the *Valiant*. Alex watched the bowsprit fly towards her like a lance, and she momentarily thought she was about to be skewered, when the ship suddenly turned to broadside, and it was when it did that that, if Alex had any doubt as to who was attacking them, it was quickly resolved. There, in the same red as the sails, passing in front of her like the opening credits of some horrible film, was the word *Gentleman* followed closely by *Ironic*.

THE THIRTY-FOURTH CHAPTER

In which a fierce battle is fought

The attack was quick and merciless. Where it had come from and how it had found them was anyone's guess, but no sooner had the *Ironic Gentleman* come alongside them, than Captain Magnanimous swung into action, literally, grabbing a rope and propelling himself on to the deck. Alex watched him barking orders, sending O'Connell to the helm and the gunner below decks. There was only so much they could do, taken by surprise in this way. De Wit and Francesca braced themselves for boarding, and Alex, trying to stay out of the way, hid herself behind the stairs to the forecastle. Peering through the steps, she watched in horror as the action unfolded in front of her.

The pirates were launching themselves on to the deck of the *Valiant*, cutlasses in their teeth and fierce glints in their eyes. Landing almost directly in front of Alex was a small man with greasy red hair who looked strangely familiar. He was carrying a large hammer in his hand. His whole body was covered with deep scars, and he was laughing wildly at nothing in particular. Alex ducked low, and he went off to join the fray.

Fighting had broken out all over the ship. Francesca was battling it out with a large man nearly twice her size, and De Wit was facing two men, the one with the red hair and the hammer, and another dressed in a white suit that the playwright Oscar Wilde might have quite liked.

At the bow of the ship, Captain Magnanimous had no fewer than eight men in his sights and was finally given some relief by O'Connell, who had passed the helm over to Shakespeare. Meanwhile Tanaka was confusing his foe by performing a series of flips across the length of the deck.

Alex felt out of her element and entirely useless. She wanted to help her friends, but at the same time she realized that her trying to help would probably have the opposite effect. She was also incredibly scared and really couldn't think of a single thing that she could do. Her only chance was to weather this particular storm and hope she would go unnoticed.

Alas, my friend, this was not to be. She had tried to keep as quiet as possible so that she would remain relatively invisible, but there was very little she could do about her smell. Because you can be quieter, and hide behind something to be less visible, but you can't turn down your smell, at least not without taking a bath. And that is how Alex suddenly found herself face to face with a large grey drooling bear of a dog, growling softly.

"Oh, hello," she said quietly. She stuck out a hand for it to sniff, but it snapped at her. "Easy, boy," she said with a quiver in her voice, "easy." The dog moved towards her slowly. Alex was quite cornered behind the stairs. It growled more loudly, revealing its long sharp teeth. And it is fair to suppose that it most probably would have torn poor Alex to shreds, had not a very loyal, and slightly seasick, friend come to her rescue. With the ferocity of a small tiger, Giggles exploded out of the hatch and, claws unsheathed, jumped on to the dog's back. It yelped pathetically. But then it turned its full concentration on Giggles, and thus began a fierce battle.

Her fear for Giggles's safety was momentarily stalled when Alex looked past where the dog had been. Alex let out a gasp. Out of the white fog that had once more blanketed the entire ship stepped forward a dark figure. A man, tall, lean and fierce, was walking with large strides purposefully right towards her. How he knew where he was going, Alex had not the faintest idea, for wrapped around his face and head was a dark black silk cloth. Instantly she recognized the terrifying figure from the photograph her uncle had taken moments before his death. It suddenly clicked that he was also the same character whose face she'd been trying to see in her nightmares. Alex pinched herself, hoping against hope that a dream was all that this was. She didn't wake up, though. Because she wasn't asleep.

As if in a trance Alex stood to meet the man. He stopped right in front of her and for a moment time stood still. And then the man asked softly, "Alex?"

"Yes."

The man raised one of his hands and placed it around Alex's neck. Now I am sure you remember from the beginning of the book that this very dangerous man had hands made of wood. Well, if you don't, this very dangerous man had hands made of wood. The grip they afforded him was so solid and unbreakable that it allowed him to close his fingers right around her neck and to lift Alex up by her chin without strangling her.

The man let out a whistle and the grey dog, who had

by now overcome poor Giggles, stopped instantly and ran over to its master. Alex looked over at Giggles, who was lying in a small furry lump, his small chest rising and falling with effort. She wanted to call out to him, but something was preventing her speech. As she was carried through the fighting, everything became a blur.

She heard yelling that the side was breached, and she saw De Wit held to the mast by a dagger through his hand. She could see Captain Magnanimous spinning to meet one new foe after the next, fighting them off with less dexterity than he had had at the beginning, sweat pouring down his face. O'Connell was cornered by the man with the hammer. And beyond that she saw Francesca, who had somehow managed to dispose of the massive creature that she had been sparring with, lying on the deck, her leg horribly injured. Their eyes met and Francesca gestured towards Alex, mouthing something. Alex squinted. With one last effort Francesca thrust her arm forward and the words "Push the button" floated over the sounds of battle. Alex moved her eyes to see the large orange button pass by her head. Not knowing why, but because it was the only thing she could do to help, Alex pushed the button. And what happened was . . . nothing. She looked back at Francesca to apologize, but she was lying still, her head face down on the wood.

And all the while the pirate carrying her moved swiftly onwards, until Alex was brought to the man in white who had just thrown the Frenchman overboard. He turned around suddenly as if the man carrying her had said something to startle him.

"My dear fellow, what have you found?" he said, his voice nasal and thin.

"It's done. Take her to the Captain," replied the soft voice of her captor. He dropped Alex hard on to the deck and, with his dog, vanished back into the fog.

"Right, then," said the man in white, giving a little sniff. "Jack!" he called to the man with the greasy red hair, who was fiercely scratching the back of his neck.

"Jack, Jack, Jack," he replied happily.

"Get everyone together. The ship's hull is stoved in. Her floating days are over. The whole vessel will be with Davy Jones in less than fifteen minutes. And," he grabbed Alex roughly by the back of her jumper, "we have the child."

"Child!" said Jack. "Okidoky!" He turned around. "Oi!" he called out to the pirates, who turned and understood.

The man in white shook his head and looked down at Alex and smiled. And quicker than you can say, "This is not what was supposed to happen," Alex was whisked back into the air, over the side of the HMS *Valiant*, and on to the deck of the most notorious pirate ship this side of the equator. A ship whose crew was as ruthless as a person not named Ruth. A ship whose captain had never been seen. A ship that was called the *Ironic Gentleman*.

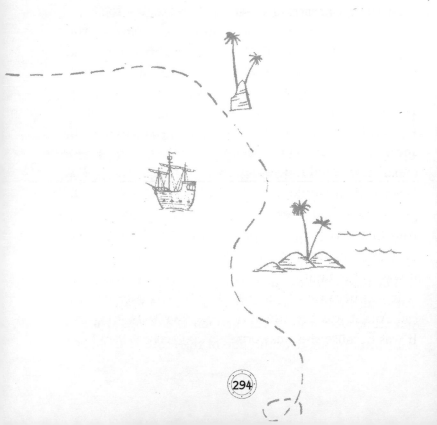

THE THIRTY-FIFTH CHAPTER

In which Alex meets the crew of the *Ironic Gentleman*

It was really depressing sailing away on the *Ironic Gentleman*, watching the HMS *Valiant* sinking lower and lower in the water and disappearing into the fog. I mean, how could it be otherwise? In very little time the HMS *Valiant* would cease to exist, as would the many people who had been so helpful and so nice to Alex. And that was a super-depressing thing to happen. But even more depressing than that was that, realized Alex, it was all her fault.

It was because of her that the HMS *Valiant* had set sail. And it was because of her that they were attacked. It was because she was cornered that Giggles had tried to save her and wound up dying on a sinking ship. The thought of Giggles made tears form in the corners of her eyes. How she missed him already. He would have scratched the pirate in white's eyes out – that would have surprised him! But now Giggles was gone; it was unbelievable. He was gone. Like everything and everyone else. And it was all her fault. Alex was secretly grateful that the pirate dressed in white was dragging her along the deck so forcefully, because she didn't think she would have been able to take a step on her own. The sadness practically paralysed her. She looked up at the pirate in white, his appearance blurred from the tears in her eyes.

The pirate in white was called Sir Geoffrey and was known by the rest of the crew as a dandy. A dandy is a man who cares very much about how he is dressed, thinks an awful lot about himself, and attempts to say witty things. Unfortunately, though, Sir Geoffrey was neither witty nor a knight. He was a decent pirate and an even better navigator, had good maths skills and could delegate. In fact, he had many qualities that were much more useful and more interesting than those belonging to a dandy, and for that reason he had been elected quartermaster. He would also have been well liked if he hadn't felt obliged to pretend to be something he so clearly wasn't.

"Well, well, well," said a strangely familiar voice. Alex looked ahead to see a large man with a bushy beard, bowler hat and a monocle emerge from the hatches before her and trip on the top step. He turned and cursed loudly down the hatch, then he returned his gaze to Alex. As he came close she noticed he was wearing white surgical gloves that, to her disgust, were covered in blood. "We meet again," he said, peeling off the gloves and tossing them overboard. "Do you remember me, Alex?" And he turned his head to peer at her through the monocle.

"You were at the house on the hill," said Alex, astonished. And then she realized something else. "You're one of the ones in the picture too!"

"Picture? What picture?"

Alex stopped talking. It suddenly occurred to her that her picture was evidence, proof that he had kidnapped Mr Underwood. She didn't want anything to happen to it. And then to her horror, she remembered that the picture was in her bag, which was on the *Valiant*, which was now at the bottom of the sea. As subtly as she could, she felt for the toothbrush holder, which to her relief, was still firmly in her pocket.

"Would you like me to take over?" asked the bearded man.

"I don't think that is necessary just yet, Dr

Brunswick," said Sir Geoffrey, wrinkling his nose. "I think we should take her to the Captain first. And if the Captain can't get anywhere with her, then, maybe, we could turn her over to you."

Now I really hate it when someone talks about me as if I'm not in the room when I clearly am. And of course, so did Alex. She also really didn't like the way in which these pirates were talking, which sounded suspiciously like they had some unpleasant plans for her. So that made her doubly uneasy. But then suddenly she had a stroke of genius. All this time she thought she was a goner. Here she was on this ship with a particular map that a certain captain was desperate to have, and she assumed that everybody must have been aware of it. But it was obvious from the conversation between the two pirates that they weren't certain that she had it. Maybe she could convince them that they had made a horrible, horrible mistake.

"Um," she said. The two pirates looked at her. "What exactly am I doing here?" she asked. She raised her eyebrows and looked as innocent as she could without feeling ridiculous. The pirates continued to look at her and then, both at the same time, burst into laughter.

"Very clever," sneered Sir Geoffrey. "But not all that clever. We know more than you think. Isn't that right, Dr Brunswick?"

Dr Brunswick smiled and took off his monocle to rub it with the edge of his jacket. "Oh, the things we know, and the fun we've had in learning them," he said. Alex remembered the bloody surgical gloves and gulped.

It was then that Alex noticed the crowd that had grown around her. She was startled to see the rest of the crew watching the interaction. She took a step backwards. "Hello," she said nervously.

"Hello!" waved Jack eagerly. "Hello! Hello!" And he scratched his ear fervently.

"How rude," said Sir Geoffrey, looking around him and shaking his head in mock embarrassment. "I completely forgot! Please allow me to introduce you to some of the members of our crew here." The crowd laughed quietly and tightened their circle.

"That enthusiastic greeter there is Jack Scratch."

"Jack!" said Jack and he pointed at his hammer. "Hammer!"

Alex smiled half-heartedly.

"And his hammer," continued Sir Geoffrey with a sigh. "I believe you met him before. He's our carpenter. He gets a bit overexcited by really almost anything, so we try not to make small talk with him. But he is excellent at taking orders. Jack!"

"Jack!" replied Jack.

"Stand on your head!"

"Jack!" he said again, and stood on his head.

"Let's see . . . who else. . ." Sir Geoffrey wandered around the crowd thoughtfully scratching his chin. "This lovely lady is Boudicca," he said, and a tall curvaceous woman with short dark red hair nodded in Alex's direction. "She is particularly adept at ripping people's limbs off. And this," he said, indicating something on the deck, "is No-Kneecaps Calvin." The crowd parted to reveal a man lying on his front holding himself up by his arms in what many a yoga master would agree was the cobra position. "Quite useless, he is," admitted Sir Geoffrey. "But freaky as heck." The crowd closed around him again.

"My name is Sir Geoffrey. I am quartermaster – and fabulous," he said, taking a small bow. "And of course you've met Dr Brunswick, ship's surgeon – and other things." Dr Brunswick winked at Alex. "Unfortunately The Wall was lost in battle. I doubt you would have liked him anyway. Really, I don't know whom to introduce next." He smiled at Alex. "Any preferences?" He stretched his arm out towards the crew, who looked at Alex eagerly.

Alex thought. "Actually," she stopped. She wasn't sure if she wanted the answer to her question.

"Go on," said Sir Geoffrey.

"Uh . . . who is the guy with the scarf over his face?" she asked, looking around to see if he was nearby. But he was nowhere in sight.

The crew started to mutter to each other and slowly began to disperse, returning to their duties. Even Jack righted himself and scurried away, whispering. Sir Geoffrey stood over Alex and frowned at her. "Senseless?" he asked.

"That's Senseless?" Alex started, remembering Coriander's description.

Sir Geoffrey's eyes widened. "You've heard of him?"

"A friend of mine told me a bit about your crew," said Alex with a shrug.

"Ah, and who would this friend be?"

"Oh, I don't think you would know him."

"I insist."

"His name is Coriander the Conjuror. He worked on the ship the *Ill Repute*, if you know it."

"I do," replied Sir Geoffrey with a slight smile. "Well, no matter about this Coriander fellow. We were talking about Senseless."

"Yes," replied Alex. "Why does he cover his face like that? How can he see?"

Sir Geoffrey laughed. "The Baron Senslesky," he said, "or Senseless, as he is more commonly known, is a very complicated individual. He's first mate and not much of a talker. He's not much of a sailor either. But he has an incredible ability to advise the Captain on exactly the right thing to do at exactly the right time. And he is incredibly, cruelly, violent."

Alex nodded. "Good to know," she said lightly. "So, um," she looked around the near deserted deck, "what now?"

"Now," said Sir Geoffrey, "I take you to the Captain."

"Right," replied Alex. She suddenly found breathing an extremely difficult activity as she remembered what Coriander had told her. About how anyone who met Steele in person never lived to speak of him. "Is that really necessary?"

"Yes," said Sir Geoffrey. "Yes, it is." He escorted Alex across the deck to the Captain's cabin. There isn't much to say about this bit. They walked. Alex was extremely frightened. Sir Geoffrey was pleased to be getting her out of his hair, which he really wanted to restyle after having it all messed up fighting. Eventually they found themselves outside Steele's door. Sir Geoffrey knocked. They waited for an answer. Then from inside they heard Steele call, "Enter!" Sir Geoffrey pushed open the door. It creaked slightly for effect, and suddenly Alex found herself in the very presence of the last person on earth she had ever wanted to meet.

THE THIRTY-JIXTH CHAPTER

In which Alex and the captain meet

Steele. The notorious Pirate Captain Steele the Inevitable was sitting at the head of a moderately sized dining table made of thick wood polished to a fine sheen. In front of the Captain was a meal fit for a king. On Steele's plate was a thick steak complemented by a pile of steaming mashed potatoes. Caramelized carrots stood in a bowl next to it along with another bowl full of broccoli. There was also a pitcher of wine, which had been half emptied. Perched next to it were the Captain's feet, the right crossed over the left.

Alex was more than shocked. But it wasn't so much because she found herself face to face with Steele after all this time, or even Steele's horrendous table manners (elbows on a table are rude enough, let alone boots you've been walking around in all day). No, the reason Alex was completely and utterly flabbergasted was that, after all the stories and everything she had heard, she just had never anticipated that Pirate Captain Steele the Inevitable would be a woman.

The complete impossibility that Steele could have been a woman struck Alex with more force than she had expected. Not that she had expected to be struck by such an impossibility, the impossibility not being possible in her mind until that very moment, but had she thought of the impossibility, then she would not have thought it would have affected her with such force.

. . .

Let me explain that better.

What I mean is this: Alex had always believed that boys and girls are capable of doing whatever they want to when they grow up. And had always assumed that every profession could be as easily occupied by a man or a woman. But she supposed that she had always thought that pirate captains would be men. Captain Hook, for example, and Blackbeard. And it was the complete shift in the mental picture she had created that had caused the shock.

So what did Steele look like, then, since we know she

didn't look like either Captain Hook or Blackbeard? She was younger than you'd expect a captain to be, too, though the explanation for this is quite simple as pirate captains are elected democratically and do not earn their posts after many years rising through the ranks in the same way as in the navy (though a certain amount of respect and experience is warranted in order to be elected – however, theoretically, it is quite possible to have a captain as young as two years old should the crew vote for it. Though what on earth the purpose of that would be, aside from novelty and momentary fame, I haven't the foggiest).

In fact, Steele looked, well, very much like her great-great-great-grandmother, with whom Alex was more than familiar, having studied her portrait in the library in the house on the hill intently and for a long time. She had that same long dark wavy hair tied loosely back in a low ponytail. Her eyes were dark brown, not green like her ancestor's, but the face was shaped very similarly. She was, to be concise, beautiful, though not typically so. Because typically beautiful women do not usually have a thin white scar crossing their face from the top of their right temple down along to the base of the left side of their neck (although Steele wore it so well that if these typically beautiful women had seen her they probably would have rushed out to have their faces sliced open by a cutlass, as had happened to Steele, just to get the look), nor are these women missing a good chunk of earlobe. She wore a long brown leather jacket, which was stitched together at the seams by thick black thread, over a plain white shirt and soft brown leather trousers. These were held up by a wide black belt with a gold buckle and tucked into black boots, the soles of which Alex could see clearly.

Pirate Captain Steele looked at Alex's expression and laughed, not unkindly.

"Ah, well, yes," she said, pouring herself another glass of wine. "You can be forgiven for assuming I would be a man. For one thing, most people assume all pirate captains are male, and for another I am known just as Steele, and, well, that is no indication at all, now, is it? It is terribly convenient actually, playing on people's, how should I put it, prejudices? Misconceptions? For years Her Majesty's Navy has been trying to hunt me down. They don't question why they are looking only at men. They don't realize there is any other way to think. Makes my life incredibly easy. Funny, isn't it?"

"I guess," replied Alex.

"Well not ha-ha funny, sort of . . . well sort of ironic funny. . . Geoffrey, what sort of funny would that be?" She turned to Sir Geoffrey.

"I couldn't say, madam, and I truly couldn't care less,"

he replied with one of his sniffs.

"Oh, go be self-important," dismissed Steele, and Sir Geoffrey swept out of the room. "I enjoy analysing what makes something funny, an interest I fear not shared by some members of my crew." With a casual flick of her wrist she sent a dish of chocolates skating across the table to Alex. It stopped a centimetre from the edge. "Chocolate?"

Alex shook her head no.

"They aren't poisoned, I assure you," smiled Steele.

Alex looked at the plate. She wasn't particularly hungry, but she was tempted. Besides it seemed rude to refuse, and she didn't want to upset the so far rather pleasant Pirate Captain Steele. She tentatively picked up a chocolate, a large one with some sort of nut in the centre. Instantly it was whisked from her hand, causing Alex to jump up from her chair. Behind her, a small dagger was sticking her chocolate to the back wall. "Except that one," said Steele apologetically, "I had forgotten about that one." Alex looked back at Steele. "Please sit down. I'm sorry to have startled you. Please sit, sit!" She extended an elegant hand towards Alex. Alex sat. "Please have another one. The rest are absolutely not poisoned, I promise." She smiled. Alex picked up another one with a cherry in the middle. "That one might be poisoned." Alex put it down. She picked up a flat square one. Steele stood up abruptly. "Do not under any circumstances eat that one!" she said loudly. Alex dropped it on to the plate. "You know what?" said Steele. "Here." And she whisked over a sealed box of chocolates. "I think you would be best to have these. Unopened, you see. Less risky."

Alex nodded, but she had by now completely lost her appetite. "I think I'll just save them for later, thank you."

"Of course," replied Steele, "whatever you want." And she sat down again. "So, Alex, do you think maybe we should just get down to business?"

Alex shrugged. "What sort of business?"

Steele smiled. "Alex, don't be coy. I hate it when people act coy. You have something that I have spent the better part of my life in search of."

"I'm really sorry," said Alex, "I have no idea what you are talking about."

"Don't you?" asked Steele, leaning forward, eyebrows furrowed. "Really?"

"No, sorry," replied Alex, her heart beating even faster now. Watching so many games of poker on the *Valiant* had taught her a little something about bluffing. Still she wasn't sure how long she could keep it up.

"Nothing at all? Nothing to do with . . . cartography?"

Alex shook her head.

"Gosh," said Steele. "I thought . . . that is . . . I was

under the impression . . . Jack!" she called out.

The door burst open and Jack fell into the room. He scratched his arm nervously. "Would you mind asking Dr Brunswick if we could relieve him of his patient momentarily?"

Jack nodded and giggled to himself as he left the room.

"Sorry about all this. It appears I have been misinformed," said Steele, picking up the salt and sprinkling some on her steak. "I'm really rather put out by it," she muttered. She sat for a few moments cutting the meat into small pieces. She took a bite of one and then looked up at Alex. "You are absolutely completely positively sure you have no idea what I'm going on about?" Alex nodded again. Her throat felt like sandpaper. "I'm talking about a map. A treasure map?" Alex offered a small shrug. "No?" said Steele. "This is so weird," she said, shaking her head. Alex heard the door open up behind her. "So weird. Look, I don't mean to keep going on about this, but I just can't understand . . . that is . . . OK. You are telling me you are not in possession of a map, possibly . . ." and she stood up and sat on the edge of the table, "printed on a lady's fan?"

Alex's heart stopped beating. Just stopped. Only for a second. She didn't die or anything, but there was definite heart stoppage there. How did Steele possibly know that bit of information? It seemed ridiculous to keep lying. And yet for some reason. . .

"No. I'm not." Her voice was thin, not like her own.

"Well, now, that is super weird." Steele laughed to herself. She gazed intensely at Alex as if she was trying to read her mind. Finally she said, "Because *he* swears you are." At first Alex didn't know who Steele was talking about as the pirate captain had not broken eye contact with her, but slowly it dawned on her that someone was standing behind her. She turned around.

"Coriander!" she blurted out before she could think.

"You admit you at least know who he is, then," said Steele.

Alex nodded feebly and stared, wide-eyed, at Coriander, who was being held up by Jack and Sir Geoffrey. He looked horrible. He was covered in bruises and cuts and strange welts shaped like nothing Alex could identify. He had lost weight, which was alarming as the last time they had met hadn't been so long ago. Coriander looked at Alex sadly. He opened his mouth to say something, but didn't.

Steele walked over to Coriander. "Dr Brunswick is quite the artist, isn't he?" She gave Coriander a pat on the shoulder and he winced. "Coriander, Coriander, Coriander. You have been very naughty lying to me," she said. "You told us that this charming young lady had the Wigpowder treasure map, and here she is firmly denying that she does. You don't, correct?" said Steele, turning to Alex once more. Before she could answer Steele added, "Alex, could you pass me the salt?"

On autopilot, Alex leaned across the table and passed Steele the salt.

"Thank you," said Steele with a smile, and she turned back to Coriander, stroking his face gently. "Someone is lying to me. I don't know who . . . OK, let's be honest here. I know who is lying to me, of course I know who is lying to me, but we are doing a bit of role-playing right now, so right now I am pretending I don't know who is lying to me. And in order to find out. . ." She licked her finger and sprinkled some salt on it. "I am going to try asking nicely. Alex, do you or do you not have the Wigpowder treasure map?"

"I. . ." replied Alex.

"Poor darling Coriander. . ." said Steele, stroking his face again with her finger. This time Coriander let out a fierce yell. "Alex, did you ever hear about the expression 'rubbing salt in a wound'? Usually it's used to mean making something that is already bad worse. Occasionally, though," and she filled her palm with salt, "it can be more literal than that. The reason the adage exists in the first place is that rubbing salt in a wound, from what I understand, is incredibly painful, isn't it, Coriander?" And she blew the salt in her hand into his face. He let out another yell.

"I have the map, I have the map!" yelled Alex, standing up.

"I know you have the map, you have the map," Steele said as Coriander began to weep quietly. "I already told you I knew that. But I appreciate your honesty. Would you like to try?" She offered Alex the salt.

"No, I want you to stop!"

Steele looked surprised. "Oh, OK, then," she said. She made a signal and Jack and Sir Geoffrey dragged Coriander out of the room. "Maybe next time," she said, sitting down at her end of the table. She brushed the excess salt from her hands on to the rest of her steak and began to eat again.

Alex watched her for a bit and then asked quietly, "Do you want the map?"

Steele looked at her. "No, not yet, maybe tomorrow we can have a look at it. It's already quite late. Lights out at eight o'clock, you know," she added.

"Really?" asked Alex despite herself.

"Oh yes, we operate under a strict code of rules. All conflicts must be settled ashore, equal shares of booty to the crew, no one can have a second helping of pudding until everyone who wants some has had their first. That sort of thing. It's all in the articles signed by every member," she said and tapped the table with her hand. She stood up, opened a drawer in the desk and pulled out a long piece of parchment.

"Here, you can read this if you want," she said, passing the parchment to Alex. She took it with shaking hands. "But now we should probably get you settled in. Unfortunately, as you are currently a prisoner, I am afraid your accommodations are not going to be all that pleasant, but hopefully in time we'll have you better situated." She ushered Alex out on to deck. The night was black. Had she not seen it in the daylight, it would have taken serious convincing to prove to her she was on a pirate ship at all, it was so dark. Then she noticed that in the distance there was a tiny speck of light.

"Dude Hector!" Steele called out. The tiny light at the bow of the ship started to move over towards Steele and Alex.

"I thought you said lights out was eight o'clock," said Alex.

"Oh, it is, but not for Dude Hector. He likes his fire, dabbles in arson, you see. It would be rude," replied Steele.

A tall lanky man appeared out of the dark. His narrow face was lit by the small flame he was playing with in the palm of his hand.

"Take Alex down to the hold," said Steele.

Dude Hector looked at Alex with hollow blank eyes. He nodded and turned and walked out into the darkness.

"Follow him," said Steele, giving Alex a gentle nudge.

Alex did so, and soon a vast darkness stood between her and Steele, enveloping the Captain so that her silhouette was only momentarily visible when she stepped through the door back into her cabin. Alex followed Dude Hector down the steps to the hold and into the small cage that was her cell for the evening. When he returned up on deck, Alex was left alone in utter darkness. Yes, as Pirate Captain Steele had said, the accommodations were most certainly not pleasant. They were wet and mouldy and squeaky animals scuttled across the floor in the dark.

Alex felt a great sadness, a weight heavy on her chest. She was so unbelievably confused and scared. Steele seemed to like her for some reason, which Alex supposed was a good thing, as strange and unexpected as it was, yet it was also quite disturbing to be treated with such kindness when Steele had proved herself at the same time staggeringly cruel. Then of course there was Coriander, who, aside from being the last person Alex would ever have imagined to have seen on the *Ironic Gentleman*, had betrayed Alex in a most astounding manner. Worst of all was to see whatever it was they had done to him. Finally, to top everything off, she was now shivering in a small cage. It was too much. It was all just too much.

Alex crumpled the parchment Steele had given her and threw it to the floor. "It's not fair," she said out loud. She wasn't sure what wasn't fair specifically, but she knew "it" wasn't.

"Who's there?" whispered a voice.

Alex froze. It couldn't be. In all the fuss, she had completely forgotten the reason for her entire journey, the thing she had wanted to find more than anything in the world. It seemed impossible that she should have been capable of forgetting such a thing, and yet somehow she had. She stood up tentatively.

Quietly and with great trepidation she said, "Mr Underwood?"

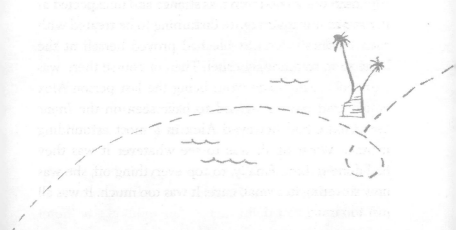

THE THIRTY-SEVENTH CHAPTER

In which we witness a reunion

There was a long silence. One of those long silences I have described many times in this book. The sort of silence where anything could happen, where you don't really realize there has been a silence, it is so full of possibility. And it was broken by. . .

"Alex?"

"Mr Underwood!" exclaimed Alex. Silent tears of joy began to replace the ones of distress. "You're alive!"

There was a shorter silence. "Alex? Is that really you?"

"Yes, yes, it's me!" laughed Alex. Her feelings tried to understand what they should be doing but gave up.

"What are you doing here? You shouldn't be here!

Alex, this is horrible!" said Mr Underwood.

"I've been trying to find you. I figured out that you were kidnapped by pirates and that I needed to go to Port Cullis, and then I met Captain Magnanimous, and he and the HMS *Valiant* took me to find you and rescue you, but things went really wrong, and I think Coriander had something to do with it, but it doesn't matter because you're alive, and you can get us out of this, and it will be OK. And then we can find the treasure! Because, oh, because, Mr Underwood, I found the map! It was in the house on the hill, and I would have come home sooner, but I was held prisoner by the Daughters of the Founding Fathers' Preservation Society, and when I finally got out you had gone, and uncle was dead and. . ."

"Your uncle is dead?" interrupted Mr Underwood.

"Oh . . . yes," said Alex, biting her lip. "Yes, he was . . . he was found under a pile of doorknobs . . . but I really don't want to talk about that right now. Did you hear the other bit, though? I found the map! We can go for the treasure now, once we escape. Right now, what we have to do is make a plan," said Alex quickly.

"Plan? What sort of plan?" asked Mr Underwood.

"An escape plan of course!"

Mr Underwood laughed a hollow laugh. "And how do you propose we escape?" he asked softly.

"Well, I don't know. I'm sure you can figure something out."

"Alex, stop, just stop," said Mr Underwood. He sounded tired and very sad. "Alex, we can't escape. Do you know where you are? Do you know who is keeping us captive? Oh, why are you here? Why did you come? Oh, how much I wish you hadn't come!"

"Mr Underwood, you don't mean that," said Alex. She was completely at a loss. This was not the reunion she had expected.

"Alex, I mean it more than I have meant anything in my life. I can't be responsible for you. If you get hurt . . . I just can't bear the thought of you in so much danger! Why couldn't you have stayed at home?"

Alex's feelings suddenly found their feet again. They knew exactly what to do, and they did it. They seethed with rage. "Because I have no home!" she shouted furiously. "Because my uncle is dead! Because you are the closest thing I have to family! Because you are supposed to make everything better! I'm not strong enough. I can't do this on my own! I'm ten and a half. I am a kid. Mr Underwood, please do something. You need to do something!" Her face was burning.

"I can't talk to you when you're like this, Alex. Either calm down, or we will have to talk tomorrow morning," replied Mr Underwood coolly.

"I will not calm down! You cannot treat this situation as though someone's misused grammar! We need to come up with a plan! We need to come up with a plan!" She collapsed on to the floor. There was no reply from Mr Underwood. Alex felt weak and very cold. She waited until her breathing had become more regular, then she said very quietly, "I brought your bike the whole way, you know. I dragged it all over the countryside. I was almost caught because of it. But now it's at the bottom of the sea, and I'm glad." She bit her bottom lip.

"Alex," said Mr Underwood, "I appreciate everything you've tried to do for me. I really do. It's unbelievable. However, what remains is the plain and simple truth that you are now in considerable danger, and the thought of it makes me ill. This was never your responsibility, any of this. What's more, you have now doubled mine. Before I only needed to take care of myself, but now I have to take care of you as well, and that is a heavy cross to bear."

Alex stared out into the darkness in silence. "Well," she said quietly, "I'm sorry that I'm such a burden to you."

"Alex, you know I didn't mean it like that. . ."

Alex shook her head. "Mr Underwood, you said you came to my town to reclaim your inheritance, and yet you spent most of your days marking papers or reading books on fencing. I had to drag you out of the house to go in search of a treasure map, even though we knew where we needed to look! Next you got yourself kidnapped, and when my uncle tried to help you, you wouldn't let him, and then you went without a struggle, and you can't deny it – there was a picture of it! And finally I find you, alive, saying that I have somehow ruined your chances at escaping when it seems to me you are more than happy to sit in the pitch-dark waiting for something to happen, either good or bad. You know what, Mr Underwood? I always thought you were a sensible kind of grown-up, always thinking and stuff, someone who always had a plan just waiting to put into some serious action, but it's not that, it's not that at all. You don't have any plans. The reason you never do anything . . . it's 'cause you're a coward!" Alex paused to take a breath. "And another thing, how can you get mad at me for getting involved, when it's all your fault that my family is in the middle of all this! I mean, my uncle gave you a place to live, and he died for it! And now as far as you're concerned I should die too!"

"I didn't say that," replied Mr Underwood. He sounded further away from her somehow.

"It doesn't matter. I don't need you. I'll escape on my own. I haven't been doing so badly myself, you know," said Alex, and she brought her knees up to her chest and hugged them tightly.

"No, you haven't," said Mr Underwood gently. There was a silence punctuated by the dripping of water somewhere. "Did you really bring my bike?" he asked.

But Alex wasn't interested in answering him. She knew what he was doing. He was trying to lighten the mood, to make her less angry, but she didn't want to feel less angry. This was a serious situation and deserved serious feelings.

"Alex?" he called out into the darkness.

Alex hugged her knees closer and rested her chin on them. She was crying again. She was so sick of crying. She suddenly felt extremely tired. When Dude Hector had locked her in her cage, she never imagined she would be able to sleep, but now she couldn't imagine doing anything else. Alex lay down in the cold wet and closed her eyes. Mr Underwood called out her name again. She didn't respond. She knew eventually he would give up. After all, that's what he was good at.

THE THIRTY-EIGHTH CHAPTER

In which Alex is made an offer

"Jack!"

Alex awoke with a start. She sat up. The left side of her body was drenched in a foul-smelling wetness from the damp floor.

"Jack!"

Alex looked up at the hatch through the bars of her cage. A silhouette of a pirate was looking down at her. When he saw that she had seen him he hugged himself and viciously scratched his back.

"What do you want?" She was in no mood for pleasantries, and anyway, being polite to a pirate was, like dinner without dessert, pointless.

"Jack!" he said again and ran down the stairs, unlocking the door to her cage. Alex stood up slowly. Every muscle in her body was aching. As Jack escorted her up the stairs, Alex took a glance down the hatch to see if she could see Mr Underwood. She caught a glimpse of a hunched figure at the far side of the hold in his own cage, but it was impossible to see his face or if indeed it was Mr Underwood and not some other poor prisoner.

Alex was greeted by a hot clear morning, and she gazed out across the water as she was ushered along towards the stern of the ship. The fog from the previous day had cleared to reveal an extraordinary coastline in the distance. Tall white cliffs rippled slightly in the atmosphere, and large waves crashed against the reef. The *Valiant* was nowhere to be seen, and Alex harboured a secret hope that somehow the frigate had managed to escape, or that at least the crew had found safety in the lifeboats and were regrouping at this very moment.

Soon Alex found herself sitting opposite Steele yet again, this time digging into a hearty breakfast of pancakes drenched in maple syrup. Alex had her own stack in front of her, and she found herself surprisingly willing to eat this morning.

"Did you sleep well?" asked Steele.

"Not really," replied Alex between bites.

Steele nodded to herself. "Understandable," she said and wiped the corners of her mouth with a napkin. "I don't suppose you read that parchment with the articles I gave you?" she said, putting her feet up on the table again.

"Well, it was kinda dark, and I didn't feel like it. Why?" Alex took a sip of orange juice.

"Just curious."

They stopped talking again as Steele watched Alex finish her breakfast. Usually Alex would gulp down her food as fast as she could. In fact, her uncle would often reprimand her for it, and try to get her to relax and take her time. But this morning Alex ate so slowly that even he would have asked her to speed up. And the reason she was doing so was that she was worried about what would happen once she had finished. She wasn't as concerned about what Steele might do or say to her. No, the problem was that Alex was deeply conflicted about her own opinion of Steele. She ought to despise her, but she just didn't for some reason. And she had a sense that quite possibly Steele liked her, too. And if that was the case, she wasn't sure what her own reaction would be to what might be put on the table when breakfast was over.

But, inevitably, Alex did finish eating, and when she

did, Steele ordered the table cleared. While members of her crew frantically removed the table settings, Steele leaned her chin on her hand, and stared at Alex. Finally, when they were alone again, Steele broke from her trance and said, "Alex, I'm not a fan of beating around the bush. I like to get right to the point."

"Me too," replied Alex nervously.

"Yes, I imagined you would. Well then, my point: the moment I heard about a young girl who was seeking out the *Ironic Gentleman*, I confess I was impressed. Few grown-ups would attempt such a thing, let alone a smaller-than-average child. And now that I have met you . . . well believe me when I say I am an excellent judge of character. There's something in you, Alex. I have a sense of incredible potential in you. And so, Alex, for that reason, I would like to offer you the opportunity of becoming a member of my crew. It will have to be put to a vote, of course, and there are contracts to sign. But with my endorsement, I can virtually guarantee you a position. That is, if you're interested."

Alex sat utterly still. "Isn't," she asked quietly, "isn't piracy, you know, wrong?"

Steele nodded thoughtfully. "Well, you know, Alex," she said, "right and wrong aren't as clear cut as all that. For example we, as pirates, tend to hurt other people physically – that can't be denied – to get what we want.

Other people hurt people psychologically. I mean, your friend Coriander is a perfect example. He's a nice enough sort of fellow, I suppose. But he's also willing to betray a friend."

Alex shook her head vehemently. "No! You tortured him!"

"There was some torture, but I can assure you that was after the fact. It is well-known that if you give the Conjuror something to drink, he just can't control himself. This is something he even knows himself, and yet he insists on keeping up with the habit, putting not only himself but others in danger, too. Do you know what the penalty is for desertion and betrayal in the army, Alex?"

"No."

"Death. We're just following the same laws as everyone else by eventually putting him to death."

"Oh, please don't!"

"Alex, we're getting side-tracked. Let's talk instead about your dear friend, Mr Underwood." Alex felt a knot tighten in her stomach. "A man who is willing to put your life on the line to protect his own. I know what you talked about last night. I know how unwilling he was to plan an escape. Why do you think that is? Because he is afraid. Of what? Of being hurt. He isn't thinking how you could be in serious danger, how he could protect you. No, he's thinking about himself. If I didn't like you as I do, that would be a death sentence. Now who is more responsible, the executioner or the judge who sanctions it?"

Alex admitted begrudgingly to herself that what Steele said rang true.

"We live in a world where the victors make the rules, but the victors do not always make good rules. How different really is the navy from pirates? The navy has punishments. The navy kills. It does whatever it takes to achieve its goals. It is the goal that makes the difference. We, the pirates, follow our hearts. You see, the pirate is a dreamer, someone who doesn't want to be tied down to what some rich person who bought their way into government tells us to do. You ran away from an expensive school to find treasure. Alex, you are already a pirate."

"No, I'm not." But she said the words with little force.

"OK, I see you're having trouble making a decision," said Steele, examining Alex's expression carefully. "Shall we offer you a trial run, perhaps? We could go find the treasure, see how all that works out, have a meeting again in a week, say?"

"I don't know," said Alex. She felt incredibly conflicted.

The door to the cabin suddenly opened. Alex turned

and felt a familiar chill creep over her.

"Senseless, excellent," said Steele, rising from the table. "Just the man I wanted to see."

Senseless entered the room deliberately, his dog Walter at his hip. "Geoffrey said you needed me," he said quietly.

"Yes, I was just about to plot a course for the Wigpowder treasure," she glanced briefly at Alex, "and I wanted some advice. You know how much I depend on your advice."

"Of course," he replied. The dog growled.

"Alex, could I have the map now? Time to get to work, I think," said Steele with a smile. But Alex couldn't move. Her fear of this man grew each time she saw him. There was something wrong about him. Something she didn't understand, aside from why he wore a scarf over his eyes. "Alex?" asked Steele again, this time with a note of warning in her voice.

"Uh. . ." was all Alex could respond.

Senseless turned and walked straight in her direction. He leaned down close to her ear. "The map," he whispered.

With shaking hands, Alex reached into her pocket and pulled out the toothbrush holder. She passed it to Senseless, who took it and brought it to Steele.

"I think," said Steele, carefully pulling the fan out of the toothbrush holder, "that maybe you should go on deck for a while, Alex."

She didn't want to leave her map alone with Steele, but she had little choice and really all she wanted to do was not be in the same room as Senseless. So Alex rose slowly, left the Captain's cabin and went out on deck.

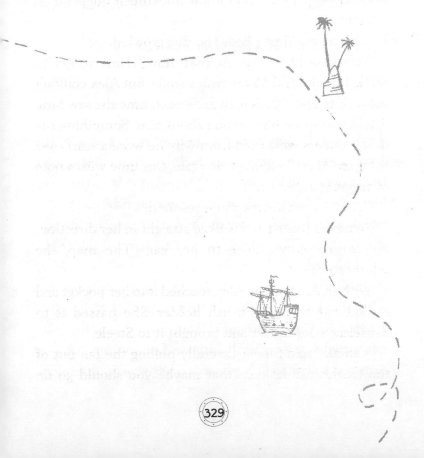

THE THIRTY-NINTH CHAPTER

In which Alex makes an important decision

It was as if they'd never seen a kid before. As she wandered around on deck feeling rather useless, Alex found herself to be a source of great interest to the crew. She was picked up and turned upside down by Boudicca, who somehow seemed impressed by the way she dangled. Then Jack ran up to her, asking if she remembered him from the house on the hill, and when she said she did, he ran away giggling to Dude Hector, who was busy cutting his shirt into tiny strips. No-Kneecaps Calvin dragged himself up to her and examined her feet with intense fascination. And Dr Brunswick scratched his beard in her general direction.

Eventually she made her way towards the forecastle and found a thin woman with horn-rimmed glasses, wearing a tweed skirt and jacket with black flat shoes, sitting on the ground, typing on a laptop. She seemed like a pleasant sort of person, at least the most normal compared with the rest of the crew, and so Alex went to introduce herself.

"Hello," she said to the young woman. "I'm Alex. I'm contemplating piracy."

"Hello, my name is Fenelle. I'm the scribe aboard the ship. I write about everything that we do or don't do."

Alex smiled and sat down next to her. She seemed nice enough.

"Say, you know Coriander, don't you?" asked Fenelle, closing her laptop and removing her glasses.

"Yes," replied Alex suspiciously.

"I used to sail with him on the ship the *Ill Repute*. He's a really funny guy, I always liked him."

"Yes, he is funny. Most of the time."

"But you know I hadn't seen him in years! So it was really just luck that I ran into him after all this time. Talk about fate!" She flattened the hair on the top of her head with her hand, smiling pleasantly. "We met by chance at the Gangrene, and then made plans for drinks the next day. He just started going on and on about you! I think he really misses adventures. He used to have great fun on the *Ill Repute*. And then when he became famous for his conjuring, he got to travel the world. Well, anyway, he just went on about you and the *Valiant* and how he'd even tried to steal a copy of the map, but you had this cat . . . what was the cat's name again. . ."

"Giggles," replied Alex, the name catching in her throat. She had forgotten all about him. How could she have forgotten about him?

"Yeah. Anyway, I can't remember all the details. All I know is meeting him was a pretty lucky thing to happen. I mean, I think you'd just set sail or something. I was on leave, I wasn't even supposed to be on the ship right now, but I thought it was far too important. So we flew to Lawless, and here we are today! I mean that's luck."

For you, maybe, thought Alex bitterly.

"Hey, can you tell me your side of the story? It would be brilliant to get another perspective on the whole thing," she said and opened her laptop again.

"Maybe later," replied Alex. "I think I need to be alone for a bit."

"OK," replied Fenelle. "Just let me know." And she went back to typing.

Alex climbed up on to the forecastle. She felt deeply depressed and confused. On the one hand, she was safe and protected by Steele; on the other, she had felt this horrible emptiness when she had heard about Coriander and the pride in Fenelle's voice that she had saved the day, and how she had used him. Though, Alex continued, how dare he be so indiscreet in the first place! She had trusted him! And what about Mr Underwood, she seethed to herself. There had been no one she trusted more, and he had let her down too.

Alex turned to look back along the ship towards the stern. She had never in her life thought that she would become a pirate. Pirates were bad people. Or so she had always assumed. But then so many of them were treating her really warmly and even seemed to like her. Steele was being more than civil. And Steele made excellent points that, really, any reasonable person could agree with.

And what made one person good and the other one bad anyway? In her long journey she had met good and bad people alike, people who were not pirates, but who had respectable jobs and were well-liked within their communities. And yet these same people could get away with the most reprehensible behaviour. Couldn't there then be good pirates and bad pirates? Couldn't she be one of the good ones?

Most of all, Alex realized, she was now homeless. There would be no way now she could return to her town, not after everything, and piracy offered a fine adventurous life. A life she had only dreamed about until recently or made up in silly baby stories. This was real life. And it was time to live it. Well, why not, she thought. Why not? Let's see how it all goes, then. Let's see what it will be like to become a pirate. Alex smiled and felt herself grow a little taller.

Becoming a pirate was actually surprisingly easy for Alex. She had already become accustomed to life on a ship from her time on the *Valiant*, so she managed to impress even Sir Geoffrey, who was overseeing her training. (This meant that he sat in a deck chair sipping lemonade from a tall frosted glass, looking at her occasionally over his dark sunglasses.)

"Well, yes, that's all well and good," he said after Alex had climbed up to the fighting top and back in record time. "But you'll never be a real pirate until you learn how to fight." He slurped on his lemonade.

"I'm very little," replied Alex. "I hardly think I'll need to fight, not just yet at any rate."

But Sir Geoffrey insisted and took it upon himself to teach her how to use a sword. Alex wasn't sure whether or not she should let on that she was an adept fencer. Something deep down was telling her to pretend otherwise, and she trusted her instinct. She thought it would also be fun, pretending to make mistakes.

However, as it turned out, pretending not to know how to fence was actually far more difficult than learning how to fence in the first place. And there was one nervous moment when she forgot herself and casually disarmed Sir Geoffrey. He looked at her intently, but only sneered, "Beginner's luck."

And in this way, over the next few days as they sailed towards the island with the treasure, Alex became one of the crew of the *Ironic Gentleman*. She eventually gave Fenelle her interview and enjoyed it very much, feeling like a celebrity. Jack would work with her, showing her how to construct things with his hammer – surprisingly, he was rather adept at using it against a nail as well as a weapon – and Alex found herself impressed with his handiwork. And once the sun would set, she and Dude Hector would sing a sad song his mother had taught him, while he delicately played with his little fire in his hands.

Because she was now a pirate, she got to sleep in a little bunk and not in the brig, and because of this she slowly started forgetting about Mr Underwood and, indeed, Coriander, who were quietly being kept below decks, and whom Steele was careful not to mention. And, anyway, it was so much easier not to think about them. By the time they finally reached their coordinates, Alex had all but made up her mind to become a full-time pirate.

There was a great group of them that went ashore to find the treasure. This was partly due to the fact that they anticipated a vast fortune and needed the manpower, and partly because everyone wanted to be a part of this historic moment. In the end only a few were left behind on the ship, including Senseless and Dr Brunswick, neither of whom seemed too put out by the arrangement.

The rest of the crew piled into the longboats and set out towards the treasure island, which, from the ship, appeared only as a dark shadow hidden behind the early morning mist. But as they approached, its outlined form became more distinct and Alex could feel a great swell of pride in her chest. She had found it. Alexandra Morningside, a kid of ten and a half, had found the elusive island of the Wigpowder treasure.

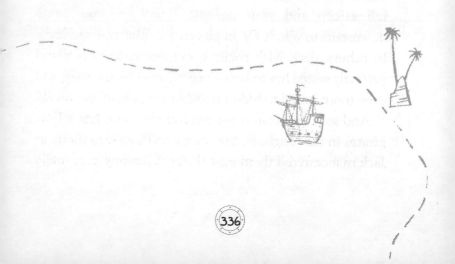

THE FORTIETH CHAPTER

In which we get to go on a treasure hunt

The island was quite exactly what you would expect a treasure island to be. The sort of place that you create late at night in your imagination when you can't fall asleep and your parents won't let you come downstairs to watch TV. In places, mountainous and leafy. In others, dark with rocky outcrops. It was an island perfectly suited not to have been charted on any map, and even more suited to hide a massive treasure in its bowels.

And so Alex sat in quiet amazement with her fellow pirates in the longboat, the waves crashing into them, as Jack manoeuvred them past the reef, landing eventually on the long white sandy beach. She quietly stared upwards towards the interior of the island as the rest of the pirates unloaded the equipment, and would have continued in her silence had it not been broken by Steele approaching her from behind.

"It's amazing, isn't it?" she said, placing a firm hand on Alex's shoulder. "For years I've fantasized about what it would be like, and now I find it is exactly as I had expected it to be."

"But more," replied Alex softly.

Steele looked down at Alex and nodded. "But more," she agreed.

Alex wanted very much to be drawn into the magnificence of the moment, to luxuriate in the special bond she had with Steele, but she couldn't help but feel slightly unhappy. Like perhaps it ought to be Mr Underwood standing over her shoulder and not the most notorious pirate captain this side of the equator. She shook her head fiercely. Mr Underwood wouldn't have appreciated it as Steele and she did. He probably would have brought his marking to do.

"Captain!" called out Boudicca. "We're set!"

Steele released Alex's shoulder, and the two of them walked to where the crew had congregated. They had each piled high on their backs a variety of interesting-looking implements, from shovels and picks to strange corkscrew-shaped scissors. Only Dude Hector carried nothing but his usual tiny flame.

"Good, good," said Steele, climbing on to a rock so she could be seen by everyone. "Before we start on this momentous adventure, I just wanted to say how proud I am of you all, my crew. It's been years of heartache and toil with very little reward. Years of murder and pillage with very unsatisfactory results. And I want to thank you for your courage through the hardship. You are all about to be rewarded beyond your wildest dreams!" There was an excited murmur in the crowd. "And as an extra special treat, I thought that, upon our return to the ship, we could have a bit of fun with the last member of the Wigpowder line. I do have my preferences, of course, but as this is a democracy, everyone have a think about it as the day passes." Alex cowered at the thought of what they might come up with, and nervously looked at the others laughing to themselves.

"For too long," continued Steele, "have those Wigpowders lorded their ancestry over us, but in a matter of hours we will show this pathetic excuse for a man who truly is the most fearsome pirate of all time. The Infamous Wigpowder's memory will be but a footnote to our accomplishments. The Infamous Wigpowder's treasure a mere drop in the well of our fortune. The Infamous Wigpowder's name like a distant echo, a song whose melody has been forgotten and whose words you can't remember!" There was a great cheer. "And Pirate Captain Steele the Inevitable and the *Ironic Gentleman*?" called out Steele above the roar. "We shall become immortal! For it is the winner who writes the history books, the winner who takes it all, the winner . . . who lives on . . . for ever!"

The noise was deafening. Had it been late at night in a small town not unlike Alex's, someone might have thought about opening a window and yelling at them to keep quiet – but then changed their mind because they didn't want to cause trouble. Alex felt decidedly uncomfortable and stood silently as the other pirates whooped and hollered and hugged each other. It was an excellent speech, Alex had to admit, using the rule of three brilliantly well and playing to baser competitive spirits. But punishing Mr Underwood? She wasn't so sure she was up for that.

Steele was gesturing to her avid followers for quiet. "Of course," she said, "of course, we can't be anything until we find that treasure, so. . ." She looked at Alex, who obligingly joined the Captain at her side. "Let's have a look, then, shall we?" And she passed the map to Alex with a smile.

Alex opened it slowly, feeling the intense stares of the

crew bearing down on her. "It, it seems straightforward enough," she said, looking over the map carefully. "We need to follow the map until we get to here." She pointed at the "X" slightly left of centre on the picture of the island. "'The Red Lagoon.'"

"Red red red red red!"

"Jack!" snapped Steele.

"Red."

Steele turned to Alex, ignoring Jack. "Is that it?"

"Well I don't know. . ." Alex was still unsure what to make of that poem at the side. With a fierce sigh, Steele grabbed the map away from Alex.

"Time for some decision making!" she announced. "Let's get on with it, people!"

She grabbed Alex by the shoulder and led her to the front of the queue. While she resented the action, Alex was still excited. After all, this was the adventure bit, the bit she had been looking forward to most. And they started into the jungle.

But after several hours of mosquitoes and the hot hazy sun on her back, Alex was feeling less inclined to keep her spirits high. She had a sense that the rest of the crew's feelings were similar to hers. She could hear them grumbling to each other and occasionally an unhappy "Jack!" would float over the crowd to where Alex and Steele and Boudicca were leading the expedition. The only person who didn't seem to lose the spirit of the moment was Steele herself. She was extremely focused, leading the group with firm determination and an excellent sense of direction.

They were rewarded for their patience six long hours later. Boudicca was cutting her way through particularly stubborn flora when she suddenly fell through the thick vines out of sight.

"Boudicca!" called out Alex. She rushed ahead and then carefully felt her way through the depression. The ground was slanting downwards, and it was tricky keeping her footing, and then suddenly the forest disappeared and she found herself standing looking down at a beautiful still lagoon of the clearest turquoise. Her breath caught in her throat as she gazed at the incredible beauty of what she had discovered. Steele joined her and then eventually the rest of the pirates lined up beside them.

They were standing at the top of a rather steep hill. The lagoon was set into the base of the valley so that the whole thing looked a bit like an open umbrella with water collected in the bottom of it. To the east extended a long, flat expanse of land that disappeared out of sight. To the west the sun was just beginning its evening descent.

"It's beautiful!" exclaimed Boudicca, sitting a few metres down the edge of the hill.

"It's too big," replied Steele angrily. She looked at the map. "This doesn't make sense. Where's the treasure?"

Alex looked at Steele's frustrated face. How could she not, even for the briefest moment, enjoy this view? "Well, I think the poem could tell us something," she said quietly. Steele looked at her then at the map again. Then she shoved it back towards Alex.

"Well then, what does it mean?"

Alex read the poem again. "I . . . I don't really know. . ."

Steele sighed loudly again then turned to the crew. "Let's set up camp down there by the lagoon," she announced and they promptly set about doing so.

Twenty minutes later several tents had been set up along the shore of the lagoon. A strong fire had been started easily by Dude Hector, and a few card games had broken out. This resulted occasionally in a small duel or fisticuffs over why someone had five aces, and would be resolved after one person had been seriously injured. Steele watched the whole thing with great enjoyment and would sometimes even point out who was cheating this particular round simply to see them go at it again.

Alex had removed herself from the activities to study the map more closely. She had wandered around the east side of the lagoon and found a nice large rock to sit on directly opposite the imminent sunset so she could watch it from a front-row seat. She looked at the map and read again:

When the earth makes its peace,
And the elements catch fire,
With a primarily high feeling
Shall you find your desire.

What could it possibly mean? she deliberated angrily. The thought was interrupted by a sudden cry.

"Look look look!" called out a distant Jack from the camp.

Alex looked over to where the pirates were congregated and saw them gazing out towards the water. And so she did too, her curiosity sparked. Instantly, she was on her feet. The lagoon, which only a moment ago had been a still turquoise, was slowly turning a pale red, reflecting the light of the sunset. That was why it was called the Red Lagoon, thought Alex. And that might be what "the elements catch fire" was referring to – it appeared as if the lagoon was as red as fire! But what about the earth making peace?

Alex had a sudden inspiration. She carefully jumped off the rock she was on and took a few steps back.

There is this saying, "the tip of the iceberg", that people use in reference to a small problem which seems big, but is nothing compared to a bigger problem which the smaller problem hints at. And the reason they refer to an iceberg is that, while icebergs seem huge on top of the water, underneath they are even bigger. And that's where the expression comes from. Well, Alex was about to experience something of the sensation in discovering the bottom half of an iceberg. She had been sitting on a rock, but what she hadn't realized was that it was merely a small outcropping at the base of a gigantic boulder. When Alex took a step to the side and looked at the giant boulder, she saw how time had eroded a small crevice in the top so that it looked a lot like two fingers making a peace sign, like the hippies used to do.

"Earth making peace," she said aloud. Suddenly everything clicked. She gazed back at the lagoon, which was getting redder by the minute. Then she gazed at the rock. It produced a long shadow extending away from the sunset, getting longer as the water got redder. Alex suddenly understood that once the water was "on fire" or had reached a certain point in the sunset, the tip of the shadow of the rock would mark where the treasure was. She had very little time.

"Captain!" she called out across the water. "Captain! I've figured it out, hurry!"

THE FORTY-FIRST CHAPTER

In which Alex uses her problem-solving skills to great effect

With a quick order, Jack had been stationed at the far end of the shadow, slowly following its progress. The rest of the pirates and Alex were standing at the edge of the lagoon by the rock watching the sunset. Alex wasn't exactly sure what they were waiting for, how they would know when the shadow had reached its mark. But she had faith that they would understand when the time came.

"You are so clever!" enthused Steele, tousling Alex's hair. "I never would have figured it out!"

Well, it takes patience, thought Alex, something Steele was quite obviously lacking.

And then it happened. The lagoon caught fire. How it had happened, none of them really knew. It probably had something to do with refracting light and mist over the water, or some invisible vapours they weren't aware of. But it didn't matter how it happened. For an instant, for longer than an instant, the water of the Red Lagoon appeared to catch fire and flames danced and played on the surface.

"It's on fire," said Dude Hector in wonder. He sat on the edge of the lagoon cross-legged and gazed into the distance.

There was a stillness as the lagoon burned. No one said anything; no one did anything. For one brief moment the Wigpowder treasure was completely forgotten and the majesty and power of nature took hold of them. And then the fire danced out. And darkness fell. And it was over.

Steele fired her pistol into the air, which was the signal for Jack to stop walking (by now he was far along the clearing, unable to hear them otherwise). Then there was a crackling sound and Dude Hector stood, carrying his small flame in his hand. He lit several torches, and suddenly, without any order being given, they all headed for Jack Scratch, who had started singing a little song he liked to call "Jack" which went a bit like this:

"Jack, Jack, Jack, Jack,
Jack, Jack, Jack, Jack,
Jack, Jack, Jack, Jack,
Jack, Jack, Jack, Jack,

Jack, Jack, Jack, Jack,
Jack, Jack, Jack, Jack,
Jack, Jack, Jack, Jack,
Jack, Jack, Jack, Jack."

He was standing in a clearing lit strongly by the moonlight. Behind him, strikingly silhouetted against the night sky, were ten very distinct palm trees in a row.

"That must mean something," said Fenelle, putting on her glasses.

Alex nodded. There was no way that such a sight could be anything but relevant to their quest. And somehow those last lines of the poem were the key.

"Well, Alex, you're on again," said Steele lightly, but Alex could hear the rage seething under the surface.

Alex did what she always did when she needed to face a problem. She sat down. With the light of the torches around her, she read and reread the last lines of the poem. It made very little sense, and didn't seem to refer to ten palm trees at all. She wracked her brain for what the lines could possibly mean. "A primarily high feeling"? It suggested that when they found the treasure they wouldn't be altogether satisfied, but that didn't seem right and definitely didn't help in finding it in the first place. Time passed. The pirates got restless and a fight broke out between Jack and his hammer. The hammer won, as it tended to. And the brief distraction was over far too soon.

And poor Alex sat still, on her own, with only Dude Hector standing over her playing with his flame and allowing her to read the map. Not that she needed his light any more; she had by now completely memorized the poem. Come on! she thought angrily to herself. Think! There was an answer, she just had to find it. Look at it like a maths question. The solution is out there somewhere. "Primarily high." She closed her eyes and thought hard. Then she opened them wide. What if, she thought slowly, what if it actually was a maths question?

She looked at the wording. "Primarily" was such a strange word and didn't even fit the rhythm of the poem. The word stuck out like a sore thumb. What if . . . what if it wasn't meant to be the word "primarily" as in "first of all", but rather the word "prime" as in "prime number", a number indivisible by anything other than itself and one. Alex shifted position. So then the "high" was in reference to . . . she looked up at the ten trees. Ten. The highest prime number out of ten! And that,

Alex knew, had to be seven. Could that be the answer? Could her school maths truly have had such a practical purpose? She looked at the trees again. The seventh tree. The treasure was buried under the seventh tree.

"I . . . I've got it," she said, nervously approaching Steele, who was lazily playing with her dagger.

Steele looked at her with raised eyebrows.

"It's . . . that is, I believe that the treasure is buried under the seventh tree," said Alex, handing the map back to Steele. Steele looked at Alex carefully and then at the map. She read the poem to herself and looked quizzically at Alex, who nodded firmly.

"Well then, let's dig under the seventh tree!" Steele rose to her feet and started to head towards it. She stopped and looked behind her at her crew. "Come on, you lazy lunkheads, d'you think I'm going to do any of the manual labour? Up, get up now!"

"Couldn't we just wait for morning?" asked Whippet, a small hunched pirate whom Alex hadn't really got to know yet. Had she known him better she might have learned that Whippet was actually from a long line of evil-doers, and had as much pedigree as a show dog. His father had been first mate aboard the *Ugly Duckling* and his mother had been a notorious cat burglar. She, in turn, was the daughter of L'Homme sans Coeur, Captain of the notorious *Elle est Morte*. And his father's father was, of course, the heinously corrupted lawman, the right dishonourable Judge Cyanide. Whippet also had two sisters, both of whom sailed on the Spanish ship *Los Diablos*. With his considerable heritage, you would have thought that he would have been a fantastic pirate. But he was the black sheep of the family – lazy, with a bad back, and not much good to anyone. Which is why it was no great loss when Steele shot him.

"Any other complaints?" she asked sweetly, smoke casually rising from the barrel of her gun.

Surprisingly, there were no other complaints, and soon they were excavating the ground beneath the seventh tree, occasionally being threatened by Steele, who was overseeing. Alex secretly crossed her fingers that she was right in her interpretation of the poem, and the more they dug, the more tightly she crossed, as they didn't seem to be getting anywhere. She hated to think what would happen if she was wrong. And so she didn't.

When Jack let out a howl of joy, though, her fears evaporated. Alex ran over to the pit, as did Steele, and they stared deep down into it.

"We've got it, Captain!" announced Boudicca.

"Yes, yes, I see that! So hurry!" replied Steele, a slight quiver in her voice.

The pirates pulled and pushed and dug deeper still and eventually a large solid treasure chest with a solid brass lock was unearthed and brought to the top of the hole. Without warning Steele fired at it with her pistol and the lock burst open. She started to dive down to open the chest, but stopped. She sat very quietly looking at it, her hands delicately tracing its edges. And she looked at her crew, who were sweaty and sandy from the dig and she smiled at them. Then she carefully lifted the lid.

It was a sight to behold. Gold and jewels glinted in the gleam of the torches, and the faces of the pirates twinkled in the reflected light. The chest was full to the top with doubloons and necklaces, the crowns of kings and the bracelets of mermaids. The wealth in that chest could buy five reasonable countries, possibly ten unreasonable ones.

"Incredible," said Fenelle.

"No. What's incredible," replied Boudicca, still inside the hole, "is that there are four more."

Alex looked over the side of the hole and was shocked to see she was right. Five chests full of the same treasure. You could purchase the world with that. There was nothing you couldn't do, no person you couldn't buy, thought Alex. She looked down at Steele and could tell she was thinking the same thing.

The rest of the pirates may have been thinking the same thing, as well. They may also have been thinking,

"Ooh, shiny!" (In fact I can assure you that that was exactly what at least Jack was thinking.) But the general consensus was pure unadulterated joy. Some began to decorate themselves in the jewellery, pointing and laughing at each other in glee. Others threw fistfuls of coins up in the air in celebration, taking no time to consider that it might hurt when they fell down again. And they hugged, and danced and laughed and everyone was just so beyond happy that I am slightly sickened to describe it if I'm honest.

Only one person sat almost perfectly still, just the slightest of motions revealed by the shifting glint on the ground from an apple-sized emerald. Alex watched Steele turn the jewel in her hand with such love, such devotion. . . And she asked herself why she, Alex Morningside, treasure seeker, did not share in the excitement of her fellow pirates. Surely this was the moment she had been waiting for all this time. Surely this was the moment she should be happiest.

But she wasn't.

"OK," Steele finally said, returning the emerald to its chest. "OK. Let's get it back to the ship."

And that bit, the getting it back to the ship part, I just don't much feel like telling you about, because it was a long tedious process due to the trunks being unbelievably heavy and the forest being unbelievably thick. But let's just say that they did get it back to the sandy beach where the longboat was waiting. And let's just say that they camped out there for the night and that they all fell into a deep sleep, exhausted from the day's events. And let's just say that when they awoke the next morning, the treasure was gone.

THE FORTY-SECOND CHAPTER

In which Alex has a relevation

lex didn't know the treasure had vanished. Like everyone else, she had been asleep when it had happened. She had been having a very unsettling dream about being tried and convicted as a pirate, then strung up on the gallows, which she supposed had something to do with the fact that her subconscious was not thrilled with her decision-making of late. So it was a great surprise to her when a bucket of water was thrown in her face as a wake-up call.

"What the. . ." she sputtered, sitting up.

"Where is it?" screamed Steele, lifting Alex on to her feet and then throwing her back down across the sand.

"What the. . ." repeated Alex, this time trying to spit the sand out of her mouth. She winced, having landed rather painfully on her side.

Steele approached and towered over her, her long leather jacket blowing in the wind. Alex shielded her eyes and looked into her face. Or rather where her face would have been had it not been eclipsed by the barrel of Steele's pistol.

"Captain," said Alex, holding her hand in front of her, "please, what's happened?" Her heart was in her throat.

"What have you done with it?" asked Steele, coldly cocking her gun.

"What do you mean? I don't know what you mean," insisted Alex.

Steele bent down and grabbed her chin, violently twisting Alex's head to the side. Alex tried to figure out what it was she was meant to see. As it stood, she was staring down towards where the sand met the water, and beyond, at the softly swaying *Ironic Gentleman* some leagues off. It must have still been early morning as the air was extremely fresh and the light extremely clear. But what she was supposed to see, in her groggy state, she hadn't the faintest.

"I don't understand," said Alex meekly, hoping that Steele would relax her grip ever so slightly. It was not to be.

"Notice anything missing?" asked Steele, squeezing harder, her nails digging into Alex's skin.

Her brain, which had up until then still been in the shower, towelled off and joined her on the beach. It whispered a tiny thought to her and then went to dry its hair. "The treasure," realized Alex, "it's not there."

Steele released her face, and Alex massaged it gently. "Very good. Very good."

Alex rubbed her eyes. "The treasure's gone." She didn't understand, she couldn't believe it. But the horror of the moment had finally dawned on her. Alex kept staring at where the treasure had been so carefully placed, and then she noticed the lifeless body of Boudicca lying nearby.

"What happened to Boudicca?"

"She fell asleep on guard duty, she had to be punished," replied Steele, standing upright again.

"You mean you did that?" First Whippet, now Boudicca. Alex was seriously reconsidering her decision to become a pirate.

"And you'll be next if you don't tell me what you've done with the treasure."

Alex stood up carefully and looked at Steele in the eye.

"Why on earth would you think I had it?" she asked.

"Because I don't trust you. Because you could very well

be working for that Mr Underwood of yours. Because you want that treasure as much as I do. I saw it in your eyes last night when it was unearthed. Now where is it?"

"This is absurd!" laughed Alex. "Even if I wanted to steal it from you, look at me. Do you honestly think I could physically move those trunks? And where could I have possibly put them? In my pocket?"

"That's what I've been asking you!" screamed Steele in her face, spit flying in Alex's eye. She made a violent gesture and Alex was grabbed by Jack and carried back to the longboat. "When we get back to the ship, I'll give you half an hour to think it over. And if at the end you still refuse to cooperate, I will have no choice but to do whatever it takes to prise that information out of you, no matter how unpleasant!"

They made their way back to the ship at a furious pace, and Alex was thrown back into the hold, somewhere she hadn't been in a long time. She had quite forgotten how horrible it was.

Alex was appalled. She stood facing the bars of her cage. Steele wasn't the only one befuddled by the whole missing treasure thing. Alex couldn't for the life of her imagine what the heck had happened to it. It couldn't have floated out to sea, it was far too heavy. It was more of a mystery than finding the treasure in the first place. She also felt a bit like a fool. The romance of being a pirate, the training, the treasure hunting, was starting to fade in the harsh reality of the casual murder she had encountered along with Steele's white-hot rage. Suddenly Alex realized very clearly that, while it was all well and good to create your own rules and follow those, it was quite another when the rules constantly changed. When the rule-maker was also judge and jury. And executioner. Piracy was a ridiculous, violent option. And she didn't want to have anything to do with it any more.

And then she heard a familiar voice.

"Alex?"

She was surprised at how often she was capable of forgetting Mr Underwood. Surprised and ashamed. What sort of friend was she? The worst kind. She was no better than Coriander.

"Don't talk to me," she said pathetically. She wasn't worth the effort, she realized. She should just let Steele kill her and get it done with.

"I need to talk to you," he said, his voice hoarse and sad.

"Please don't. I'm a horrible person. Please don't."

"Alex."

"I said don't!"

Her words rang out in the air and there was a long silence. Then Mr Underwood spoke again.

"There was a man here for a while," he said, "named Cumin. . ."

"Coriander," replied Alex automatically.

"That's it. He wasn't well, very sick, they were starving him, I think. I'm afraid, well, I'm afraid he died yesterday. But he wanted me to tell you something. He wanted me to tell you that he was sorry. He wouldn't say what for, only that you would understand and that he hoped someday that you would forgive him."

Poor foolish Coriander, thought Alex, poor foolish man. Of course she forgave him, there never was really any question of that. She began to cry. She cried for Coriander. She cried for Whippet and Boudicca. She cried for Giggles and the crew of the HMS *Valiant*. And she cried for her uncle. Oh, how hard she cried for that man with the tiny spectacles and the nicely pressed suits with brown shoes and his long white beard. She cried harder than she ever had in her short life, and she knew that she would never stop. She would cry for ever and ever, until Steele put her out of her misery.

"Alex," pleaded Mr Underwood softly, "Alex, don't cry, I can't bear it."

"I'm sorry," she said. "I'm sorry for everything. Everything is my fault. I am so sorry, please, please. . ." she begged, not Mr Underwood, but something else. She didn't know what. "Please, I am so very sorry." And she collapsed under the weight of her sadness.

She wept like this for the full half hour Steele had

given her, and when the pirate captain came, she found Alex curled in a little ball on the floor.

"Feeling sorry for lying to me?" asked Steele.

"Leave her alone," commanded Mr Underwood softly.

Steele turned to the dark. "What, in the same way you have?"

"If you hurt her, I swear. . ."

But Steele just laughed. "Oh, Mr Underwood, please. Don't start trying on some noble mantle. It just looks ridiculous on you."

"You will regret it. If you take her to visit that. . ."

"It's OK, Mr Underwood." Alex looked up and, with a sniff, staggered upright to meet Steele. "I don't know where the treasure is. Kill me if you have to, but I don't know where it is."

Steele leaned close to Alex and smiled coldly. "Oh, I will."

She made a signal and Jack unlocked Alex's cage. "But first we need to get that information out of you." And she placed a hand on Alex's cheek, wiping away a tear with her thumb. Guiding Alex out of her cage, Steele walked her along the dark of the hold. As she handed her over to Jack, she said, "Tell me, Alex, when was the last time you had a doctor's appointment?"

THE PENULTIMATE CHAPTER

In which everything comes to a head

Alex had not yet been to the surgery, which was safely hidden in a part of the hold far away from the prison. She didn't much like what she was looking at. The place was lit by a single lamp dangling above a rough wooden plank covered with a white sheet. Or at least what at one time had been a white sheet, the stains on it masking any evidence of its earlier days. Framing it on three sides were three teetering cabinets full of foul-looking medicines and other stranger things, like the ear of a fox and the toenail of a Zamboni driver.

Jack dropped Alex down on the sheet-covered plank and stepped to her right-hand side, scratching his nose.

She lay there obligingly, her sadness weighing her down better than any restraints. She didn't really know what he was waiting for until she saw the familiar large outline of Dr Brunswick facing the far wall. What he was doing, she couldn't tell, but she had a distinct suspicion it wasn't pleasant.

"Hello there, Alex," he said without turning around. He picked up something silver that glinted momentarily in the light of the lamp and then vanished as it fell with a crash to the floor. "Blast!" He picked up the object with a jerk. "Butterfingers," he muttered to himself.

"Butterfingers!" giggled Jack.

"Shut up! Just shut up!" the doctor yelled at him, before turning to look at Alex. Even though he wore a surgeon's mask covering both his mouth and nose, Alex could tell by the creases around his eyes that he was smiling apologetically. He approached her left side and looked down at her through his monocle.

"Being this big, sometimes I don't always have control over my body. Always falling over things, dropping things. Makes me really mad, so I'm sorry for the outburst. Anyway, I understand you have been rather difficult with the Captain, little Alex," he said. "And it is my job to teach you about sharing. Kids should always know about sharing." Dr Brunswick extended his hand over Alex and Jack passed him a pair of surgical gloves.

He deftly put them on, snapping the base of each one on his wrist with a resounding crack. Then he reached into his pocket and pulled out a small torch. Holding Alex's face roughly, he examined her eyes, ears and throat, then turned it off and placed it back in his pocket.

"You're in excellent health, which is important. I hate working with the sick; it's disgusting."

Alex suddenly felt her despair slowly morph into terror as she watched Dr Brunswick roll over a small table on which sat a dozen or so very unpleasant-looking implements, sort of miniature versions of what they had unearthed the treasure with the night before. She tried to sit up, but Jack pushed her down by her shoulder.

"Don't worry," said Dr Brunswick, "I know this is a pirate ship, but I do keep all my instruments sterilized. You'll have very little risk of infection."

"Dr Brunswick?" squeaked Alex.

"Yes?" he said, examining a long blade with serrated edges.

"What exactly are your intentions?"

"My intentions? It's not about my intentions, but yours. Do you intend on telling us the truth?"

"Of course!"

"Well then . . . why don't you start by revealing where you've put the treasure."

"But I haven't done anything with the treasure! I

haven't touched the treasure," Alex insisted.

"I'm afraid that's not good enough," replied Dr Brunswick. He picked up what looked like a small trident and nodded. "This will do nicely."

He looked carefully at Alex and bent over her, thinking hard and touching the tip of the trident with his forefinger. "I think," he said, "I think as long as you stay very still. . ." And he lowered it in the general direction of her left eye, his hand shaking.

There was a blood-curdling scream. Not from Alex. Nor from Dr Brunswick or even Jack. The scream had come from somewhere on deck. Both of the pirates stood upright and looked at each other. Without pause, Jack raced out of the room, and Dr Brunswick quickly followed behind, grabbing his sword off the wall and knocking over his table of instruments as he did so.

The terror from just a few seconds earlier lingered on and Alex lay still for a few seconds watching the lamp sway overhead. She couldn't believe it. Never in her wildest dreams could she have thought she would ever have been in such a perilous position. She ran through a list of everything she had been through since the day at the house on the hill, and a cold shiver ran up her spine. When she thought about it, it was truly a miracle that she had got this far unscathed. And it was nothing but luck that had saved her now, dumb blind luck.

She finally sat up. The sounds on deck were fierce, but difficult to place. If she had thought it possible, she would have guessed the *Valiant* had returned and had attacked the *Ironic Gentleman*. But it didn't sound like a battle. There was only one way to find out what was going on.

Alex slid off the table on to her feet and made to move towards the stairs, when she heard a low growl. She took a few steps back into the surgery, and, following her into the light was that monster of a dog, Walter, baring his teeth in her direction. Which could only mean one thing. One incredibly terrifying horrific thing.

The prospect of being tortured had been truly frightening. To describe how frightened she had been would only in turn make you, dear reader, equally as frightened. Which is why I didn't. And which is even more why I won't describe how she felt when she realized she was alone in a small enclosed space with Senseless, something that scared her more than any strange small sharp object held in the hand of a clumsy maniacal doctor.

"You'll never guess what's going on up there," whispered Senseless as he entered the room.

Alex slowly tried to inch away from him, but she found herself with the table at her back.

"Your year-six teacher has decided to take on the entire crew of the *Ironic Gentleman*." He slowly approached her and she could feel Walter drooling on her foot. "Which is probably the stupidest thing I've ever seen." He paused for a moment and then laughed quietly to himself. "Or not," he added.

Alex looked at Senseless. She couldn't speak for fear.

"In a matter of minutes, he'll be dead. The Captain is very unhappy at the moment. I doubt she's in a merciful frame of mind. I must admit I certainly am not." There was the sound of metal scraping metal and Alex found herself staring at the tip of his sword. Light from the lamp slid down the true edge.

With great effort Alex managed the barely audible whisper, "What do you mean?"

"I don't like children. I don't see their purpose. And as far as I'm concerned you've more than served yours. Enough with this stalling. Let's just be rid of you."

Alex's whole body began to shake. She listened intently to the noise upstairs. Was it possible that Mr Underwood was up there taking on the pirates? It seemed rather unlikely. Nonetheless the possibility had stoked the flame of hope in her, a flame that had all but burnt out.

"Any last requests?" asked Senseless.

Alex tried to think hard of some way to outwit him.

Of something she could do or say, so she could run up on deck. But she couldn't. She was out of ideas. There was only one thing she could think of, one thing that her morbid fascination wouldn't let go of.

"Can I see behind the scarf?" she asked ever so softly.

There was a pause and Alex watched the sides of Senseless's mouth twitch.

"If you insist," he said, amusement playing in his voice.

Without moving the sword a centimetre, he reached up with his left hand and pulled off the scarf. Alex gasped at what she saw. At the man with no eyes, no nose and no ears. She had never seen anything like it, and, truly, why would she have? He looked hideous: his skin was pasty white and the few wisps of hair on his head were pressed on to his skin like worms. It was the worst thing Alex had ever seen, and she cowered against the plank. Senseless was laughing. He was thoroughly enjoying the moment and while he had lost the rest of them, it appeared as though he had retained his sense of humour.

Alex wished she hadn't asked him to show her something so disgusting. What was she thinking? People hid things for good reasons. What was she expecting to see? The most distinguished Roman nose of our time and eyes the colour of sapphires? She looked up at him again, and then she suddenly had a very striking thought.

"Are we quite finished now?" he asked, still amused.

Alex didn't answer, but not because of her paralysis – rather because she was trying to make sense of what she had just realized.

"Let's end this, shall we? If only you had been there the night I killed your uncle, all this could have been averted."

Alex looked up at him sharply.

"What did you say?" she asked.

"Do you even remember him?" asked Senseless. There was a sound of mocking in the question. Alex didn't answer but glared at him. "Well then, you know that he died, surely?"

"Yes, I do. He was found under a shelf of doorknobs. Did you do that?"

"Of course I did, didn't I just say that? The way he begged when we took Mr Underwood, it was just miserable, like some pathetic dog. So I put him out of his misery."

"You are a horrible, horrible person!" shouted Alex, rage filling her.

"Oh, please, you're just a child. What do you know about anything?" replied Senseless, touching the tip of his sword to the underside of her chin.

Alex was still shaking, but now with anger. "What do I know?" she seethed. "Well, let's see. I know the difference between right and wrong. I know that there are good people and bad people in this world, and that it takes a lot of work distinguishing between them. But I know I've figured out you are a bad person, not just because you are about to kill me, but because you killed my uncle, my old defenceless uncle, for no reason whatsoever."

Senseless began to laugh quietly.

"You know what else I know? I know that pirates are not fun romantic characters from adventure books, but hardened criminals with the maturity of infants, who, when they don't get their way, hurt someone else. And I know that adventures are only fun in retrospect, that at the time they are hard and tiring and you get hungry, and that there are more important things than treasure . . . like the people you care about." She paused for a breath. "I know that being afraid of something, or someone –" she gazed at Senseless – "doesn't necessarily mean the person is actually someone to fear." Alex stopped briefly and listened to Senseless laugh more and more loudly. "And I also know something else," she said quietly.

The tip of the sword dug deeper into her skin. "That's enough now."

"I also know," said Alex, looking right into his eye sockets, "that you can't see me."

The laughter stopped. With one quick flick of the wrist she beat away his sword and jumped on to the table. She watched him flail his weapon in her general direction but she jumped easily over it, like when you skip a rope. Walter the dog began to bark and jumped up beside her, but she grabbed a few bottles off one of the shelves and threw them at him, hitting him square in the jaw and sending him flying off the table. Suddenly Senseless grabbed her wrist, pulling her down into a squatting position, and aimed the sword between two of her ribs.

"You think you're so smart," he hissed and pulled back to lunge at her.

"That's because I am," she replied and grabbed the cabinet on which were sitting the fox ear and toenail of the Zamboni driver. She pulled at it hard and jumped back. It fell with great accuracy on top of Senseless and made a hearty thud when it landed.

Alex stood on the plank for a silent moment panting. She didn't know if he was dead, but he certainly wasn't getting up any time soon. Suddenly she noticed that the noise above had vanished. In a flash of panic, Alex grabbed Senseless's fallen sword and ran out of the surgery up on deck. What she saw surprised her more than anything in her adventure so far.

Mr Underwood was holding a sword, standing in the

middle of the deck surrounded by a dozen or so fallen pirates, with the rest of the crew cowering on the fringes. Facing him a mere metre away was Steele, pointing her pistol at his head.

"No!" cried out Alex, running to Mr Underwood.

"Alex, you're still alive?" asked Steele casually, still focused on Mr Underwood.

"Don't shoot!" she begged.

"Give me one good reason not to," replied Steele.

"The articles! You said that all fights were to be settled ashore."

"Well, yes. But I don't think someone who has single-handedly tried to take over my ship deserves such courtesy."

Alex looked up at Mr Underwood. He looked very much as he always had. He was skinnier than before, and paler, but he was still wearing that sweater of his and the white tennis shoes. And his floppy hair still fell in his eyes.

"Kill her," said Steele quietly. And Alex turned just as Sir Geoffrey lunged at her with his sword. Never when she had been practising in the safety of the gym at Wigpowder-Steele had she anticipated needing to fence for real. Luckily for her, she had been taught by a man who evidently could take on an entire pirate ship by himself.

She parried Sir Geoffrey easily with a bind and lunged forward. He reeled from the shock, but took instant stock of the situation and just managed to defend himself. They continued fighting until Alex realized she had been simply toying with him, trying to make the fight last longer as she did with some of her fellow pupils. What was needed now was the kill, or in this case, a nice swift swipe to his right arm and upper thigh. In an instant, Sir Geoffrey was down for the count.

"Where on earth did you learn that?" asked Steele. The momentary distraction allowed Mr Underwood to disarm her.

"Guess," he said, pointing his sword at her chest.

Alex beamed with pride. She truly had the best year-six teacher in the world.

Steele looked at Alex. "I was right about you, wasn't I?" she said. There was a distinct look of pride in her face. As if somehow she was secretly responsible for everything Alex was capable of. "I feel terrible," she continued with a sad smile, "I should never have threatened you like that, or for that matter handed you over to Dr Brunswick. If you come back to me, I can guarantee that will never happen again. Partly because, of course, Dr Brunswick has been thrown overboard, but also because you are just too special to lose."

"I don't think so," replied Alex ruefully.

"No, think about it," said Steele quickly. "I could teach you everything I know. You would become my prized pupil. We would sail the world accomplishing feats that others have only dreamed of. Every day would be an adventure. There would be nothing we couldn't do. We would be known far and wide as the most fearsome pirates this side of the equator. Imagine the way the entire world would fear you and I!"

"Me." Alex said it without thinking.

"Pardon?"

Alex looked at Mr Underwood and then back at Steele. "It's 'me', not 'I'. 'Me'."

"Well, whatever. . ."

"No," said Alex, approaching Steele, "not 'whatever'. It's 'me', not 'I'. A very clear grammatical error."

"What difference does it make?!" shouted an exasperated Steele.

"Every difference in the world!" matched Alex. "You make these fancy speeches, you think you're just so eloquent, you love to feign elegance. But you're neither. You're just a pirate. With a bad temper."

With a roar Steele produced her dagger secretly sheathed up her sleeve and went to charge Alex, but Mr Underwood intervened with a thrust of his sword. Alex watched as Pirate Captain Steele the Inevitable fell as in slow motion on to her knees. The sword had gone clear through her torso, and she looked down at it in contempt.

"What? No. This is wrong," she said and looked up at Mr Underwood, who slowly took a few steps away from her. "This is not supposed to happen. You're a school teacher! I'm Pirate Captain Steele the Inevitable. Captain of the most deadly pirate ship this side of the equator. I was supposed to win! It was my right! It was my right!" She squeezed her eyes tight then opened them again. "You've made a horrible mistake," she spat at Alex.

"I don't think so," replied Alex, holding on to Mr Underwood.

Steele shook her head in disbelief and said, "The Wigpowders won? They actually won? That was not supposed to happen." She took a difficult breath. Then she shook her head and looked up. "So . . . what happens now for the great Mr Underwood?" They made eye contact.

"I guess . . . I go back to work. . ."

"Ah yes, marking all those 'What I Want to Be When I Grow Up' papers." She smiled broadly. "I always hated that assignment. My teachers always graded me very low."

"Why, what did you put?" asked Alex, curious.

Steele raised an eyebrow at her and fell lower on to the deck.

"Well, a pirate, obviously!" She fell on to her side and laughed. She laughed and laughed and laughed until she stopped. And then that was it. And Pirate Captain Steele the Inevitable was gone.

THE LAST CHAPTER

In which the loose ends are tied

Alex turned to Mr Underwood and looked at his tired face. Then she hugged him tightly. She hugged him for a long time, never wanting to let go. And when she finally did, he crouched down to look her in the eye.

"I'm so sorry for the way I talked to you that time," he said, his eyes misting with tears. "I was just scared. The thought of you getting hurt was unbearable. It wasn't that I didn't care about you. It was, in fact, for the exact opposite reason that I got so angry. I wasn't sure if I would be able to protect you, and I would have told you that, but you wouldn't let me."

"I know, I'm sorry!" said Alex, her eyes misting as well. She felt so stupid and so guilty for having even thought what she had thought about Mr Underwood. He was one of the good ones. One of the best ones.

"And then, when I heard that Steele was going to have you killed, I had to do something. I wish I'd done it sooner. I wish I hadn't wallowed in self-pity for so long. Will you ever be able to forgive me, Alex?"

"Of course," she said, the words catching in her throat, and she threw her arms around him again and hugged him even more tightly than before. He picked her up and held her close.

"Alex," he said, setting her down softly, "I've been doing a lot of thinking in that dark hold. And I was wondering if maybe . . . that is, only if you think it's a good idea . . . if you wouldn't mind . . . if I adopted you. I know it's really soon after your uncle and everything, but I mean if you were interested. . ."

"Really?" she asked quietly.

"I mean only if you want to."

"Would you, you know, take care of me and stuff?"

"I guess that would be my job, yes." He nervously ran his fingers through his hair.

"'Cause I really think I need to take a break from making all the decisions for a while."

Mr Underwood laughed. "I can't imagine you'd ever

really stop being the independent person you are, Alex. But if you ever need help, I promise, I'll be there for you."

Alex nodded. "Then I think I would be up for that," she said with a big grin, which Mr Underwood returned with one of his own. Alex wiped away the tears on her face. And to break the slightly embarrassing silence, asked, "Say . . . so . . . how did you manage to escape anyway?"

"Oh, I guess," Mr Underwood smiled to himself, "having lived with your uncle and working in his shop, well, I couldn't help but learn a thing or two about the nature of doorknobs. Especially ones made with very outdated locking mechanisms that can easily be overcome by manipulating the spring-bolt." And he held up the handle to his cage.

Alex took it in her hand and shook her head. Then she looked up at Mr Underwood. He shrugged. And they both started to laugh in a way that wasn't so different from crying.

"Ahoy there!"

The two of them turned around, and Alex started to laugh even harder with a big smile this time.

"Captain!" she called out and ran to the deck rail.

Alex thought that there couldn't have been a more beautiful sight in the world than what she was seeing that moment. The HMS *Valiant* was floating by them on gigantic orange water wings. The whole of the crew had gathered on the starboard side and were waving happily. There was much cheering as well.

"You pushed the button very well!" called out Francesca over the noise, indicating the wings with a big grin. She was leaning on a crutch, and her head was bandaged tightly. "Is it not the most useful of my buttons?"

"It is!" laughed Alex. "By far!"

The crew of the HMS *Valiant* anchored their ship beside them and moored it to the *Ironic Gentleman*. They were so close they could easily swing from one ship to the next. Magnanimous sent some of his crew to round up the remaining pirates and put them in the hold of the *Valiant* and meanwhile sat with Alex and Mr Underwood on the *Ironic Gentleman*. After a brief but enthusiastic introduction and the telling of their adventures, Magnanimous smiled that incredible smile of his and whistled.

"That is most impressive," he said. "Most impressive. But I think," and he pointed to De Wit on his ship, who disappeared into the hold, "I think you still haven't had your happy ending."

Alex and Mr Underwood exchanged puzzled looks. While they waited for De Wit's return, Alex had to ask,

"How did you find us, Captain?"

Magnanimous smiled. "You still had Heather's excellent copy of the map in your bag. We must remember to thank her when we get back."

Alex smiled at that thought. She was very excited that she would get to see Heather again soon.

"Captain!" called out O'Connell, and Captain Magnanimous looked back towards the *Valiant*. Alex and Mr Underwood followed his gaze.

"Holy sweet cherry orchard tree," said Alex with a gasp.

Congregated along the deck rail, like a group of suspected criminals in a line-up, were all five of the Daughters of the Founding Fathers' Preservation Society. And behind them stood O'Connell and De Wit, holding a giant treasure chest between them.

"We caught these little dears in a rowing boat. We don't quite know who they are or how they found the stamina, but it would seem that they are responsible for stealing the Wigpowder treasure from you. We have all five trunks with us and are taking the old ladies in for questioning," explained Magnanimous.

"How do they do that?" gasped Alex.

"Don't I know them?" said Mr Underwood, remembering hard.

"No, seriously," said Alex standing up at the rail. "How

do you do that?" she called across to them. "How can you possibly have followed me, and what's more how could you have managed all that treasure?!"

"I don't have to answer to you, urchin," replied Poppy with a sneer. "And I haven't done anything wrong. We found that treasure fair and square!"

"No, you didn't. You stole it!"

"And it was stolen from others who probably in turn stole it from others. They can't lock us away for that!"

Alex thought hard. "No, they can't. But they can lock you away for stealing both the takings and the wine from the house on the hill! Not to mention kidnapping!"

"Hey," said Mr Underwood, snapping his fingers, "aren't they the little old ladies from the house on the hill?"

"She just said that," snapped Poppy.

Captain Magnanimous nodded his head and the Daughters of the Founding Fathers' Preservation Society were trooped downstairs to join the pirates. They didn't much like being held with pirates, but the pirates felt far worse being with them. It started small with being told to tuck in their shirts and to take a bath. But when it was discovered that not a single one of them had called their mothers in the last five years, you could almost feel sorry for the poor pirates. They were made to give endless foot massages, and hold their ball-and-chains high above their heads for hours. And if they so much as grumbled, Poppy did her infamous pug-dog impression, and poked them hard with her pen.

Meanwhile. . .

Back on the deck of the *Ironic Gentleman*, a very important conversation was taking place.

"So what remains is to decide what to do with the treasure," Magnanimous was explaining.

"Well," said Mr Underwood. "I don't really know. I've never really had much use for treasure. The idea of it was far more intriguing than the reality. Alex?"

"I don't care much for treasure any more. Do whatever you want with it," she replied, sitting back down next to Mr Underwood.

"May I offer a suggestion?" asked Captain Magnanimous.

"Please."

"I've been doing a lot of thinking, and, considering what I know about you, Mr Underwood, I thought quite possibly an excellent idea would be to take the money to start your own school. . ."

"Oh, I don't know. . ."

"Wait, hear me out. I was thinking what was lacking in many schools was a sense of adventure in the classroom, a sense that learning can be an exciting thing. I, for one, dreaded going to my school. We had a very strict teacher who left shortly after I went to sea as a cabin boy. Her name was . . . Mrs Swinsky, I believe. Quite a nasty woman. I pity the poor students who had to face her next. But I digress. Being a sailor and liking nothing so well as I do the sea, I thought that what you could do is maybe take the *Ironic Gentleman* and convert it to a floating school. A school on a ship. So that if you were studying Zimbabwe, say, instead of reading about it in a book, you could visit it. Of course," he added, "it's just an idea."

Alex looked at Mr Underwood. It wasn't just an idea, it was a marvellous idea. With the treasure they could fix up the ship, so it was suited for students, turn the brig into sleeping quarters, let's say. And they would never want for supplies, having an endless source of finances. She only wondered if Mr Underwood saw it that way too.

"Captain Magnanimous, you are just about the most –" he searched for the word – "the most generous person I've ever met. Giving us this treasure and this ship."

"To the victor go the spoils," said Magnanimous modestly.

Mr Underwood looked at Alex, who was fidgeting nervously in her seat.

"Let's do it," he said. "Let's do it!"

And so it was that in a few short hours, both the HMS *Valiant* and the *Ironic Gentleman* set sail for Port Cullis, the latter helmed by a beaming De Wit, using his one good hand. Several other crew members had joined them for the trip as well, including Shakespeare and O'Connell, who approached Alex with big smiles.

"We wanted to give you something," said O'Connell.

"Yes, please, take him off our hands," replied Shakespeare.

And he held out a bandaged but rather feisty Giggles.

"Giggles!" cried Alex, grabbing him and holding him tight. "You're all right!"

"Of course he's all right!" replied Shakespeare with a grimace. "It's the rest of us you should be worried about," and he held up his hands, which were also bandaged. Giggles raised his usual eyebrow at him, and then snuggled into Alex's shoulder happily.

"That's not all, though," said O'Connell with a laugh at Shakespeare, and he presented Alex and Mr Underwood with their rucksack and bicycle respectively.

"You really did bring my bike," said Mr Underwood in astonishment.

"Yes, I did," replied Alex proudly, giving the seat a pat. She opened her bag to find its contents just as she left them, even the toothbrush and toothpaste and floss given her by Heather. Reaching down to the bottom she produced her camera. "I can't wait to develop these," she said, "I doubt anyone has pictures quite like them anywhere."

Mr Underwood laughed. "I'm sure they will be truly unique," he said, placing a hand on her shoulder. "But now, Alex, I feel a little left out. Everyone else seems to know of your great adventure but me. We have a fair bit of time before we reach Port Cullis. Do you think you could possibly indulge me with one of your amazing stories?"

Alex nodded enthusiastically and they found a comfortable seat at the bow of the ship. "Well," she said, Giggles purring on her lap, "it begins like this." And with a private grin, as if she knew the punch line to a great joke, she launched into her story. There was no need for hyperbole or exaggeration; it was more than exciting in and of itself.

So that, I am sad to say, is the end, my friend, but let's not finish just yet. Let us take a last moment to enjoy the view of the two ships sailing away over calm seas. The blue and gold of the frigate the HMS *Valiant*, with the orange of the water wings, and the red and black of the brig infamously known as, or I suppose now it will simply be famously known as, the *Ironic Gentleman*. Let's watch as they sail further and further away towards the horizon. There they go, my friend, right into the sunset. And even though it happens to be overcast at the moment, let's pretend it isn't, because it's just that much nicer.

THE "THE END"

In which there is no more left to tell

Yet more excitement than is still probably good for you. . .

Timothy Freshwater was always told he was too smart for his own good. But he wasn't too smart to do some good for a dragon forced to take on the form of a human slave.

Pursued by maniacal black cabs and Canadian ninjas, and confronted by a fleet of Chinese pirate junks and its dangerous commander, the Man in the Beige Linen Suit, the last thing Timothy expects is to be aided by the crew of the *Ironic Gentleman* and an annoying new ally, a girl called Alex.

Look out for Adrienne Kress's next amazing story.

ADRIENNE KRESS

Adrienne Kress is a writer and actress born and raised in Toronto, Canada. She graduated from the University of Toronto with an honours BA in theatre and then moved to England to study at the London Academy of Music and Dramatic Arts.

As well as her passion for acting, Adrienne has a passion for writing. In high school she won an award for her work, and in university she studied with top Canadian playwright Djanet Sears. A play she wrote as a result of that experience was performed at the Edinburgh Festival Fringe to excellent reviews and sold-out houses. Adrienne currently lives in Toronto. *Alex and the Wigpowder Treasure* is her first novel.

The journey begins...

Duke

The Illustrious Hotel

Dr Brunswick

Mr Underwood

Alex

Singing waiter

Coriander

Heather

Gigg

PORT CULLIS